# THE LAST GUNFIGHTER
# SLAUGHTER

# THE LAST GUNFIGHTER
# SLAUGHTER

## WILLIAM W. JOHNSTONE
### with J. A. Johnstone

## PINNACLE BOOKS
### Kensington Publishing Corp
www.kensingtonbooks.com

PINNACLE BOOKS are published by

Kensington Publishing Corp.
850 Third Avenue
New York, NY 10022

PUBLISHER'S NOTE
Following the death of William W. Johnstone, the family is working with a carefully selected writer to organize and complete Mr. Johnstone's outlines and many unfinished manuscripts to create additional novels in all of his series like The Last Gunfighter, Mountain Man, and Eagles, among others. This novel was inspired by Mr. Johnstone's superb storytelling.

All Kensington titles, imprints, and distributed lines are available at special quantity discounts for bulk purchases for sales promotions, premiums, fund-raising, educational, or institutional use. Special book excerpts or customized printings can also be created to fit specific needs. For details, write or phone the office of the Kensington special sales manager: Kensington Publishing Corp., 850 Third Avenue, New York, NY 10022, attn: Special Sales Department; phone 1-800-221-2647.

PINNACLE BOOKS and the Pinnacle logo are Reg. U.S. Pat. & TM Off.

ISBN-13: 978-0-7860-2002-7
ISBN-10: 0-7860-2002-4

First printing: March 2009

10 9 8 7 6 5 4 3 2 1

Printed in the United States of America

# Chapter 1

Frank Morgan eased back on the reins and brought the big, golden-hued stallion he was riding to a halt. Behind him, the two horses he was leading came to a stop as well.

The big, wolflike cur that had been loping alongside bounded on ahead, though, darting into the brush in pursuit of some small animal Frank hadn't seen.

Frank had reined in at the top of a long, twisting ridge that overlooked a broad plain. Behind him was an even broader valley. In the distance to the south and southwest he saw flashes of blue that he knew came from the Pacific Ocean.

"That's it," Frank said to the horse. Like most men who spent a lot of time in the saddle, he was in the habit of talking to his mount. "That's where we're headed, Goldy. Los Angeles."

Frank had been there numerous times over the years, beginning when he was a relatively young man and the settlement was little more than a sun-baked pueblo.

Now Frank was a man in advancing middle age, and Los Angeles was a real town. No, more than that, he reflected.

It was a *city*.

Streets that looked like a maze crisscrossed the valley in front of him. They were lined with houses and with brick business buildings, some of them several stories tall.

Buildings weren't the only things that had sprouted since Frank was here last. Tall wooden structures jutted up in scores of locations scattered all over the city. They were oil well derricks, and Frank had seen numerous others as he crossed the San Fernando Valley.

Nor were oil wells the only thing multiplying around here. Had to be thousands of people living down there, Frank reflected as he thumbed back the wide-brimmed, high-crowned Stetson he wore. No, more likely tens of thousands, he amended. Just thinking about it was enough to give a man who didn't like crowds the fantods.

Luckily, Frank was the sort of man who was comfortable wherever he went, from big cities like Chicago and San Francisco and Denver to small frontier settlements such as Buckskin, Nevada, the place he had left a week earlier.

Not that Buckskin was all that small anymore, he reminded himself. It had gone from being a ghost town the first time he saw it to a regular boomtown as the old silver mines located nearby began to produce again.

Frank had spent a pleasant, if somewhat hectic, time as the marshal of Buckskin before coming to the realization that it was time for him to move on again. Years before, someone had dubbed him The Drifter, and the name fit. He'd been fiddle-footed too long to settle down permanent-like.

Besides, the good folks of Buckskin deserved a marshal who didn't have bloodthirsty varmints trying to kill him all the time.

A rangy, muscular man with a face a little too rugged to be called handsome and dark hair shot through with strands of silver, Frank Morgan had been roaming the West for most of the thirty years or so since the end of the Civil War. He had first made his name as a fast gun in his home state of Texas, and that reputation had followed him ever since, no matter where he drifted.

The days of the Wild West were fading now as the century waned and a new century loomed in only a few more years. The sprawling, modern city that was Los Angeles was proof of that. It had changed a great deal from the raw frontier settlement it had once been.

From time to time, Frank Morgan had tried to change, too, but he'd never been successful at it. He was still the same man he had always been.

A gunfighter.

According to some, the last gunfighter.

He lifted the reins and hitched his horse into motion. "Come on, Stormy," he said to the rangy gray stallion he was leading along with a packhorse. "Hey, Dog, we're leaving."

The big cur known only as Dog emerged from the brush, licking his chops over the critter he'd just dined on. Some unlucky rabbit, Frank thought. Dog fell in alongside Frank and Goldy again as they began making their way down the ridge. The sure-footed Goldy picked his way along the trail with ease.

Frank had come to Los Angeles on business of a sort. No one looking at this rugged rider in worn trail clothes would take him for a rich man, but in truth, Frank had enough wealth to rival all but the biggest mining magnates and railroad tycoons. He had inherited half of the vast Browning financial empire from his late wife Vivian.

Being rich had never interested him all that much, though. As long as he had enough money for supplies and ammunition as he roamed, he was happy. So he had several firms of lawyers in Denver and San Francisco who managed his holdings for him.

He was here in Los Angeles as a favor to one of those attorneys, Claudius Turnbuckle. Turnbuckle had come to Buckskin to help him out there, and when the lawyer had asked Frank to ride down to Los Angeles since he was leaving Buckskin anyway, Frank had agreed.

It seemed that Turnbuckle's law partner, a man named John J. Stafford, had traveled from San Francisco to southern California to handle a case for one of the firm's clients, and he had run into considerable trouble there—the sort of trouble that Frank Morgan was uniquely suited to handle.

Gun trouble.

Frank had the name of the hotel where Stafford was staying. That was all he really knew. The lawyer was expecting him, though, and would fill him in on everything when they met.

Frank intended to reserve judgment until then

about what he would do. Despite the reputation he had—especially among nervous lawmen who didn't want shootouts on the streets of their towns—Frank had never hired out his gun. He sometimes helped out folks who needed his help, that was all.

His other killings had been strictly in self-defense. He always tried to turn away the ambitious young gunnies who came after him looking to make a name for themselves. His efforts were seldom successful, though, and then Frank was forced to slap leather to save his own life.

Because even though he didn't want to kill anybody, he wanted to die even less. That was just common sense.

The residential streets on the outskirts of town were wide and dusty. As Frank rode along them leading the two horses, a couple of kids wearing short pants and caps left off playing some sort of game and started trotting alongside him.

"Hey, mister!" one of the youngsters said. "Are you a cowboy?"

"Damn, that's a big hat," the other one said. "He must be a cowboy."

Frank grinned down at them. "I've done some cowboyin' in my time," he admitted. "Used to work on a ranch in Texas when I was a youngster my own self."

"Look at his gun," the second kid said. "You ever shoot anybody with it, mister?"

"Every now and then. But only when I have to."

"Are you Wild Bill Hickok?"

Frank shook his head. "I'm afraid not. Bill Hickok's been dead almost twenty years, I'm sad to say."

"Was he a friend of yours?"

"Not really. I met the man a time or two, but I wouldn't say we were friends."

In fact, Hickok had once warned Frank to get out of Abilene, when the famous pistoleer had been serving as marshal of that wild cow town. Frank had gone along with Hickok's carefully worded "suggestion," not because he was afraid of the man but because even by then, he had learned that it was easier to avoid trouble than to seek it out.

He was human, though, human enough to have wondered every now and then how he and Wild Bill would have stacked up against each other if it had come to a draw. Hickok had been fast, no doubt about that. Fast enough to be in the same league as Ben Thompson, Smoke Jensen, Luke Short, Falcon McAllister, and that bunch.

Curious or not, Frank was just as glad that he had avoided that particular showdown.

"Wow," the first kid said now. "You knew Wild Bill Hickok! How about Wyatt Earp?"

Frank nodded. "Him and his brothers, and Doc Holliday, too."

Fact of the matter was, he had heard that Virgil Earp was living somewhere here in southern California now. Frank figured to look him up and say hello if he got the chance.

"Were you in Tombstone for the big gunfight there?"

Frank shook his head. "Nope. I missed that one."

If he had been there, he thought, he probably would have sided with the Earps and Doc. They could be a mite on the shady side at times, but Frank knew he wouldn't have been able to abide the Clantons.

"Have you *ever* been in a big gunfight?" one of the youngsters persisted.

"Probably not any you've heard of."

"Aw, he ain't a real gunfighter," the second kid said to his buddy. "He probably ain't even really from Texas."

"Hey, mister, is that a dog or a wolf?" the first kid asked, abandoning his efforts to find out if Frank was somebody famous.

"He's a dog. Might have a little wolf in him, though."

"Can we play with him?"

Frank shook his head. "Wouldn't be a good idea." Dog had been pacing along, warily eyeing the youngsters, but he hadn't growled at them or ruffled his fur . . . yet. "He's not a real playful sort."

"We see coyotes sometimes. They come down outta the hills. Mostly they stay away from folks, though."

Frank nodded. "So I've heard."

The first kid asked, "Did you come here to kill somebody?"

"I told you, he ain't a real gunfighter," the second kid said, slugging his friend on the arm.

"Ow! What'd you do that for?"

"'Cause I felt like it!"

A second later, the two youngsters were rolling around in the dusty street, wrestling and grunting and swearing. Frank grinned, shook his head, and rode on.

The houses were being replaced by businesses now. Frank spotted a squat, thick-walled adobe building with a sign over its open door that read CANTINA.

He wasn't much of a drinker, but he had been on the trail long enough so that a cool beer to cut the dust in his throat sounded pretty good. He angled Goldy toward the building, and stopped at the hitch rail in front of it.

When he had tied the horses to the rail, he told Dog, "Stay," and went inside, grateful for the cool dimness after being in the blazing California sun.

The place wasn't very busy. A couple of men stood drinking at the bar. Only one of the tables was occupied. The lone man who sat there lazily dealt himself a solitaire hand. He looked like a professional gambler, but his threadbare suit and old hat had seen better days.

Frank moved to the bar and ordered a beer from the chunky Mexican bartender. He left a good space between himself and the two other drinkers, who were dressed like cowboys.

But he was close enough to hear the sudden whispers, and when he glanced over, he saw one of them nudging the other in the ribs with an elbow. They both looked at him and then looked away.

Then he heard one of them say "Morgan" and "gunfighter," and he tried not to sigh.

That hadn't taken long. Not long at all.

# Chapter 2

More than once, Frank had been the subject of dime novels, and while the scribblers who wrote those lurid little yellowbacks usually didn't have much idea what they were talking about, the artists who provided the covers for them sometimes worked from photographs of the novels' subjects.

So even though they usually drew him with the sort of menacing scowl on his face that he seldom if ever displayed in real life, he was at least recognizable from those book covers. Cowboys loved those dime novels, despite knowing how much hokum was crammed between their covers.

Now that he'd been recognized, Frank's hope was that the two waddies down the bar would just want to talk to him and hear about any gunfights he'd been involved in, like those youngsters outside. Most grown men still had a little boy in their nature that they would never outgrow.

The worst thing would be if one or both of those hombres fancied themselves fast on the draw and eager to prove it by bracing a known gunfighter, especially one as famous as Frank Morgan.

It was out of his hands now, so Frank sipped the beer the bartender set in front of him and waited to see what was going to happen.

The beer was a disappointment, somewhere closer to warm than cool, and on the bitter side. It was wet, and that was about the best thing Frank could say for it.

The actions of the two young cowboys were disappointing, too. They threw back the whiskeys they had ordered and then turned to swagger along the bar toward Frank. He knew the attitude all too well.

"Hey, mister," one of them said. "My amigo here claims that you're Frank Morgan, the fella they call The Drifter. Is that right?"

If he lied, chances were they wouldn't believe him. He wasn't in the habit of lying either.

"I'm Morgan," he said without looking at them.

From the corner of his eye, though, he saw the elbow nudge that passed between them. "Told you," the second cowboy said. "Told you I seen his picture on books."

They sidled closer. The first one said, "I hear that you're a famous gunfighter, Mr. Morgan. I'd be plumb honored if you'd let me buy you a drink."

Frank gave them a taut smile. "I'm much obliged, boys, but I'm not much of a drinking man." He hefted the beer mug in his left hand. "This one will do me just fine, and then I have to be moving on. I just stopped for a minute to wet my whistle."

The first cowboy frowned. "Well, that's not very friendly of you," he declared.

"I didn't stop to make friends."

The second man put a hand on his friend's arm. "Come on, Lonnie. You don't want to horn in where you ain't wanted."

The cowboy called Lonnie shook off the hand as his frown deepened into a scowl. "Listen, Mr. High-an'-Mighty Morgan, all I wanted to do was buy you a drink."

"I said I was obliged," Frank told him. He drained the rest of the beer in the mug.

"You know *why* I wanted to buy you a drink?" Lonnie went on.

"Just being friendly, I suppose."

"I figured it'd be a nice thing to do, buyin' one last drink for the man I was about to kill!"

There it was, the challenge that Frank had known was coming. Lonnie hadn't been trying to be friendly at all. He'd just wanted to goad Frank into a fight, believing that he could best the man he considered a washed-up has-been still living on his reputation.

It might have been funny, if it wasn't so dumb and tragic.

And so damn common.

"I'm not looking for trouble," Frank said. "I've had my drink, and now I'll move on."

He had to look up John J. Stafford, Claudius Turnbuckle's law partner, but that was his business, not Lonnie's.

"You're not goin' anywhere, Morgan," Lonnie said. "Not until you and me have it out."

Frank shook his head, a small, barely perceptible side-to-side motion.

"I've got nothing against you, kid, and you've got no reason to draw on me."

"No reason?" Lonnie echoed. "How about to show Barclay here, and ol' Pedro, that I'm faster'n you?"

The man dealing solitaire, whose name evidently was Barclay, didn't look up from his cards, but he drawled, "Don't kill anybody on my account. I'm not even really paying attention."

Pedro the bartender leaned over the bar and held out his hands as he said, "Please, Señor Lonnie, no shooting. The floor, she is dirt so she cleans up easy, but it's no good for business when people get killed in my cantina."

"Shut up," Lonnie said. "This old man insulted me."

"Now how'd I do that?" Frank asked. "By not taking that drink you wanted to buy for me?"

"By thinkin' that you're faster'n me! I can't let you get away with that. I'm the fastest draw around here, and I'm gonna prove it!"

*Hell,* Frank thought, *why do they always have to say the same damned thing?*

He started turning toward Lonnie, still holding the empty beer mug in his left hand. Without warning, that hand moved quicker than the eye could follow, smashing the mug against the right side of Lonnie's head and knocking the young cowboy's hat flying. Lonnie's knees unhinged. He crumpled to the hard-packed dirt floor.

His friend let out a surprised yell and took a fast step back. The young cowboy's hand dropped to the butt of his gun in what appeared to be a purely instinctive move.

He froze with his fingers wrapped around the Colt's walnut grips, because Frank's .45 was already out and leveled. The cowboy's eyes widened in shock as he found himself staring down the revolver's barrel.

"Don't draw, son," Frank said in a quiet voice.

As if the Colt had suddenly turned scalding, the cowboy let go of it and jerked his hand away from it. "D-don't shoot, Mr. Morgan," he said as his face turned pale under the permanent tan of a man who worked outdoors all day.

"I don't intend to if I don't have to," Frank told him. "What's your name?"

"J-Jeff, Mr. Morgan."

"Well, now, Jeff," Frank said, "I'm going to walk out of here, get on my horse, and go on about my business. That all right with you?"

Jeff managed to nod.

"When I'm gone, you might want to help your friend up and take him back to whatever spread you boys work for. I didn't want to hurt him at all, but I figured an aching head was better than a bullet in the brisket."

"Y-yes, sir." Jeff gulped. "I never . . . never even saw you draw, Mr. Morgan! It was like . . . the gun was just there in your hand, without you havin' to do a thing."

"You tell Lonnie that when he wakes up." Frank started to lower his Colt. "All right if I holster my gun? You don't want to try your luck, too?"

Jeff shook his head vehemently. "No, sir!"

Frank nodded and pouched the iron. He looked at the bartender and said, "I'm sorry about busting that mug. I'll pay you for it."

"No need, Señor," the man said, shaking his head. "I'd rather have to pick up busted glass than have to haul out some young fool's ventilated carcass."

"I insist," Frank said. He used his left hand to take a double eagle out of his pocket and lay it on the bar. "For your trouble, amigo."

Pedro shrugged. "If you insist . . ." The gold coin disappeared with an adroit motion of the bartender's hand.

Frank turned away from the bar, adding to Jeff, "Tell Lonnie I'm sorry I had to knock him out."

As Frank passed Barclay's table on his way out of the cantina, the gambler said, "I'm surprised you didn't kill that young fool. I was ready to hit the floor in case any wild shots started flying."

"There wouldn't have been any wild shots," Frank said.

Barclay chuckled. "No, probably not." He paused, then went on. "You have the look of a man who's weary of killing, Mr. Morgan."

Frank had gotten weary of it so long ago that he couldn't even remember how long ago it had been. So he just nodded and moved on toward the door. He heard a groan and a mutter of voices as he went out. Lonnie was starting to come around.

As Frank reached for Goldy's reins to untie them from the hitch rail, he muttered a curse. He had meant to ask somebody in the cantina where he could find the Nadeau Hotel. That was where John J. Stafford was staying. The confrontation with Lonnie had made it slip his mind entirely.

He would ask someone else, he decided. There

were plenty of people on the street. Los Angeles was a busy place.

He had just pulled Goldy's reins loose from the rail when an angry shout sounded. Lonnie burst through the cantina's door, jerking away from Jeff, who was trying to hold him back. Frank saw the gun in the young cowboy's hand, heard the roar of the shot, saw Colt flame bloom from the weapon's muzzle as he crouched and turned and dropped the reins.

The bullet missed, whipping past Frank close enough so that he heard the flat, slapping noise of its passage through the air. His gun was already in his hand again, and he fired as Lonnie tried to bring the revolver down from being kicked up by the recoil of the missed shot.

Lonnie didn't get a chance for a second shot. Frank's slug punched into his chest and knocked him backward into the arms of a shocked Jeff, who caught him and held him up.

"Oh, God!" Jeff cried as Lonnie shook and blood trickled from the corner of his mouth. The gun slipped out of his grip, hung for a second with one finger in the trigger guard, and then fell to the ground at his feet. His eyes rolled up in his head and he went limp. He would have fallen if not for Jeff supporting him.

Jeff stared at his friend's slack face, then looked at Frank and said, "You killed him!"

Barclay came up behind them. "The young idiot didn't give Morgan any choice in the matter."

"He didn't have to kill him!"

"That's where you're wrong, kid," Barclay said. "If

you're dumb enough to throw down on The Drifter, then somebody's gonna die." He looked at Frank, who was already replacing the spent shell in the gun's cylinder. "And chances are it's not gonna be an old curly wolf like Frank Morgan."

# Chapter 3

Figuring that it would be easier and simpler to deal with the authorities now, rather than make them hunt him down later to question him about the shooting, Frank waited at the cantina for the law to show up.

"I'll testify that you acted in self-defense, Mr. Morgan," Barclay said.

"So will I, Señor," Pedro added.

They were standing outside the cantina by the hitch rail, along with a considerable crowd that had gathered in response to the shots. People stood around watching solemnly as Jeff sat in the doorway with the dead Lonnie's head cradled in his lap. Jeff looked grief-stricken, but he wasn't making any move to try to avenge his friend's death.

A short time later, a couple of blue-uniformed men drove up in a wagon. Los Angeles had a regular police department like the big cities back East, Frank recalled, rather than a city marshal and deputies like most frontier communities. The officers climbed down from the wagon, and one of them demanded, "What happened here?"

It seemed pretty obvious to Frank, but he supposed the officers had to follow procedure.

Barclay spoke up, saying, "That young fella there with the bullet in his chest tried to kill this gentleman." He nodded toward Frank. "As you can see, that was a mistake."

"*Sí,*" Pedro added. "He followed Señor Morgan outside and started shooting."

The second officer glanced sharply at Frank and said, "Morgan? That wouldn't be Frank Morgan, would it?" Despite the blue serge uniform and felt cap, he had a rawboned, sunburned look about him, as if he would have been more at home on horseback and in trail clothes.

"It would," Frank said with a nod. "Do we know each other, friend?"

The policeman grinned. "No, we never met, but I was in Cheyenne some years back when three men braced you in the Gold Room. All three of 'em hit the floor within a couple of seconds of each other, as I recollect. You'd plugged each of 'em dead center."

Frank shrugged. "With three-against-one odds, there wasn't time to get fancy. I just aimed for the biggest targets."

"And hit 'em," the policeman said.

His companion looked annoyed. "Damn it, Randolph, you almost sound like you admire this . . . this gunslinger. I've heard of Frank Morgan. He's nothing but a cheap, hired killer."

Frank felt a surge of anger, but suppressed it. Arguing with the law wouldn't accomplish anything except to delay him from getting to the business that had brought him here.

"That shows what you know," the officer named Randolph said. "You moved here from Philadelphia. You don't know anything about the West except what you've read in *Leslie's Illustrated Weekly.*" He stuck a hand out to Frank. "Glad to actually meet you, Mr. Morgan. I'm Ben Randolph."

"Glad to meet you, too, Ben," Frank said as he shook hands with the man. He nodded toward Lonnie and Jeff. "Is there going to be trouble about this?"

Randolph shook his head. "I wouldn't think so, what with these two other fellas testifying that you shot back in self-defense."

"Blast it—" the officer from back East began.

"Don't mind him," Randolph said with a wave of his hand. "I'll fill out the report. You may be called to the inquest, but as long as we know where to find you, that'll be fine."

"I'll probably be staying at the Nadeau Hotel," Frank told him.

"You know how long you'll be in town?"

Frank shook his head. "I'm afraid not." That would depend on exactly what sort of trouble Stafford needed him to handle. "A few days at least, I reckon."

"That ought to be all right. I'll talk to Chief Glass myself and let him know the situation."

"I'm much obliged," Frank said.

The other officer was still upset and grumbled something about kid gloves, but Randolph silenced him with a glare. He took a notebook and a pencil from his pocket and began writing in it as he asked Barclay and Pedro to tell him again what happened.

While that was going on, Frank walked over to the doorway and hunkered on his heels next to Jeff and Lonnie. "I'm sorry about what happened," he told Jeff. "You know I didn't want to kill him."

"I . . . I tried to hold him back," Jeff said. "But he was so mad I couldn't stop him. Still, couldn't you have . . . I don't know . . . winged him or something?"

"Maybe," Frank allowed. "And maybe I would have missed and his next shot would have killed me or some innocent person walking by in the street." His voice hardened. "I said I was sorry and I meant it, but when you start throwing lead around, you've got to figure that somebody's liable to throw it back at you."

Jeff didn't say anything in reply to that, but his eyes burned with anger. In addition to whatever trouble Stafford was about to ladle onto Frank's plate, he knew that he would also have to keep an eye out for this youngster impetuously trying to even the score for his dead amigo.

Maybe Jeff would have more sense than that. Frank hoped so.

He stood up and went back over to where Randolph had finished talking to Barclay and Pedro. The officer patted the pocket where he had put away the notebook and said, "I reckon I've got all the information I need, at least for now. You're free to go, Mr. Morgan."

The other officer still looked like he didn't care for that decision.

Frank nodded and said, "Thanks. Can you tell me how to get to the hotel?"

"The Nadeau, you said?"

"That's right. I guess it's been built since I was here last. I recall the Bella Union and the Lafayette Hotels, but not the Nadeau." Frank paused. "Say, it's not named for old Remi Nadeau, is it?" The French-Canadian immigrant had established one of the first freight lines in the area, using mule-drawn wagons to haul goods from Los Angeles to San Pedro and back.

Randolph laughed. "It's more than named for him. Remi sold his mule teams a dozen years ago and decided to go into the hotel business with the profits. The Nadeau is the biggest and best hotel in the city. Four stories!"

Frank had seen taller buildings in Chicago and Boston, but he had to admit that four stories was pretty impressive, especially in a town that had started out with one-story adobes. Randolph told him that the hotel was located at the corner of First and Spring Streets and added, "It even has an elevator."

"Well, I'll have to take a look at that, all right," Frank said. "I'm much obliged, Officer."

"You're welcome. You take care now, Mr. Morgan."

Having a representative of the law treat him so pleasantly was a nice change, Frank reflected as he mounted up and rode toward downtown Los Angeles on Goldy, still leading Stormy and the packhorse. Dog padded alongside. The big cur let out a growl from time to time. He didn't like crowds.

The Nadeau was so big that it occupied an entire city block. A concrete sidewalk ran all the way around it. Frank didn't know much about architecture, so he didn't know what to call the style in which the hotel was built. To him it was just a big, ugly brick box.

He left the three horses at a stable across from the hotel's rear entrance. The hostler agreed to let Dog stay there, too, while Frank went into the hotel . . . but he wasn't too happy about it.

"Critter looks more like a wolf than a dog to me," the man said with a worried frown. "He's not gonna attack any of the horses or my customers, is he?"

"Not unless I tell him to," Frank said. "And I don't plan to do that." He handed the hostler a ten dollar gold piece. "I may be staying here for a while, so consider that just a starter."

The man's attitude improved considerably at that. "Thanks," he said. "We'll take good care o' your horses, mister."

"And the dog," Frank said.

"Yes, sir. And the dog, too."

Satisfied for the moment, Frank crossed the street, which here in downtown was paved with cobblestones. Instead of going in through the hotel's rear entrance, he walked all the way around to the front. That put him closer to the desk so he could ask for John J. Stafford's room.

The Nadeau's lobby was full of potted palms, crystal chandeliers, polished hardwood floors, overstuffed furniture, and people coming and going. The men wore suits and looked stuffy and prosperous; the women were mostly pretty and sported big hats, bustles, and flowery, flowing dresses. With his rough, dusty trail garb, old Stetson, and well-used .45, Frank felt a little like a turd in the middle of a plate of cookies.

Judging by the sneer on the desk clerk's face, he

felt the same way about Frank. "Yes?" he asked curtly as Frank stepped up to the desk. "Can I help you?"

"I'm looking for Mr. Stafford," Frank said, keeping his voice and expression mild. If he was going to let himself be annoyed by every jackass in the world, he wouldn't have time for much else.

"Which Mr. Stafford?"

"John J. You have more than one staying here?"

The clerk didn't answer the question. Instead, he glanced over his shoulder at the board where guests' keys hung and said, "Mr. Stafford isn't in his room at the present time. Would you like to leave a message for him?"

"You happen to know where he is?"

"Even if I did, I wouldn't be at liberty to divulge Mr. Stafford's whereabouts to . . . to a person of your . . ."

The clerk let his voice trail off and swallowed as he saw the flinty look that came into Frank's eyes. Frank couldn't keep his irritation from showing, and he didn't care anymore whether he did or not. He'd already had to kill some stupid kid today, and he wasn't in a very good mood.

"Just tell me where to find Stafford," he began, then stopped as a voice behind him asked, "Did I hear my name?"

Frank turned and saw a tall, blocky man with thinning brown hair and prominent side whiskers, wearing a gray tweed suit and a bowler hat. The man's eyes widened. He stuck out his hand.

"My God, sir, you must be Frank Morgan! Claudius wired me that you were coming. It's good to meet you. I'm John J. Stafford."

"Pleased to meet you," Frank said as he shook hands with the lawyer.

"I was just on my way into the hotel's barroom to have a drink. I've been out visiting my clients, and it's a rather dusty buggy ride back into town. Would you care to join me?"

"I'll pass on the drink," Frank said, thinking back to the beer he'd had in the cantina, "but I wouldn't mind a cup of coffee."

"I'm sure that can be arranged." Stafford put a hand on Frank's arm. "Come along, Mr. Morgan."

Normally, Frank didn't care for being touched like that. He let it go this time, though, sensing that Stafford didn't mean the gesture to be insulting or domineering. The two of them walked across the lobby to an arched doorway that led into the barroom.

Stafford signaled to the bartender for a drink and added, "I'd like to get a cup of coffee for my friend here, too, George."

"Sure thing, Mr. Stafford," the man replied.

Stafford led Frank to an empty table in a corner of the well-appointed room. "Did you have any trouble on the way here?" he asked as they sat down.

"Nothing I couldn't handle," Frank said with a shrug. He took off his high-crowned hat and placed it on the table. He didn't want to go into the details of the shooting with the lawyer.

"Well, I hope that you can help me handle the trouble that I've run into here," Stafford said. "I wasn't sure about bringing in a . . . a . . ."

"Gunfighter?" Frank suggested with a faint smile on his rugged face. "I don't know what Turnbuckle told you, Mr. Stafford, but I'm not a hired gun if that's what you're thinking."

"Not at all, not at all. But it's true Claudius convinced me that you might be able to give me a hand with this case, Mr. Morgan."

"I'm not a lawyer either," Frank pointed out. "Not even close."

"I'm aware of that . . . but you are a man who knows what to do when all hell breaks loose, aren't you, Mr. Morgan?"

The blunt question brought a chuckle from Frank. "I reckon that's true," he admitted.

"Did you come into the city from the north?"

Frank wasn't sure what that had to do with anything, but he nodded. "On horseback."

"Then you must have seen all the oil derricks in the San Fernando Valley as you rode through it, as well as here in town."

Frank nodded again and said, "I did. I'd heard folks had started drilling for oil around here, but I didn't expect to see derricks all over like that."

A grim look came over Stafford's face as he leaned forward and said, "Those oil wells, Mr. Morgan, are the gateways to that very hell I was talking about!"

# Chapter 4

Frank didn't know much about oil. His son, Conrad Browning, who was the managing partner in the business empire they jointly owned, had mentioned a time or two that they ought to look into drilling for oil, maybe in Texas. It might be lucrative someday, Conrad claimed. But that was just about the extent of Frank's knowledge.

However, he couldn't quite bring himself to believe that oil wells were gateways to hell, despite the fact that they smelled a mite like brimstone. He said, "I'm afraid you're going to have to explain that, Mr. Stafford."

That explanation was delayed for a moment as the bartender arrived with a cup of coffee for Frank, a drink for Stafford, and a glass of water. Evidently, the man already knew what Stafford's poison was, because he hadn't asked.

"Thank you, George." The lawyer picked up the drink and took a sip, then closed his eyes in appreciation for a second. "Nothing like some fine cognac to make a man glad that he's alive."

Frank could think of several things that would make *him* gladder to be alive, but he didn't say anything. He just waited for Stafford to resume, which the lawyer did after a moment.

"People have been drilling for oil in the San Fernando Valley on a limited basis for nearly twenty years now. They've been fairly successful, but there was never really a boom until a few years ago when a driller named Lyman Stewart sank a well that produced fifteen hundred barrels a day. That started a boom in the valley. It spread here to the city when a couple of prospectors named Doheny and Canfield dug a well with picks and shovels and wound up tapping into an even larger oil field." Stafford shook his head. "My clients aren't here in the city, though. The boom here is Los Angeles's problem. What I'm concerned with is happening up in the valley."

Frank realized that like most lawyers, Stafford was in love with the sound of his own voice. He said, "Who are your clients?"

"Our firm represents several of the prominent ranching families in the San Fernando Valley. Some of them, such as the Monteros, established ranches there long before California was even part of the United States."

"Ah," Frank said. "The Californios." That was the term by which the old families referred to themselves. Many of them had settled here while Spain still controlled the area, even before Mexico had broken free from its European parent.

Stafford nodded. "Exactly."

"Why do they have lawyers from San Francisco instead of Los Angeles?"

"Because the Monteros ranch has been here since Los Angeles was little more than a wide place in the road. When they needed assistance with legal matters, they had to go to San Francisco to find it. Francisco Montero retained the firm of Turnbuckle and Stafford more than twenty years ago, and we've always provided him with good service."

"So you're working for the ranchers in the valley . . . doing what?"

Stafford downed the rest of his cognac and followed it with a sip of water. "They're being crowded," he said. "Oil wildcatters are moving in all around them, and in some cases, actually on their range. The drilling disrupts ranch activities, the excess oil seeps into streams and ponds, and some of the ranchers have even lost cattle."

"Rustling?" Frank asked with a frown.

"The drillers have to eat." Stafford shrugged. "According to the ranchers, they regard the local herds as a source of free beef."

"I suppose a cow might get butchered every now and then like that," Frank said, "but it doesn't seem to me like a setup for widespread rustling."

"It's becoming more prevalent all the time," Stafford insisted. "And the problem is actually worse than that. Some of the riders for the various ranches have been ambushed. Several men have been wounded, and my clients are convinced that it's only a matter of time until someone is killed." The lawyer looked grim again as he added, "So am I."

Frank leaned back in his chair and took a sip of the excellent coffee. What Stafford was telling him was an old story with a new twist. Frank had seen dozens of range wars across the West, sometimes between rival cattle spreads, sometimes between cattlemen and encroaching farmers or sheepherders.

This was the first time, though, that he had heard of a range war between cattlemen and oil drillers.

"You're sure the drillers are behind the trouble?" he asked.

"There have been several out-and-out brawls between the two sides, followed by shootings the next day. No other explanation makes sense."

Frank nodded slowly. "I guess not. What have you advised your clients to do?"

"Actually, I've been urging them to get into the oil business themselves. Beat the wildcatters at their own game, if you will." Stafford shook his head. "They're very resistant to the idea, though. I was out at the Montero ranch today, talking to Dolores Montero, and when I suggested again that she consider drilling, I thought for a moment she was going to have me thrown off the place."

"I thought you said a fella named Francisco Montero owned that ranch."

"He did until he passed away last year. Señora Montero is his widow. She runs the ranch now. And since it's the largest one in the valley, she carries a lot of influence with the other cattlemen, too. If I could get her to go along with the idea . . ." Stafford sighed and shook his head. "But I don't think that's going to happen. She's too set in her ways."

That didn't surprise Frank. Most older folks were like that, and getting a mite long in the tooth himself, he knew that from experience. He had tried to break his own pattern of drifting by settling down in Buckskin, and in the end it just hadn't worked.

"What is it you want me to do?" he asked.

"I need proof that the drillers are rustling cattle and ambushing the riders who work on the ranches. The Montero spread would be a good place to start, since the bulk of the trouble has been there."

"And you want me to get that proof?"

Stafford spread his hands. "I need an experienced man who can handle himself. I've spent my career in offices and courtrooms. I can't go gallivanting around the range on horseback. And when it comes to handling a gun . . . well, let's just say that I'm no Frank Morgan."

Frank didn't doubt that. He said, "So what you want is for me to be a sort of range detective for you?"

"Exactly!"

"And if I can find that proof you're looking for, what will you do with it?"

"The local law hasn't given me a bit of help with this matter," Stafford said. "I suspect that the county sheriff and the chief of police may be in the pay of the oil speculators. If they're not actually being paid off, they're at least being influenced by the wealth of the men involved."

"Seems to me like those big ranchers would have some influence, too," Frank pointed out.

"In the past, yes," Stafford said. "But the amount of money that oil might produce for the area in the long run is astronomical compared to the value of the ranches. The city fathers know that, and so do the local lawmen."

That seemed unlikely to Frank, but he realized

that he didn't know enough about the situation to make a valid judgment. Maybe Stafford was right. Maybe oil was the coming thing, and raising cattle would fade into insignificance, at least in southern California. Frank didn't believe it for a second, but he supposed it could happen that way.

"At any rate," Stafford continued, "I need some evidence that the law can't ignore, and I'm counting on you to obtain it for me, Mr. Morgan. If you can do that, I'll take the proof to the authorities, and they'll be forced to take action against the drillers."

That seemed to be the only course still open to Stafford, Frank thought as he mulled over the lawyer's words.

He didn't have any stake in this dispute himself, other than the fact that he considered Claudius Turnbuckle a friend, and Stafford was Turnbuckle's partner. After a moment, he said, "All right. I'll see what I can do."

A smile appeared on Stafford's face, replacing the hangdog expression that had been there a second earlier.

"Excellent! Now, about your fee—"

Frank stopped him with an uplifted hand. "Whoa, there, Counselor. Nobody said anything about a fee."

Stafford's smile disappeared, and a puzzled frown replaced it. "But you've come all this way, and you've agreed to take on a job that may well prove to be dangerous. Surely, you deserve some sort of recompense for that."

"I agreed to come down here as a favor to Turnbuckle. That's why I'm taking on the job, too. But like I told you, I'm not a hired gun."

"But . . . but . . ."

Having someone turn down an offer of money clearly had thrown Stafford for a loop. In Stafford's experience, folks just didn't do that sort of thing.

Confronted with Frank's level stare, though, all he could do was nod and accept what Frank had to say.

"Very well. But the least you can do is allow me to take care of your expenses while you're here. I have a room reserved for you here in the hotel, and I'll pay for it along with all your meals and supplies and whatever else you need."

Frank nodded over the coffee cup. "Now, that offer I'll take you up on, Counselor."

"If you don't mind my asking, how are you going to proceed with your investigation?"

"It's too late in the day to do anything until tomorrow. I thought I'd take a ride out to the Montero spread and have a look around. I reckon you can tell me how to get there?"

"Of course. In fact, I have a map of the valley that I'll give you. It has the location of the Montero ranch and all the other ranches marked on it."

Frank nodded. "Sounds like it'll come in handy all right."

"If you'd like, I can ride out with you and tell Señora Montero why you're here—"

"Might be better not to," Frank said with a shake of his head. "Have you told anybody that I was on my way down here?"

"No, I don't believe I have."

"Let's leave it that way," Frank suggested. "Might be easier to find out what I need to know if nobody knows I'm looking for it."

Stafford thought about that and began to smile again as he nodded. "Yes, I see what you mean," he said. "You prefer to remain incognito. That means—"

"I know what it means," Frank said. He wasn't as well educated as Stafford, but he always carried at least one book in his saddlebags and figured he was as well read as the lawyer, if not more so.

"Yes, of course. I meant no offense, I assure you." Stafford leaned back in his chair and sighed. "I have to tell you, Mr. Morgan, I feel much better now. I'm confident that you'll get to the bottom of this and help me put a stop to all the lawless behavior that's been going on around here."

"We'll see," Frank said.

# Chapter 5

Stafford insisted on having dinner with Frank in the Nadeau Hotel's excellent dining room. That was all right with Frank, who used the time to have the lawyer fill him in on the other ranchers in the San Fernando Valley who were having trouble with the oil drillers.

"I told you the Montero ranch is the largest and most successful. Next would be Jorge Sandoval's ranch. The Sandovals have been in the valley almost as long as the Montero family. Then there's old Edwin Northam's place. He was an English sailor who jumped ship in San Pedro back in the 1850s, made his way to the San Fernando Valley, and wound up owning a ranch there."

Those were the three biggest ranchers in the valley, Stafford explained, but his clients also included Ben Patterson, Dave Guthrie, Augusto Lopez, and Jaime Castillo. All of them had fairly successful spreads, Stafford explained, but not on the same level as the Montero, Sandoval, and Northam ranches.

"And they've all had trouble with the drillers?" Frank asked.

"To one extent or another. No one has lost as much stock as Señora Montero, but some of those smaller ranchers don't have as much stock to lose. And their riders have all clashed with the oilmen here in town. This is where both sides come to drink, so you can well imagine there have been some con-frontations."

Frank could imagine it, all right. Nothing made a cowboy proddy like being shot at or having cows widelooped.

Stafford pushed aside the plates he and Frank had emptied, and unrolled the map to point out the locations of the various ranches. Frank had ridden through the San Fernando Valley earlier in the day and made a mental note of the landmarks, as he was in the habit of doing, so he had a pretty good idea where all the places on the map were.

Frank glanced around the dining room. "See anybody here from either side?" he asked Stafford.

"You mean someone who works for the drillers or the ranchers?"

"That's right."

Stafford studied the other diners for a moment and then shook his head. "No one that I recognize."

"Let's keep it that way," Frank told him. "In fact, now that dinner's over, it'd probably be best if we went our separate ways and kept some distance be-tween us."

Stafford looked like he didn't understand what Frank was getting at, but then his expression cleared.

"Ah! You don't want people to know about the connection between us."

"That's right." Frank drained the last of the coffee from his cup and reached for his hat. "Tell the clerk at the desk that I'll pick up my key in a little while. I'm going to check on my horses before I turn in."

"And you'll ride out to the Montero ranch tomorrow?"

"That's the plan." Frank smiled. "I might even ask Señora Montero for a job."

"Oh, that's a fine idea! I hadn't even thought of that. That way you'd have a reason to be in the valley without anyone knowing why you're really there."

Frank nodded. Stafford was starting to catch on.

Frank stood and settled the Stetson on his head. "I'll see you later, Counselor," he told Stafford, "but probably not until I have something solid to report."

"Very well. Thank you, Mr. Morgan. I pride myself on being a pretty good lawyer, but I'm afraid I'd about reached the extent of my abilities with this case."

Frank nodded, tipped a finger to the brim of his hat, and walked out of the dining room.

Instead of leaving the hotel through the front entrance and walking all the way around it this time, he followed a hallway toward the rear of the building and stepped out into the warm southern California night through a door back there.

A lantern burned in the livery stable across the street where he had left Stormy, Goldy, Dog, and the packhorse, but the light had been turned low. Frank started toward it, crossing the street, which was empty of traffic now that night had fallen.

Frank was halfway to the stable when the hairs on the back of his neck suddenly prickled. He knew better than to ignore the warning. He might not have been consciously aware of it, but his senses had picked up something that wasn't right.

Following his instincts, he darted to the left, at the same time reaching for his gun. Colt flame bloomed in the darkness to his right, at the corner of the stable. Frank heard the roar of the shot and the bullet ripping through the air next to his ear at the same time.

His revolver was already in his hand. He brought the heavy six-gun up in a smooth, unhurried motion that was still almost faster than the eye could follow. The .45 bucked against his palm as he pulled the trigger. The gun blasted twice as Frank aimed at the muzzle flash he had seen.

Before the echoes of those shots had a chance to die away, Frank dived forward, rolled, and came up running. The bushwhacker fired again, but the shot went well wide of Frank. He didn't hear the bullet whip past him this time.

It was too dark in the alley next to the livery stable for him to see whether or not he had tagged the gunman with his return fire. If the man was hit, the wound wasn't bad enough to knock him out of the fight. Two more shots sounded as Frank lunged toward the stable door.

The door was open a couple of feet. Barely slowing, Frank lifted a foot and kicked it open more. He dashed into the wide aisle that ran down the center of the big, vaulting cavern of a barn.

Dog stood in that aisle, fangs bared in a snarl and

the shaggy fur on his back standing up. Frank snapped, "Outside, Dog! Hunt!" as he ran toward the stable's back door.

Dog disappeared out the front, moving fast and low to the ground. Frank's idea was to get out the back of the barn and trap the bushwhacker in the alley with Dog on one end and him on the other.

It might have worked if the gunman hadn't had a horse with him. As Frank shouldered through the back door and turned toward the corner of the barn, he heard a swift rataplan of hoofbeats.

Biting back a curse, he legged it toward the corner, hoping to get there before the fleeing bushwhacker, but the man had reacted too fast. He burst out of the alley on horseback, leaning low in the saddle and spraying bullets around him as he emptied what must have been a second six-gun, since he hadn't had time to reload.

Frank hit the dirt again as slugs whined over his head. He triggered another shot, but in this bad light, aiming at a swiftly moving target, it would have been pure, blind luck if he'd hit anything.

The bushwhacker never slowed down.

Dog ran past Frank, giving chase. As fast as the big cur was, though, he couldn't keep up with a galloping horse. Frank whistled, signaling to Dog to give up the pursuit and come back. Dog did so reluctantly, angry growls still coming from his throat.

Frank stood up and dusted himself off, whipping his Stetson against his trouser legs. Light from the lantern in the stable spilled out through the open back door. Frank turned and studied his clothes in its glow.

Luck had been with him tonight. He hadn't been hit by any of the bushwhacker's shots, and he hadn't landed in any horseshit when he went diving to the ground those two times.

Thumbing fresh rounds into the Colt's cylinder to replace the ones he had fired, Frank went back into the livery stable. The elderly hostler he had talked to earlier peered out through a narrow gap around the office door. The man's eyes were wide with fear.

"Is the shootin' over?" he asked.

"It appears to be," Frank said.

"Are you hurt, mister?"

"No. Whoever that hombre was, he wasn't a very good shot. Not good enough anyway."

The office door opened wider. The hostler stepped out, using his thumbs to pull his suspenders up over his long underwear. He must have turned in already when the shooting started, and had grabbed his pants and hurriedly pulled them on.

"You don't know who was shootin' at you?"

Frank shook his head. "Nope. All I know is that he wasn't an amigo of mine." A grim chuckle came from The Drifter. "Not a very good one anyway."

The old-timer ran a trembling hand over his whiskery jaw. "I don't like a bunch o' shootin' around my place," he said.

"I don't care much for it myself." Frank slid the now-reloaded Colt back into its holster and turned toward the stalls. He wanted to make sure nobody had bothered his horses.

Considering how ornery both Stormy and Goldy could be whenever anyone but Frank came around them, anybody who tried anything funny with them would probably regret it.

Sure enough, both the gray stallion and the golden-hued one were fine, as was the packhorse. Frank had already seen Dog in action, so he knew the big cur was fine. When he was satisfied that no one had tried to hurt his animals, he turned back to the hostler and flipped a coin to the man.

"I don't think any of the bullets flying around hit the barn, but that ought to cover the damage if you find any."

"Thanks, mister. I'm much obliged. You're gonna stay here, ain't you, until the law shows up? Somebody must've reported those shots."

Dealing with the Los Angeles police for the second time today didn't appeal much to Frank, but he nodded in answer to the old-timer's question. Despite the low opinion of him most lawmen had, he tried to cooperate with the authorities whenever he could.

Just as the elderly hostler predicted, several blue-uniformed officers trotted up a few minutes later, already with guns in their hands. Frank had told the old-timer to turn up the wick in the lantern, so there was plenty of light in the barn. He didn't want the officers to get trigger-happy and start shooting at shadows.

"What the hell happened here?" one of the men demanded. "We got reports that a war had broken out."

"Another Bear Flag Rebellion?" Frank asked dryly. When that just brought scowls from the officers, he went on explain that he had been crossing the street between the hotel and the livery barn when someone started shooting at him from the alley.

"Are you hurt?"

"No, the shots missed."

"And I reckon you shot back at whoever it was."

"Seemed like the thing to do at the time," Frank drawled.

The officer who was handling the questions nodded. "Sounds like a robbery attempt to me. The gunman probably planned on killing you, then looting whatever he could from your corpse before help got here." The officer looked critically at Frank's clothes. "Although it doesn't seem to me like he chose his victim very well. No offense, mister, but you don't strike me as a rich man."

"Just a drifter," Frank said, trying not to smile.

# Chapter 6

When the police were gone, the hostler said, "They got it wrong all the way around, didn't they, mister?"

"What do you mean?" Frank asked.

"That policeman figured you for a saddle tramp, but you ain't. Those two stallions you brought in are fine horses, and your gear ain't fancy, but it's good quality. And you're stayin' at the Nadeau, which that fella didn't even think to ask you. So I'd say you got considerably more'n two nickels to rub together."

Frank smiled. "You're an observant man, amigo."

"That ain't all he got wrong," the old-timer went on. "If'n that bushwhacker was just out to rob you, he wouldn't've kept firin' once his first shots missed and you started throwin' lead back at him. He'd've took off for the tall and uncut. No, sir, he didn't want your money. He wanted you dead."

"He lit a shuck after a minute," Frank pointed out.

"Only after you got into the barn and he figured out you was tryin' to cut off his escape route. Smart fella, cuttin' his losses that way."

Without confirming or denying the hostler's guesses, Frank shrugged. "Whatever you say, old-timer."

The man squinted at him. "I say I seen you before, a good while ago. In Tascosa maybe. Ever been there?"

"I have."

"You didn't tell me your name, but a fella who looked a mite like you cleaned out a saloon in Tascosa, oh, fifteen, maybe sixteen years ago. Sound familiar."

It did, but Frank just smiled. "That's too long ago for me to remember."

"Whatever you say . . . Mr. Morgan."

Frank slipped him another coin. "How about let's just keep that part quiet?"

The hostler closed his bony hand around the coin. "I seem to've forgot all about Tascosa. The mind plays funny tricks on a fella when he gets to be my age."

"I'm obliged," Frank said. He left the stable and went back across the street to the hotel.

John J. Stafford was waiting in the lobby for him. The lawyer hurried over when he saw Frank and said, "I heard some shooting a little while ago, and there's a rumor going around the hotel that someone was killed at the livery stable behind the hotel."

"Nobody was killed," Frank said.

"But it *did* have something to do with you?"

"Just a robbery attempt that didn't work out for the hombre who tried it." If that was what the police wanted to believe, Frank was willing to go along with it.

But just to be on the safe side, he continued. "Did you give anybody in the hotel my name when you reserved that room for me?"

Stafford shook his head. "No, I just had them hold it and charge it to my account."

"Let's keep it that way," Frank suggested. "The fewer people who know who I am, the better."

Stafford sent suspicious glances around the lobby. "I understand," he whispered in a conspiratorial tone.

Frank didn't know whether to laugh or sigh and shake his head.

He settled for having Stafford claim the room key for him, then headed upstairs to get some shuteye. He looked at the elevator as he passed it—the first one in Los Angeles, according to what he'd heard about the Nadeau Hotel—and decided that he wasn't comfortable getting into a little barred cage that moved up and down between floors. He took the stairs instead.

Definitely old enough to get set in his ways, he told himself with a smile.

Frank was up early the next morning, practically before anyone else was stirring in the hotel. He was the first customer for breakfast in the dining room, and cleared out before any other hotel guests showed up.

He had explained his plans to Stafford the night before, so he didn't see any need to wait and talk to the lawyer again. Instead, he went out through the

Nadeau's rear entrance again and crossed the street to the livery stable.

Nobody shot at him this time. That was a definite improvement.

A different hostler was on duty at the livery stable this morning, not quite as old but almost as gnarled as the man who'd been there the night before. He was sleepy-eyed and indifferent, not seeming to care who Frank was.

Frank saddled Stormy himself, as he usually did. He trusted the care he took in such jobs more than he did anybody else.

Most of the time on the journey down here from Nevada, he had ridden Goldy, so the big gray stallion was fresher. Stormy was ready to hit the trail, too, as he proved by frisking like a colt as Frank rode him out of the stable with Dog trailing behind them.

Frank grinned at the horse's spirit, and let Stormy have his head for a few minutes. Like his master, Stormy was getting older, but that didn't mean he was washed up.

In the gray light of dawn, the oil derricks sticking up all over the city looked like a bizarre forest of some sort. They rose fifty or sixty feet in the air, four-sided, broad-based structures that tapered to a more slender shape at the top.

The derrick sides with all their cross-braces reminded Frank of the way railroad trestles were built. He also rode past large, round wooden tanks where the oil pumped from the ground was stored.

At this hour, the streets were quiet as far as pedestrians and horse and wagon traffic were concerned, but the air was full of noise from the donkey engines that powered the drills. Walking beams rose and fell with a clatter and a thump, and drillers called out to each other as they worked. Smoky lanterns provided light for the men to see what they were doing. They worked around the clock in their quest for the black gold that flowed up out of the earth.

The flaring lights, the raucous shouts, and the stench of sulphur in the air made Frank feel a little like he was riding through the outskirts of Hell. He was glad when the road he was following angled up the slopes of the Santa Monica Mountains and he was able to rise above the clamor and the stink.

The sun was up by the time he made his way over the mountains and started down into the broad San Fernando Valley. Some of the valley had been converted into farmland, but this was still prime ranching country, as it had been for most of the past two centuries.

Now that Frank knew what to look for, though, he saw that there were even more oil derricks here than he had realized when he rode through the area the day before. They weren't as thick as they were in Los Angeles itself, but he could see dozens of them from where he was.

As he neared the base of the mountains, he saw a wagon coming toward him, too, being pulled by a team of mules. Ten men were in the wagon, he noted, two in the driver's seat and eight riding in the back. The overalls they wore were heavily stained, and their hands and faces were smudged with black, too. Frank moved Stormy to the side of the road to let the vehicle pass.

But instead of driving on, the man handling the

reins hauled back on them and brought the mules to a stop. He glared at Frank—at least, Frank thought he did; it was hard to read expressions with all that grease smeared on their faces—and said, "Look, fellas, it's one of those damned cowboys."

Frank had done plenty of cowboying in his younger days, before he'd gotten a reputation as a fast gun, but he hadn't worked as a ranch hand for a long time. He supposed that to these drillers, though, anybody on horseback wearing a Stetson was a cowboy.

He gave them a nod and said pleasantly, "Mornin', boys. Heading into town?"

"Don't tell him anything," snapped the man seated beside the driver. "You know you can't trust any of those cow-stinking bastards."

Frank felt a surge of anger. He thought about telling them that he hadn't come over here to the valley looking for trouble . . . but of course, that was exactly what he had done.

He hadn't figured on running into it quite this soon, though.

"I reckon you're not from these parts, mister," he said. "And by these parts, I mean west of the Mississippi. So I'm not going to take offense at those careless words of yours."

"I don't give a damn if you take offense or not," the driller said. Even though he was sitting down, Frank could tell that he was a big man, tall and broad through the shoulders, with blocky fists almost as big as hams. "Who do you ride for, that Mexican bitch?"

Frank supposed he was talking about the widowed Dolores Montero. It angered him even more to hear a man speak so disrespectfully about any woman. The fact that Señora Montero had lost her husband fairly recently made it even worse.

Still, it was obvious that the driller was trying to pick a fight with him, and Frank was determined not to let that happen. He didn't want to draw attention to himself until he had a chance to find out more about what was going on here in the valley.

"I think I'd better just mosey on where I'm headed," he said as he lifted Smoky's reins.

"Hold it!"

The driller's harsh cry made the other men stand up in the back of the open wagon. Dog let out a growl as the feeling of tension and hostility in the air thickened even more.

The driver looked like he was starting to regret stopping the wagon and directing the unfriendly comment toward Frank. He said to the man beside him on the seat, "Better take it easy, Hatch. You know what Mr. Magnusson said about not starting any trouble."

"I'm not starting any trouble," the man called Hatch rasped as he made a curt motion toward Frank. "It's those damned cowboys who've caused all the problems."

Still hoping to head off a ruckus, Frank said, "For what it's worth, friend, I don't ride for any of the spreads in the valley. I'm just passing through."

That was stretching the truth a little, of course. Frank had a reason for being here, and as part of that reason, he planned to ask the foreman on the Montero ranch for a riding job. But these drillers didn't have to know that.

Frank's words didn't do any good anyway. Hatch put one grease-coated hand on the wagon seat and vaulted down from it, landing lightly on the ground for such a big man. Frank saw that he wore laced-up work boots, and from the looks of the big bruiser, he had probably done some stomping with them in the past.

He advanced on Frank now, saying, "Get down off that horse, you son of a bitch. I'm gonna teach you a lesson. The days of you cowboys ridin' roughshod over everybody else are over!"

Dog growled, his hackles rising. One of the men in the back of the wagon called, "Better tell that dog of yours to behave himself, mister, or we won't be responsible for what happens."

Frank glanced at the man and saw that he had produced a pistol from somewhere inside the greasy coveralls. That angered Frank even more. He didn't like anybody pulling an iron on him—or on Dog.

The Good Lord hadn't burdened him with much back up in his nature either. He might try to skirt around a confrontation when it suited his purposes, but damned if he was going to run from one.

"Sit, Dog," he told the big cur in a flat, hard voice. "Stay."

Dog didn't like it—his continued growling made that obvious—but he obeyed the commands.

Frank swung down from the saddle and let Stormy's reins dangle to the ground, knowing that the big stallion wouldn't go anywhere. As Hatch stood there with a smug grin on his dirty face, Frank reached down and untied the thong that held his holster to his thigh. Then he unbuckled his gunbelt, coiled it, and hung it on the saddle horn. He took off his Stetson and set it on top of the gunbelt.

"Mister, are you sure you know what you're doing?" the driver of the wagon asked with a worried frown.

"I reckon I do," Frank said as he began to roll up the sleeves of his faded blue shirt. "I'm about to quiet down a loudmouthed bully."

That comment made Hatch's grin disappear. "I'm gonna enjoy this," he said.

"Hatch, you better not kill him," the driver warned. "You know how upset Mr. Magnusson will be if you do."

"I won't kill him," Hatch said as he lifted his big fists. "But I'll make the shit-stompin' son of a bitch wish he was dead."

And with that he lunged at Frank, swinging his hamlike right hand in a sweeping blow that would knock The Drifter's head clean off.

# Chapter 7

At least, it might have if Frank had stayed where he was and the punch connected.

But instead, Frank weaved to the side so that the fist shot harmlessly past his head. Missing like that threw Hatch off balance. The driller stumbled forward a step.

That brought him within range of the hard left that Frank hooked to his stomach. Hatch grunted when the blow landed, but other than that, he didn't seem bothered by it. He tried to wrap his arms around Frank.

Knowing that he couldn't afford to get caught in a bear hug from the bigger, heavier man, Frank twisted away, jabbing a right into the middle of Hatch's face as he did so. Hatch's head was rocked back. Frank drove another left into the driller's belly, again with no noticeable results.

All right, so the man had a cast-iron stomach. But he had to have some other weakness, Frank told himself. Every man did.

With his friends yelling encouragement to him,

Hatch waded in, swinging wide, looping punches that Frank avoided without much trouble. Frank continued to pepper Hatch's face with short, sharp punches. Blood began to leak from Hatch's nose, mixing with the oil smudges on his face and making a mess.

Hatch shouted, "Stand still, damn you!" He changed his tactics, employing more strategy than Frank expected from such a bruiser. He feinted with a left and then shot out a straight right that caught Frank in the chest.

The blow landed solidly and made Frank stagger back a couple of steps. Roaring, Hatch tried to capitalize on that momentary advantage. Again, his arms reached out to draw Frank into a bone-crushing hug.

Still a little breathless from the punch, Frank had the presence of mind to duck under the arms. He grabbed Hatch's right arm, pivoted, and threw his hip into the man in a wrestling move that an Indian had taught him years earlier. Hatch's own weight and momentum worked against him, and he let out a startled yell as he found himself flying through the air.

That yell was cut off a second later when Hatch slammed into the ground on his back. The driller hit the hard-packed dirt of the road with such force that he actually bounced, Frank saw as he stepped back.

His hope was that after a fall like that, Hatch wouldn't get back up for a while. But luck wasn't with him. Hatch rolled over, pushed himself to his hands and knees, rumbled something incoherent as he shook the cobwebs out of his head, and then lurched back onto his feet.

Frank had had time while Hatch was climbing

upright to kick the man in the brisket, but he'd never been one to fight dirty like that. Besides, if he had, the rest of the drillers probably would have ganged up on him in outrage. As it was, so far they'd been willing to let Hatch carry the flag for them.

At least, Hatch was starting to show some effects from the thrashing Frank was handing to him. His nose continued to bleed, and his eyes were beginning to swell. They were probably turning black, too, but Frank couldn't tell about that with all the oil on Hatch's face.

With his chest heaving, the driller said, "I was just gonna . . . teach you a lesson, cowboy . . . but now I'm gonna . . . squeeze the life outta you!"

"Hatch, no!" the driver yelled.

"Shut up, Rattigan!" Hatch bellowed. "This ain't your fight!"

He came at Frank again, slugging wildly once more. Frank parried and dodged most of the blows, but one of them clipped him on the side of the head and made the world spin crazily for a second. His vision blurred.

It cleared just in time for him to see Hatch's huge fist coming straight at his face. Frank didn't have time to dodge to either side, so he dropped instead, falling to one knee.

Then as Hatch lurched toward him, Frank powered forward, burying his head and shoulder in the driller's belly. Frank kept his legs driving ahead. He wrapped his arms around Hatch's thighs and lifted, and once again Hatch left the ground and came crashing down on his back.

Frank didn't give him a chance to recover this

time. Instead, he landed on top of Hatch, planted a knee in his belly, and smashed a right and then a left into the man's jaw. Hatch's eyes rolled up in their sockets. He shuddered once and then lay still, out cold for the moment.

Breathing hard, Frank pushed himself to his feet. He turned toward the wagon and saw the other drillers staring at him in amazement. It was possible they had never seen Hatch defeated before.

"Am I going to have trouble . . . with any of the rest of you hombres?" Frank asked, pausing in the middle to draw a breath into his body.

A couple of the men looked like they wanted to climb down from the wagon and take up the battle, but the driver, Rattigan, said, "Damn it, that's enough! I'm still in charge of this crew, and I'm telling all of you to sit down."

"But he knocked Hatch out!" one of the men protested.

"Then I'd say he's earned the right to go on about his business in peace," Rattigan snapped. "Besides, Mr. Magnusson gave us clear orders when we went off shift. We were supposed to stay out of trouble. I don't know about the rest of you, but all I'm interested in right now is cleaning up, getting some sleep, and then maybe a drink or two to wash down a good meal."

The man who had complained scratched his head and said, "I got to admit, that sounds pretty good. But what do we do with Hatch?"

"Some of you get down and throw him in the wagon. I imagine he'll come to by the time we get over the mountains."

While the drillers were picking up Hatch's limp

form and loading it in the wagon, Frank got a rag from his saddlebags and wiped his hands and face as clean as he could. They had gotten smeared with oil while he was grappling with Hatch.

There was nothing he could do about the stains on his clothes. He hoped there was a Chinese laundry in Los Angeles that could get them out.

"Worried because you got a little oil on you, mister?" Rattigan asked. "It won't kill you, you know."

"I'm not worried about that at all," Frank said. He put the rag away and reached for his hat. "If I was you, I'd be more worried about my friend going around looking for trouble."

"We haven't had to look for it. It keeps coming to us, and I suppose it will as long as you damn cowboys keep taking potshots at us and destroying our rigs."

A frown creased Frank's forehead. "I hadn't heard anything about that."

"Then you must not have been paying attention," Rattigan snapped. He turned his head to look at his companions. "You got Hatch loaded back there?"

"Yeah," one of the drillers replied. "Looks like he's startin' to come around a little."

"Good. I was afraid for a minute there that this cowboy had killed him."

Frank didn't waste his breath correcting Rattigan about him being a cowboy. He just said, "Hatch will have a headache, but he ought to be all right when he wakes up."

Rattigan snorted. "Don't act like you care, mister. We know you don't give a damn about any of us drillers. You'd just as soon see all of us dead."

Frank didn't feel like arguing. He buckled on his

gunbelt and stood at the side of the road beside Stormy and Dog as Rattigan slashed at the rumps of his team with the wagon's reins. Grudgingly, the mules leaned into their harness and the wagon lurched into motion.

All the drillers glared at Frank as the wagon rolled past him. He returned a cool, steady stare and didn't mount up until the vehicle was a good fifty yards up the road toward the mountains. He hadn't seen a rifle in the wagon, and he was well out of range now of the only handgun he'd seen.

"Those fellas were sure on the prod," he said to Stormy and Dog when he had swung up into the saddle. While he didn't doubt what Stafford had told him about the drillers being to blame for the trouble in the valley, it was obvious that the hostility went both ways.

He rode on toward the Montero ranch, giving the oil derricks he passed a wide berth. Rattigan had mentioned a man named Magnusson and indicated that the drillers worked for him. Frank wondered how many of the wells he was passing belonged to Magnusson.

When he came to a long, tree-lined ridge, he knew he was getting close to the ranch. He was probably on Montero range already, he told himself as he thought back to the markings on the map Stafford had shown him.

Not surprisingly, when Frank topped the ridge, he spotted a large number of cattle grazing on the grassy hills that rolled gently away to the north and west. He reined in and rested his hands on the saddle horn, leaning forward in the leather to ease his back.

It was mighty pretty country he saw in front of him. Not too many trees, but plenty of grass. Canyons in the foothills on both sides of the valley would offer some shelter in case of bad weather, but Frank knew that the climate here was usually some of the most pleasant to be found anywhere. It was easy to see why the Californios who had settled here when Spain still ruled the region had picked this valley for their ranchos.

While he was stopped on top of the ridge getting the lay of the land, Frank fished a spare shirt out of his saddlebags and put it on in place of the oil-stained one. He couldn't do anything about the jeans he wore. He would have to put up with them being dirty until he got back to town.

Feeling more presentable, he stowed the stained shirt away and rode on. He hadn't gone very far when several men on horseback emerged from some trees and came toward him. He could tell that they carried themselves with a certain wariness, and considering the history of trouble in the valley, he didn't blame them.

There were four men, Frank saw as they drew closer, a couple of vaqueros in charro jackets and broad-brimmed sombreros. The other two riders were gringo, wearing dusty range clothes.

All four men were well armed. One of the vaqueros packed two irons, the belts crisscrossing around his hips, and the others sported one revolver apiece. Winchesters jutted up from saddle boots on all four mounts, though.

Frank kept riding until he was about twenty yards from the men; then he reined in to wait for them to come to him. They did so, fanning out so that they faced him in a wide-spread line. If any gunplay broke out, not even The Drifter would be able to drop all four men before one of them ventilated him.

Smart, he thought . . . and it showed that they were used to trouble.

He kept Stormy's reins in his left hand and raised his right, palm out, to show them that he wasn't looking for a fight.

"Howdy," Frank called. "You fellas from the Montero ranch?"

"What business is it of yours?" one of the gringo cowboys asked in a suspicious tone. "Who are you, mister?"

"Name's Frank." He didn't offer anything except the front handle. "Thought maybe I'd talk to the ramrod and see if the spread's hiring right now."

One of the vaqueros said something in low, rapid Spanish. Frank caught enough of the words to know that the hombre was commenting on how old he was.

"I can still make a hand," he said sharply.

The other cowboy pointed and said, "From the looks of that grease on your jeans, you been makin' a hand on one of those damned drillin' rigs."

"Not hardly," Frank said with a shake of his head. He jerked a thumb over his shoulder. "I had a run-in back up the road with a whole wagonload of drillers. One of them climbed down and said he was going to teach me a lesson. I reckon he was the one who got taken to school, though."

Smiles played briefly over the faces of the men, but then they looked cautious again. "You happen to catch the name of the man you tangled with,

Señor?" asked the vaquero who had said something about Frank being old.

"His name was Hatch."

That raised their eyebrows. "You beat Hatch in a fair fight?" one of the cowboys asked.

"I did."

"How do we know you're tellin' the truth?" the other cowboy asked.

Frank's voice hardened, as did his expression. "Because I'm not in the habit of lying," he said.

"No offense, mister. We believe you. Don't we, boys?"

The others nodded.

"It's just that we've had a passel of trouble around here lately," the man went on. "Stock rustled, cowboys bushwhacked, water holes poisoned . . . you name it, it's been happenin'. And those damn oil drillers are behind all of it. So you can't blame us for bein' a mite leery of a man with grease on his pants, even one wearin' a Stetson like yours."

Frank shrugged. "No offense, I reckon. If you hombres want to point me toward the ranch headquarters, I'd be much obliged."

"We'll do better than that. We'll take you there."

Frank knew they probably hadn't been on their way to the hacienda, but they insisted on providing him with an escort. Of course, what they really wanted to do was keep an eye on him. He couldn't really blame them for that.

The riders swung around and pretty much surrounded Frank as they continued along the road from Los Angeles. Despite their vigilance, they were friendly enough, and Frank quickly learned their names. The two white cowboys were Thackery and Bullard; the vaqueros were called Santiago and Lupe, short for Guadalupe.

"I heard talk in Los Angeles about the trouble you've been having up here," Frank said truthfully enough. "Sounds like things have gone to hell since those oil drillers came in."

"There's been drillin' in the valley for a long time," said Bullard, the older of the two cowboys. "Never like it's been the past couple o' years, though. Damn derricks sproutin' up all over like weeds. If you've been to town like you said, then you know it's even worse there."

Frank nodded. "You can't hardly see the houses because of all the derricks."

Thackery said, "That's the way it'll be out here in the valley if the drillers have their way. They're tryin' to crowd out the ranchers who've been here for a hundred years or more. They don't give a damn about cattle and horses. They just want that damned stinkin' oil."

"Folks use the stuff for a lot of different things now," Frank pointed out.

"And they got along just fine without it for a lot of years before that," Thackery argued. "As far as I'm concerned, we don't need it. We can get along without it."

Maybe that was true, Frank thought, but once people got used to having something, they never wanted to give it up. Folks had worn animal skins and lived in caves once, too, but he didn't figure anybody wanted to go back to those days.

The ranch headquarters came into view. A large

group of buildings sprawled along the bank of a narrow creek, including a massive barn, a number of adobe shacks that were probably used for storage and a blacksmith shop, a long, low adobe building that had to be the bunkhouse, and the hacienda itself, a huge, beautiful house of whitewashed adobe with red tile roofs in the Spanish style on the various wings. Looking at it, he found it easy to believe that the Montero family had been the leading citizens in the valley for a long time.

"Who's the foreman?" Frank asked as they approached the buildings.

"Pete Linderman's the ramrod," Bullard replied.

"Think he's looking to take on another hand?"

Bullard shrugged. "Couldn't say. We lost a boy yesterday, so he might. Even if Pete wants to hire you, though, Señora Montero will have the final say."

That surprised Frank a little. He had figured that after the death of her husband, the old widow would have turned over the day-to-day details of running the ranch to the foreman and the crew.

They had to pass the bunkhouse to get to the hacienda. As the group of riders rode past, several men emerged from the building, no doubt drawn by the hoofbeats. They looked curiously to see who the stranger was accompanying the Montero hands.

That was when one of them suddenly clawed his gun out of its holster and ran forward, shouting, "That's him, damn it! That's the gunslingin' bastard who killed Lonnie!"

*Jeff,* Frank thought as he looked at the distraught young man charging toward him.

Now *that* was a stroke of bad luck for you.

# Chapter 8

Even though Frank hoped to obtain the cooper-ation of the folks on the Montero spread, he wasn't going to just sit there and let Jeff run up and shoot him, as the young cowboy seemed intent on doing. Frank's hand started to move toward the butt of his Colt.

But before he was forced to draw, one of the men who had come out of the bunkhouse with Jeff lunged after the youngster and grabbed his collar. He slung the cowboy roughly to the ground and then kicked the gun out of Jeff's hand.

"You damn fool!" he burst out. "You think Morgan was just gonna sit there and let you plug him? I swear, Jeff, sometimes you're so stupid I think I should've let him blow a hole in you."

"Aw, Pete," Jeff said as he lay there in the dust nursing his aching wrist where the man had kicked him. He sniffled back tears. "He killed Lonnie."

"Because Lonnie was an even bigger idiot than you and drew on Frank Morgan." The man turned to Frank, who had reined in along with the other riders, and gave him a curt nod. "I'm obliged to you for not ventilating this loco young pup, Mr. Morgan."

"I'm glad I didn't have to," Frank said honestly. "I reckon you'd be Pete Linderman, the ramrod hereabouts?"

The man nodded again. He was stocky, with the permanently bowed legs and ruddy face of a man who spent most of his life in the saddle. Graying blond hair showed under his battered Stetson.

"Yeah, I'm Linderman. I won't say it's good to meet you. What are you doin' out here anyway?"

Bullard spoke up. "He said he was lookin' for a job, Pete." The old puncher's hand rested on the butt of his gun. "He didn't tell us he was a gunslinger, nor that he was the one who killed Lonnie."

Linderman hooked his thumbs in his gunbelt and regarded Frank curiously. "Why's The Drifter lookin' for a job like any grub-line rider, especially here?"

Frank shrugged his shoulders casually. "A man's got to eat," he said. "As for Lonnie, I didn't have any idea he rode for the Monteros. And if Jeff told you the truth about what happened yesterday, you know that he didn't give me any choice. I tried to handle it without having to shoot him."

"Yeah, I reckon," Linderman said in clipped tones. "Lonnie was a hothead, right enough. Thought he was fast on the draw and was anxious to prove it." The ramrod's voice grew even harder. "But he was one of us. You can't expect us to welcome you with open arms, mister, no matter what happened."

Frank knew Linderman was right. This was going to complicate the chore he had agreed to take on for Stafford.

Just then, a new voice cut through the warm morning air. It belonged to a woman, and it demanded, "What's going on over there, Pete?"

Everyone looked around, including Frank. He saw a tall, lithe figure striding toward them. The woman carried herself with a confidence that bordered on arrogance.

If beauty counted for anything, she had good reason to be confident. She was strikingly attractive. Tight, black leather trousers hugged her legs and hips. She wore a matching black vest over a bright red silk shirt. Thick, wavy hair as dark as midnight tumbled around her shoulders.

Frank was old-fashioned enough that the sight of a woman in trousers bothered him a little, but he had to admit that this lady managed to make it look good. At first glance, he thought she was in her twenties, but as she came closer he saw that she was older than that, with a few lines of experience around her eyes and mouth that did little if anything to detract from her beauty.

From the imperious way she sounded and the way she carried herself, she had to be one of the Monteros, Frank decided. Probably the daughter of old Francisco and Dolores.

Linderman reached up and touched the brim of his hat as he said, "This is nothin' you need to concern yourself with, ma'am. This fella showed up lookin' for a job, but I was just about to tell him that we don't need any more hands right now."

A slight frown creased the smooth, golden tan forehead. "But what about Lonnie?" she asked. "We need someone to replace him, don't we?" She looked at Jeff. "And what are you doing lying on the ground, Jeff?"

The young cowboy was still holding his injured wrist, so he lifted both arms to point at Frank. "He's the one who killed Lonnie! He's Frank Morgan, the gunfighter!"

The woman's gaze swung back to Frank. "Is this true?" she asked in a cool, unfriendly voice.

Frank nodded. "I'm afraid so."

"You got in a gunfight with a young man who was still wet behind the ears and killed him?"

"Only after he took a shot at me," Frank said, letting his own voice get a little chillier. "I give you my word, miss, I didn't set out to kill Lonnie. He forced me into it."

She looked at Jeff again. "Is he telling the truth?"

"Well . . ."

Linderman spoke up, saying, "I reckon it's true enough. Morgan walloped Lonnie and then tried to leave without any shootin', but Lonnie threw down on him." The ramrod spat in the dust. "Can't expect a man to just stand there and let somebody blaze away at him."

"No," the woman said, "I suppose you can't." She faced Frank. "Very well, Mr. Morgan. I agree with Pete that hiring you wouldn't be wise, but hospitality demands that we not turn you away empty-handed. Feel free to water your horse and your dog, and you'll stay for lunch."

Frank nodded. "I'm obliged to you, Señorita, but maybe you'd better check with your mother and make sure it's all right to be handing out invitations like that."

She smiled, and Linderman chuckled. He said, "I'll take care of his horse for him, Señora Montero."

Frank hoped that his face didn't betray just how surprised—not to mention foolish—he felt just then. Dolores Montero's status as a widow had caused him to think of her as an older woman, but as he considered the matter now, he realized there was no reason she had to be.

"Thank you, Pete," she said to the foreman. "Well, Mr. Morgan? Are you coming in?"

"Yes, ma'am." Frank swung down from the saddle and handed Stormy's reins to Linderman. "I'm obliged for the hospitality."

"Don't make more of it than it is," she snapped. "I'd extend the same invitation to almost anyone . . . except perhaps that snake Victor Magnusson."

There was that name again, Frank thought. Even though his plan to get a job on the Montero ranch hadn't worked out, maybe he could still get some information from this young woman about the trouble going on in the valley. He could always reveal to her that he was working with Stafford, but he thought he might be better off using that as his hole card.

Dolores Montero turned and walked toward the sprawling adobe ranch house, providing an interesting view in those snug leather trousers. Frank paused before following her to tell Linderman, "Better keep an eye on that stallion. He gets it into his head sometimes to take a nip out of somebody's hide."

Linderman grunted. "Thanks for the warning. Is that dog gonna tear my throat out if I get too close to him?"

"Not unless I tell him to," Frank said.

Even though it wasn't the middle of the day yet, the air was growing hot. Frank was grateful for the coolness generated by the thick adobe walls as he stepped into the house behind Dolores Montero.

"Would you like a drink?" she asked him.

"It's a mite early in the day for that. I'd take a cup of coffee, though, if you've got any handy."

"Of course." She raised her voice. "Pilar!"

A heavyset woman who looked more Indian than Mexican came into the room a moment later. "Señora?" she asked.

"A cup of coffee for Mr. Morgan," Dolores said, "and I'll have one, too."

*"Sí, señora."*

Frank was looking around the room while his hostess talked to the servant. It was a very masculine place, all dark wood and heavy furniture and thick, woven rugs on the floor. Mounted on the wall above a massive fireplace was the head of a bear, its mouth open so that its teeth showed in a menacing snarl.

"My husband's grandfather killed that bear," Dolores said. "In those days there were many of the creatures around here. They were very dangerous. But Francisco's grandfather slew that one with a single shot from a pistol. God was smiling on him that day."

"I'd say so," Frank agreed.

"Francisco," she repeated. "That is your name, is it not, Mr. Morgan?"

"Well, I've always gone by Frank, but I reckon it's pretty much the same thing."

"You were shocked to find that the Widow Montero was so young." It wasn't a question.

Frank shrugged. "No reason you shouldn't be young."

"I was not my husband's first wife. He outlived her by a number of years. Unfortunately, he outlived all of their children, too. So in the end, I was all he had."

Frank couldn't help but wonder how she had come to marry the old ranchero. Had she been a poor young woman, out to marry a rich old man because of his money? One of the servants here on the ranch maybe, who was now the mistress of the place and seemed quite at home in the role?

That was none of his business, he reminded himself, and had nothing to do with why he was here.

"And in the end, I was not enough for him," Dolores went on, which further puzzled Frank because just by looking at her, it seemed that she would be enough woman for any man.

Before she could say anything else, Pilar reappeared with a silver tray containing two cups of thick, black coffee. She set the tray on a brilliantly polished hardwood table with thick, ornately carved legs. Dolores said, *"Gracias,"* then picked up one of the cups and offered it to Frank.

*"Muchas gracias,"* he said as he took it. He waited until she had her cup and then sipped the coffee. It was as potent as it appeared, which was just fine with him. He had always liked his coffee strong enough to get up and walk around on its own hind legs.

"So tell me, Mr. Morgan," Dolores said when she had taken a sip from her own cup, "what really brings you out here? I cannot believe that a famous man such as yourself would truly be seeking a job as a vaquero."

"Everybody's got to eat," he said, using the same answer he had given Linderman. Dolores didn't appear to be any more convinced than her foreman had been, though.

"You don't get any income from the dime novels that are written about you?"

"Not a penny," Frank said with a smile. "All those stories are made up anyway. I'm surprised you even know about them."

"Such stories are popular in the bunkhouse, I'm told. I see them from time to time, but I'm afraid I've never read one."

"You're not missing much," Frank said.

"I stay busy taking care of the ranch. I feel I owe that to my late husband. Salida del Sol has been in his family for many generations."

"Sunrise," Frank said, translating the Spanish name.

"Named by Francisco's great-great-grandfather because he first saw the land here by the light of the rising sun one morning, when he came here to settle and establish a ranch. It's been known by that ever since."

"I like it," Frank said with a nod. "It suits the place."

A fierce expression appeared suddenly on Dolores's face. "It is my home," she said, "and I will defend it to the death. If that barbarian has hired you to force me out with your gun, you'll find it's not so easy a job!"

Frank set his coffee cup on the table and held up his hands. "Hold on there, Señora," he said. "Nobody's hired me to do anything of the sort. Like I keep telling people, I'm not a hired gun—"

Before he could go on, the heavy front door of the house swung open again, and Pete Linderman stepped inside. Frank knew right away from the foreman's urgent manner that something had happened—or was about to happen.

"Sorry to bother you, Señora," Linderman said, "but somebody's comin'."

Dolores glanced at Frank. "Another visitor so soon. Who is it, Pete?"

Linderman's face was grim as he answered, "Looks like that son of a—I mean, it looks like Victor Magnusson . . . and I expect he's huntin' more trouble!"

# Chapter 9

Dolores's gaze swung quickly back to Frank. "Magnusson!" she breathed.

"I tell you, I don't have anything to do with the man," Frank insisted. "I've never even seen him before."

"Of course," Dolores said, not sounding convinced at all. "Well, you're about to see him now."

Frank swallowed the irritation he felt. First, Magnusson's drillers had mistaken him for one of the Montero ranch hands, and now, Dolores Montero herself seemed to think that he had been hired by Magnusson to wage some sort of campaign of terror against the ranch.

"Exactly who is this hombre Magnusson?" he asked.

Dolores sniffed, as if to say that she believed he knew good and well who Magnusson was. But she said, "Victor Magnusson is the most successful wildcatter in the valley. He has wells all over . . . but he insists that the largest pool of oil is under the Montero range, and he wants it!"

"If he's right and the oil really is down there," Frank said, "why don't you go after it yourself?"

That was the suggestion Stafford had made to his clients, including Dolores, and it sounded like a good one to Frank.

She gave him a withering look. "This is a cattle ranch, not an oil field. I don't want anything to do with that foul stuff."

"Life doesn't always give you a choice," Frank said with a shrug.

Pete Linderman still stood there just inside the door with his battered Stetson in one hand.

"What do you want me to do, ma'am?" he asked. "The boys and me can run Magnusson off if you like."

Dolores frowned in thought for a second and then shook her head.

"Not unless he starts trouble," she declared. "If he just wants to talk, I'll talk to him."

Linderman looked like he thought that was a bad idea, but he wasn't going to argue with the mistress of the Montero ranch. He nodded and said, "*Sí, señora.*"

The ramrod turned and left the house. Dolores said to Frank, "My apologies, Mr. Morgan. It appears that lunch may be delayed."

"That's quite all right," Frank told her. I'm a mite curious about Mr. Magnusson myself."

She gave him a still-skeptical look and then went to the door, which Linderman had left open. Frank followed, settling his hat on his head again.

They went through a flower-bedecked courtyard and out a black wrought-iron gate in the adobe wall that surrounded the hacienda. Frank spotted the buggy rolling toward the ranch house, its wheels and the hooves of the two horses pulling it kicking up a spiral of dust behind the vehicle. The man at the reins appeared to be alone in the buggy.

Whatever Victor Magnusson's failings, a lack of courage didn't appear to be one of them. He was riding straight into the stronghold of his enemy all by himself.

Pete Linderman stood near the bunkhouse with several of the hands, including Jeff. Frank saw the young cowboy casting furtive, angry glances at him, and his mind went back to the ambush attempt on his life the night before.

Jeff had to be the leading suspect in that shooting. No one else had had any reason to throw lead at him from that dark alley.

And yet for some reason, Frank didn't feel that Jeff had been the bushwhacker. No doubt the youngster bore a grudge against him, but Jeff just didn't strike Frank as the sort who would try to shoot a man from hiding. Jeff was rash enough to come at an enemy out in the open, as he had done when Frank rode up a short time earlier.

Magnusson drove the buggy into the yard between the hacienda and the bunkhouse and brought the two horses to a halt. They looked like good sturdy animals, Frank thought. Like most Westerners, he was in the habit of assessing the horseflesh he saw.

Victor Magnusson seemed to be a pretty sturdy animal himself. When Magnusson stepped down from the buggy, Frank saw that he was tall and brawny in a brown tweed suit. His shoulders stretched the fabric of the coat. A darker brown hat was crammed down on fiery red hair. A spade beard of the same blazing shade jutted from a pugnacious jaw.

Frank was reminded immediately of illustrations he had seen in books depicting the fierce Viking rovers of ancient times. Victor Magnusson looked like he ought to have a horned helmet on his head and a broadsword in his hand.

He started toward Dolores Montero, but Linderman got in his way.

"Hold on there, Magnusson," the foreman said. "What's your business here?"

"I want to talk to Señora Montero," Magnusson snapped in a deep voice. "And don't try to tell me she's not here, because I can see her right there!"

He flung out a big hand and pointed toward Dolores.

"I'm the foreman here," Linderman went on stubbornly. "You got a question about the ranch, you can talk to me."

Magnusson glared and looked like he wanted to push Linderman out of his way, but he controlled his anger with a visible effort and said, "I want to talk to her about that man right there."

Again he pointed, this time at Frank, who didn't care much for it.

"You mean Morgan?" Linderman asked.

"I don't know what his name is, and I don't care. All I know is that he viciously attacked and injured one of my men a little while ago. I was on my way out from town when I ran into a wagonload of my drillers coming off their shift. The injured man was in the back of the wagon. They said he was attacked by a Montero cowboy, and that man matches the description!"

Linderman shook his head. "You've got it wrong, Magnusson. Morgan doesn't work for us. Never has, and likely never will."

Under the red mustache, Magnusson's mouth curled in a sneer. "He looks right at home to me."

Frank had listened to enough of this. He stepped around Dolores and strode toward Magnusson.

"Linderman's right," he said. "I don't work for Señora Montero. It's true that I rode out here thinking that I might get hired, but that's not going to happen."

He came to a stop directly in front of Magnusson and only a few feet away from the man. Magnusson was several inches taller than Frank and considerably heavier, but the driller called Hatch was bigger, too, and Frank had whittled him down to size.

Although to tell the truth, after that little dustup, Frank hoped he wouldn't have to tussle with Magnusson. He was already sore from the battering he had taken.

"As for what happened out there on the road," Frank went on, not giving Magnusson a chance to interrupt, "your men told you their version, and it doesn't exactly match up with the truth."

Magnusson's already flushed face grew even more ruddy, almost matching his beard.

"Are you callin' my men liars?"

"If they say that I attacked them, they are," Frank stated without hesitation. "I moved aside to let the wagon pass. I wasn't looking for trouble."

There was that pesky stretching of the truth again.

"Your men are the ones who stopped and provoked a fight," he continued. "Hatch got down from the wagon and started throwing punches. I didn't have much choice except to throw some of my own back at him."

Jeff stepped forward and said, "You seem to get in a lot of jams where you don't have any choice but to hurt somebody, Morgan."

Linderman turned his head and glared at the young cowboy. "Hush up, kid," he snapped.

Magnusson frowned at Frank. "What's he talking about? Just who are you, mister?"

Jeff ignored Linderman's warning glower and called, "He's Frank Morgan! He's nothin' but a nogood, murderin' gunfighter!"

So much for keeping quiet about who he really was, Frank thought bitterly. Now the leaders on both sides of the dispute in the valley knew his identity.

"Frank Morgan, eh?" Magnusson said. "I've been in the West long enough to hear plenty about you, Morgan, and none of it good. It's said you've killed more men than Billy the Kid, John Wesley Hardin, and Ben Thompson put together!"

Frank shook his head. "I don't keep count of things like that. I just do what I have to to stay alive."

"Well, you'll find that attacking my men was a mistake," Magnusson blustered. "I'm going to swear out a warrant for your arrest!" He flung out a hand again as he went on. "By God, I may not have been able to prove yet that the Montero ranch hands are responsible for all the deviltry going on in the valley, but I've got ten witnesses to testify against you, sir!"

"You mean ten witnesses to lie for you," Frank said.

Magnusson chewed his mustache in rage for a second before he said, "We'll just see about that!"

"Mr. Magnusson," Dolores Montero cut in coolly, "Mr. Morgan is my guest, and I'm not going to stand by and see him abused and insulted this way. If you don't have anything else to say, I'll thank you to leave."

"I'll leave when I'm good and ready!"

That wrathful answer was a mistake, especially directed at the mistress of this ranch. Linderman and the other members of the crew stepped forward, their faces set in angry lines, their hands close to their guns.

Magnusson was outnumbered, outgunned, and just flat out of luck if the cowboys attacked him. That prospect didn't seem to worry him, though. He stood his ground and continued glaring at Frank and Dolores.

After a moment, Dolores lifted a hand just enough to signal to Linderman and the others that they should stay back. They stopped their advance, but clearly didn't like being reined in. They wanted to give Magnusson a thrashing and then toss him off the ranch.

Frank could sympathize. Big, arrogant, blustery hombres like Magnusson always made him itch to throw a punch or two as well.

"You've overplayed your hand by hiring a gunfighter, Señora," Magnusson said after the strained silence had gone on for several seconds. "The law won't have any choice but to be on my side now."

"The law was already on your side," Dolores said. "The sheriff has done nothing about all the shots your drillers have taken at my men. He doesn't even try to track the cattle your men steal from my herds!"

Magnusson drew himself up straighter, and his beard seemed to bristle even more.

"My men are not thieves! How dare you—"

"I dare because this is *my* ranch!" Dolores shouted as she stepped forward and jabbed a finger into Magnusson's broad chest. "I dare because I give the orders here, and I'm ordering you now to get off Montero range, Magnusson! Get off, or I won't be responsible for what happens!"

They stared daggers at each other from a distance of a foot or less for a moment that seemed to stretch out longer. Finally, Magnusson growled, "All right, I'll go. But this isn't over yet, Señora. Not by a long shot!" He glanced at Frank as he started to turn away from Dolores. "You'd do well to remember that, Morgan!"

"I intend to remember everything that's happened here today, mister," Frank drawled. "And I've got a good memory for jackasses."

Magnusson's hands clenched into fists. Frank thought for a second that the wildcatter was going to take a swing at him, and he thought wearily that if that happened, he supposed he and Magnusson would have to go around and around, too.

Or maybe not, because Linderman and the other cowboys might actually pitch in to help him. Right now, it was probably a toss-up which of the two of them the Montero hands hated more, him or Magnusson.

Magnusson stalked back to his buggy, though, and climbed up into the vehicle, his movements stiff with anger. He jerked the reins loose from where he had tied them around the brake and slapped the lines against the backs of the team, then hauled hard to turn the horses as they started moving. With his back ramrod-straight, Magnusson drove away from the hacienda.

"Well," Dolores said a moment later as the breeze shredded the dust left behind by the buggy's departure, "I seem to have been wrong about you, Mr. Morgan. You're not working for Victor Magnusson after all."

Frank smiled. "Not unless he's putting on a mighty good act."

Dolores shook her head and said, "That man couldn't put on an act like that. That would require intelligence and subtlety, two things in which Victor Magnusson is sorely lacking!"

She glared after the buggy, which was dwindling in the distance, for a moment, then went on. "Don't take this to mean that anyone on this ranch has grown fond of you, Mr. Morgan. There's still the matter of what happened to Lonnie." She paused and shrugged. "But Jeff made it clear that Lonnie started the trouble. I'll make sure Pete and the rest of the men understand that you're not to be harmed while you're on Montero range . . . at least not by anyone who works here. I can't speak for interlopers such as Magnusson."

"I'll take my chances with him," Frank said.

"We all take our chances with life, don't we?" she mused. With a toss of her head, she turned toward the house. "Come along. Pilar should have lunch ready soon."

# Chapter 10

Frank and Dolores went back into the hacienda. She took his hat this time, since he was going to be staying for a while, and hung it on a set of antlers mounted on the wall near the door for that purpose.

The servant woman Pilar appeared, and told Dolores in Spanish that the meal was ready in the dining room. "This way," Dolores said to Frank.

She led him into a large, airy room dominated by a long, heavy hardwood table. Tall windows looked out on a garden courtyard built in the center of the hacienda. Water trickled from a fountain into a pool in the middle of the courtyard. The pool was surrounded by bright flowers, and ivy climbed sinuously up the walls surrounding the courtyard.

It was a beautiful setting, but it also had an air of barbarity and even decadence about it. The pool looked like it ought to have nymphs dancing naked in it, Frank thought. He had seen a few illustrations like *that* in books as well.

Pilar already had the food on the table: warm tortillas, beans, strips of roasted beef, chilies . . . There was nothing fancy about the fare, but it looked good to Frank.

Tasted good, too, he discovered as he and Dolores sat down and began to eat. Pilar appeared again and filled glasses with dark red wine.

Frank enjoyed the food and enjoyed the company as well, although Dolores was still a bit cool and reserved. She wasn't going to forget that he had killed one of her ranch hands, no matter what the circumstances had been.

"Tell me about the trouble you've been having," Frank prompted.

"Why? Not to be rude, but our problems are no business of yours, Mr. Morgan."

He shrugged. "Call me curious, I guess." He reserved judgment on whether or not to tell her about his connection with Stafford. He added with a smile, "And call me Frank, too."

"I think I prefer Mr. Morgan."

"As you will, Señora."

After a moment, she said, "Our troubles began even before my husband's death. Victor Magnusson and other wildcatters approached Francisco and attempted to make arrangements to drill for oil on our range. He refused, of course, telling them the same thing I told you—this is a rancho, not an oil field. And then he threw them out."

"I reckon Magnusson didn't want to take no for an answer. Probably didn't care much for being tossed out on his ear either."

Dolores shook her head. "He was furious. He said that he was only trying to be polite, that he could drill wherever he wanted because much of the land

that comprises Salida del Sol was granted to the
Montero family by the King of Spain. The legality of
those land grants as far as the American government is concerned is still a matter of some dispute."

"So Magnusson regards most of your ranch as
open range?"

"*Sí.* There is a smaller area here around the hacienda that Francisco filed on again, once California became part of the United States, but he saw no
need to file such claims on land the Montero family
had been using for generations."

Frank nodded. That sort of thinking had backfired
on many a cattle baron and helped to start more than
one range war across the West, he mused. Earlier
generations had felt like the land was theirs by right
of usage, and they didn't need any pieces of paper
from the government to back up those claims.

The government saw things differently, though,
and so did the opportunists who had swooped in to
put an effective end to the open-range era.

Victor Magnusson was a different sort of oppor-
tunist. He didn't want to run his own cattle or sheep
on Montero range. He wanted what was underneath
that land.

But maybe he was just as ruthless as the interlopers
had been in other places. Maybe when it came to getting what he wanted, he was willing to do whatever it
took.

"Not long after that, Francisco died," Dolores
went on.

"If you don't mind talking about it, what happened
to him?" Frank asked. "Was he sick?"

She shook her head. "No, despite his age, he was

still a vital, healthy man. But he was thrown from his horse and struck his head on a rock. Pete found him shortly after it happened, but there was nothing anyone could do."

A frown creased Frank's forehead. "You're sure it was an accident?"

"You think someone might have killed him?"

"He'd already had a run-in with Magnusson. I saw for myself what that hombre's like when he's got a burr under his saddle."

Dolores smiled sadly and shook her head. "In my grief over Francisco's death, I would have gladly blamed Magnusson. But Francisco lived for a short time after Pete brought him back here, and he told me himself how the buzz of a rattlesnake in the brush had frightened his horse. Francisco was an excellent rider, but even he could be taken by surprise. When the horse leaped away from the snake, he was thrown off."

"That's a real shame. You have my sympathy and my condolences, Señora."

"Some time has passed," Dolores said. "The pain is not as great as it once was. But I still miss Francisco, and I will every day for the rest of my life."

Frank nodded. He had lost loved ones, too, and not a day passed that he didn't think about them. So he knew how Dolores felt.

She took a deep breath and resumed the story. "As I said, things had begun to happen even before Francisco's death. Magnusson moved one of his drilling machines onto Montero range, in one of the canyons northwest of here. When Pete and some of the men rode over there to tell him to get out, they were confronted by guards with rifles. That could have been a very bad day, a bloody day. Pete was cool-headed enough, though, to keep our men from going for their guns. Not long after that, our cattle began to disappear, and shots were taken at my men as they went about their business on the ranch."

"Anybody been killed?" Frank already knew from Stafford that wasn't the case, but he wanted to hear all of it from Dolores, too.

"No, Dios be praised. Several men have suffered wounds, though. It cannot be tolerated."

"Has anybody tried to track the bushwhackers?"

"Of course. But they retreat into the foothills, where the canyons are rugged and a trail is easily lost."

"And Magnusson keeps moving in more and more drilling rigs."

Frank saw the sudden weariness in her eyes as she nodded. He could tell that she was getting tired of fighting.

"Yes, he encroaches more and more on our land. I have complained to the sheriff, but he says that until the matter of ownership is settled in the courts, there is nothing he can do."

There might be some validity to that stance, Frank thought, but he would have been willing to bet that Magnusson and the other wildcatters had something to do with the sheriff's decision not to get involved, too. He made a mental note to ask John J. Stafford how the court cases involving Spanish land grants were coming along. Frank had always stayed away from lawyers and legal matters as much as he could, but he knew how these things could stretch out interminably.

And while that was going on, Magnusson was sinking his claws deeper and deeper into Montero range.

Frank took a sip of wine, then said, "I appreciate you indulging my curiosity this way, Señora."

"You are a guest in my home," Dolores said, as if that explained everything. And to an extent, it did, Frank thought.

"I hope you won't think me rude if I ask you to tell me more about your husband."

A smile curved her full red lips. "You mean how a woman such as myself wound up married to a man more than thirty years older? Such things are common, you know. A rich old man, a young woman . . ."

"I meant no offense, Señora, I assure you."

"And I take no offense, Mr. Morgan. You know nothing of us here in the valley. My family and Francisco's family have been friends for many years. For generations."

Frank nodded, knowing that the old California families had a tendency to intermarry.

"My name was Dolores Sandoval."

"Related to Jorge Sandoval?"

"You know the name then?"

"I've heard it," Frank said with a shrug, not mentioning that it had been Stafford who told him about Jorge Sandoval.

"Jorge is my brother."

"He owns a ranch here in the valley, too, doesn't he?"

"That's right. And he believed that once Francisco was gone, Salida del Sol would belong to the

Sandovals as well." Dolores took a sip of her wine. "He was wrong."

"You didn't want to merge the ranches?"

"Why would I wish to do that? Salida del Sol is the largest, most prosperous ranch in the valley."

"It would be even bigger if it was joined with your brother's ranch," Frank pointed out.

"I could not do that to Francisco," she said with a shake of her head. "This is Montero range. It will always be Montero range."

"Even though Don Francisco is the last of the Monteros?"

She set her wine glass down and gave Frank a cool stare. "A guest has responsibilities, too. One of them is not to pry too deeply in his host's affairs."

"My apologies, Señora," Frank said. "But when you married Don Francisco, surely your brother had in mind—"

"You think my brother *sold* me to Francisco in exchange for Salida del Sol?" she asked with a flare of anger. "That would make me no better than a common whore!"

"I've insulted you. That was not my intention. You have my sincere apologies—"

"I care nothing for your apologies, Señor Morgan. Your opinion is meaningless to me. And I know nothing of any arrangements made between my brother and Francisco. All I know is that this is Montero range, and I am a Montero, and I intend to fight for it until my dying breath!"

With her full breasts rising and falling and her eyes bright with anger, Frank thought she was lovelier than ever. Of course, he had no business thinking such things, he reminded himself. He was considerably older than her, too, although the gap between them was only about half of what it had been between Dolores and Francisco Montero.

Given everything he had learned today, and the fact that Dolores was already aware of his name and reputation, Frank didn't think there was any point in withholding the rest of the truth from her any longer. He said, "I'd like to help you fight for this range, Señora Montero."

"I have no need of a hired gunfighter!"

Frank sighed. "I keep telling folks I don't hire out my gun, but for some reason they don't want to believe me." He leaned forward in his chair. "I'm offering to help as a friend."

"A friend? I never met you until today."

"No, but I'm friends with a man named Claudius Turnbuckle," Frank said.

"Turnbuckle?" Understanding began to dawn on Dolores's face as she repeated the name. "He is a lawyer?"

"That's right. He's John J. Stafford's partner. And I'm a client of Turnbuckle and Stafford, just like you."

"But you are . . ." She let her voice trail away, hospitality making it difficult for her to finish what she had started to say.

Frank finished it for her. "A gunslinger and a saddle tramp?" he said. "Appearances can be deceiving, Señora. The important thing is, I'm here, and I'd like to help you put a stop to your troubles."

"You came here to California to help me?"

"That's right."

"And yet you begin by killing one of my men. Shooting him down like a dog."

"Not hardly," Frank said. "He had a gun in his hand and he was shooting at me. Like I told you—"

This time she finished his sentence. "I know, you had no choice. And I think perhaps I believe you, Mr. Morgan. I know how rash and reckless Lonnie could be, how quick to anger. His friends know that, too, but they may not be able to forgive you anyway." She shook her head. "I cannot hire you."

"I'm not looking for wages."

"I cannot even make a pretense of it. The men would never accept it. And there is enough trouble on Salida del Sol these days."

Frank thought it over and finally nodded. "All right. But can you use your influence to get all the ranchers in the valley together? I understand that Stafford represents most if not all of them."

"Why do you desire such a meeting?"

"I'd like to talk to all of them, find out just what's been happening on their ranches." Frank rasped a thumbnail along his jaw. "I'm starting to get an idea of what's going on around here, but I'd like to get all the information I can."

"If you truly want to help, I can tell you what you need to know. Victor Magnusson is to blame for the trouble. The other wildcatters may be involved in it with him, but he is the ringleader."

"You're probably right," Frank said, "but I'd still like to talk to the other ranchers."

"Very well. I will send word to them. Where should this meeting be held?"

"How about here? Looks like you've got a nice big barn out there that would hold plenty of people."

She considered the suggestion for a moment and then shrugged. "'Sta bueno. When?"

"The sooner the better. Tonight?"

"I will see what I can do. Where can I get in touch with you if I'm not able to arrange the meeting?"

"I'm staying at the Nadeau Hotel in Los Angeles. So is Stafford. You should be able to find one of us there."

"Very well. We have, as you Americans say, a deal."

"Shake on it?" Frank suggested with a smile.

"I don't think so," she replied coolly. "I'm still not sure I fully trust you, Mr. Morgan."

"Maybe we can do something about that, too," Frank said.

# Chapter 11

Since he'd had a good meal and had made some progress of a sort with Dolores Montero, Frank didn't see any reason not to head back to town until it was time to return to Salida del Sol for the meeting with the other ranchers that evening. Assuming, of course, that Dolores was able to set it up on such short notice.

He thanked her for her hospitality and left the hacienda, heading out to the barn to pick up Stormy and Dog.

Pete Linderman was the only one inside the cavernous structure when Frank entered. He sat on a keg, whittling. He glanced up at Frank, and gave The Drifter a curt nod as he folded the knife and put it away.

"Morgan. Enjoy your dinner with the señora?"

Frank suddenly wondered if Linderman was interested in Dolores Montero. Women who had inherited ranches had been known to wind up marrying their foremen. Dolores had probably leaned on Linderman a great deal in the days following her husband's death. Likely, she still did.

If not for the fact that Don Francisco had lived long enough to tell his wife what had happened, Frank might have suspected that Linderman had had something to do with the ranchero's death.

"It was a fine meal," Frank replied. "Pleasant company, too."

"Better than you have any right to expect, considerin' what you did." Linderman stood up. "I sent Jeff out onto the range with some of the other men and told them to keep an eye on him, not let him double back toward the ranch. Are you leavin'?"

Frank nodded. "Heading back to Los Angeles."

"Probably be a good idea if you stayed there, or anywhere else except here."

"Well, now," Frank said, "that's going to be a problem, because I'm riding back out here this evening."

Linderman stared at him for a long moment without speaking. Then the foreman exploded, "Son of a bitch!"

Frank's face hardened and his hands wanted to clench into fists.

"I don't take kindly to be called that, Linderman," he said.

Linderman shook his head. "I'm not calling you that, Morgan. I'm just surprised, that's all. I wondered if she might try to hire you. I reckon she did."

"Señora Montero, you mean?"

"Who else?" Linderman looked like he had a bad taste in his mouth. "I don't blame her for gettin' a little desperate. If we keep on havin' problems with Magnusson and his bunch, it might get bad enough so she has trouble hangin' on to the ranch. This place means the world to her. But to hire a gunslingin' killer . . ." Linderman shook his head. "It don't set right with me."

"It doesn't set right with me for folks to think they know the truth about me when they don't," Frank snapped. "For what it's worth—and I don't owe you any explanations, Linderman—Señora Montero didn't hire me. Didn't even try to."

Linderman looked a little relieved.

"But that doesn't mean I'm through with Salida del Sol," Frank went on. "I offered to help her with her problems, and she accepted."

Linderman's eyes widened with surprise. "What! I thought you said—"

"She didn't hire me," Frank cut in. "Not unless you count a good meal as the only pay I'll get. Seems to me like she's in a bad fix here, and I'd like to help out."

"Out of the goodness of your heart?" Linderman's tone made it clear how unlikely he believed that to be.

"Because I don't like to see a woman being taken advantage of. And to tell you the truth, because I didn't much cotton to Victor Magnusson."

Linderman grunted in agreement. "Yeah, he rubs me the wrong way, too." He studied Frank for a moment. "So now we've got a gunfighter on our side."

"I'm going to poke around and see what I can find out about your troubles." Frank didn't mention his connection with Stafford. If Dolores wanted her men to know about that, she could tell them.

"You won't have to poke very much. Magnusson's to blame for all of it, him and those other wildcatters. But mostly Magnusson."

"If I can get proof of that, the sheriff will have to act."

Linderman gave a disgusted snort. "The sheriff's in Magnusson's hip pocket. Those oilmen are bringin' a lot of money into this area. The authorities aren't gonna go against 'em."

"With enough proof, they won't have any choice."

Linderman looked like he would believe that when he saw it with his own eyes, and not before.

Frank went on. "It would sure make things easier if I could count on you and the rest of the crew not to interfere with what I'm doing, Linderman."

The foreman shook his head. "I make no promises except this one, Morgan—I'll steer clear of you, and I'll tell the rest of the boys to steer clear of you. But I can't guarantee that they'll listen to me, especially Jeff. He and Lonnie were pards for a long time, ever since they were kids."

"Then he ought to know how Lonnie was."

"Knowin' and carin' are two different things," Linderman said with a shrug. "Like I said, I'll do what I can . . . but you'd better keep an eye on your back trail, Morgan."

"I always do," Frank said.


He rode out a few minutes later, after explaining to Linderman about the meeting that would be held there at Salida del Sol that evening. The foreman was still unfriendly, but he promised that he would see to it the other ranchers in the valley got the word.

As he rode back through the valley, Frank became aware of the unnatural smells and noises that filled the air. A constant scent of brimstone lingered, and the clanking and clattering and rumble of engines sounded, instead of the lowing of cattle and the songs of birds and the rustling of small animals in the brush.

Dog looked up at Frank and whined softly as he padded along. "I know, Dog," Frank told the big cur. "Things sure as hell aren't like they used to be around here. This was a mighty pretty place ten years ago, and before that, too, of course." He shook his head. "But once things change, they hardly ever go back to the way they used to be. You can mourn the past, but you can't change it."

Dog just whined again.

"I know," Frank said with a laugh. "You didn't ask for any homespun philosophy, did you?"

Things were even worse on the other side of the Santa Monicas, because there were more drilling rigs in Los Angeles proper. Seemed like everybody's front yard or backyard had one of the tall wooden derricks in it. They were about to crowd out the homes and businesses on some streets. The racket was hellish, and so was the smell.

"How do you stand it?" he asked the hostler when he reached the livery stable behind the hotel and began unsaddling Stormy.

"The smell, you mean?"

"That and the noise."

"That's the smell o' money, mister," the man said. "And the noise might as well be coins bein' minted."

Frank put his saddle on a stand and shook his head. "Folks are willing to put up with a whole lot just for money."

"Story o' the world, ain't it?"

"I reckon." Frank told Dog to stay and then headed for the hotel.

The same clerk was on duty behind the desk who had been there the previous afternoon, but this time when Frank asked him if Mr. Stafford was in, the man responded politely and a little nervously, "Yes, sir, Mr. Morgan. I believe I saw him go into the bar a short time ago, sir."

"Thanks," Frank said with a nod.

"Anything else I can do for you, Mr. Morgan?"

"No, I don't reckon there is." Obviously, someone had filled the clerk in on Frank's reputation. He was probably worried that a gunfight would break out right there in the lobby.

It might liven things up a mite at that, Frank thought with a wry smile as he walked into the barroom.

He spotted John J. Stafford sitting at a table in the corner and started in that direction. Stafford saw him at the same time and lifted a hand in greeting. The lawyer had a glass in front of him full of what appeared to be the same stuff he had been drinking the day before. It was a little early in the day for cognac, Frank thought, but to each his own.

"Are you about to ride out to the Montero ranch?" Stafford asked as Frank pulled back a chair and sat down at the table.

Frank shook his head. "Nope. Already been there."

"Already? You must have started very early."

"I've never been one for burning daylight," Frank said. "Everything you told me was right. The ranchers out in the valley seem to be in a bad way, with those oil wells crowding in all around them."

Stafford leaned closer to him and frowned in the somewhat dim light of the barroom. "Is that a *bruise* I see on your face?"

Frank chuckled. "I wouldn't be surprised. I had a little run-in with some of Victor Magnusson's drillers. A while later, I met the man himself. It wasn't a very friendly meeting."

"My God, what happened? Were you injured?"

"Nothing to speak of, just a few bumps and bruises, like the one you noticed. I got in a ruckus with a fella named Hatch."

"Good Lord! Hatch is a monster! And you fought him with your fists? Why didn't you just—"

"Shoot him?" Frank finished when Stafford's question came to an abrupt halt. "As far as I could see, he was unarmed. Gunning him down would have been murder."

Stafford took a handkerchief from his pocket and mopped his forehead where beads of sweat had broken out. "I meant no offense, Mr. Morgan," he said. "It's just that Hatch is considerably larger than you, and he's beaten men within an inch of their lives on several occasions."

"I was able to whittle him down to size," Frank said.

"And what about Magnusson? You said that you met him, too?"

"He came out to Salida del Sol while I was there. He was looking for me, in fact. He'd heard about my ruckus with Hatch and figured that I worked for Señora Montero. She set him straight on that."

"You weren't able to get a job on the Montero ranch, as you planned?"

Frank shook his head. "That idea sort of blew up in my face. They found out who I am." He explained about Lonnie and Jeff and everything that had happened the day before. He concluded, "I think Señora Montero was sort of intrigued by the idea of hiring a fast gun to deal with Magnusson, but in the end she wouldn't do it . . . not that I would have hired on to kill him anyway." Frank paused. "By the way, you didn't tell me that the señora was so much younger than her late husband."

"Nor that she was so attractive," Stafford said with a smirk on his face. "She's a lovely woman."

"And *you're* old enough to be her father, too," Frank pointed out.

"Yes, ah, ah, of course," the lawyer said. "I didn't mean to imply—"

"Never mind," Frank said. "Señora Montero's looks don't have anything to do with her problems. I persuaded her to let me help her anyway, even though she didn't hire me. I told her about my connection with you."

Stafford nodded. "Good, good. Might as well put our cards on the table, I suppose, since your original idea didn't work out. What are you going to do now?"

"First thing is to have a meeting with all the other ranchers," Frank said. "They're going to be at Salida del Sol this evening, unless the señora lets me know different. I want to talk to all of them and get a better sense of everything that's going on in the valley."

"That sounds like a fine idea. Should I attend this meeting with you?"

Frank nodded. "That probably wouldn't hurt. You represent most of them, don't you?"

"All of them except Edwin Northam."

"They might be more inclined to trust me if their own attorney is there vouching for me. Can you be ready to go in a couple of hours?"

"Of course."

Frank nodded and pushed himself to his feet. "Your buggy's in the stable behind the hotel?"

"That's right."

"I'll see you over there then in two hours."

"What are you going to do in the meantime?"

Frank glanced down at his oil-stained jeans. "Figured I'd clean up a mite and see if there's a laundry around here that can get these stains out. I got them wrestling around with Hatch."

Stafford shook his head and said, "I still can't believe you were able to defeat that brute in hand-to-hand combat."

Frank rubbed his jaw. "Well, it's not a waltz I'd care to repeat any time soon," he said.

# Chapter 12

Stafford was waiting at the livery stable when Frank got there a couple of hours later. He was wearing clean trousers, and had left the oil-stained jeans at a laundry down the street, where the pigtailed proprietor had promised that he could get the stains out.

The lawyer was already sitting in his buggy, ready to go. Dog sat a few yards away with his tongue lolling out, and Stafford eyed the big cur warily.

"The hostler tells me that animal belongs to you," he said to Frank. "Is that true?"

"He and I are old trail pards, all right," Frank replied with a smile and a nod.

"Is he safe? Does he bite?"

"Only folks who need bitin'."

Stafford swallowed hard. "Well, I'd appreciate it if you'd keep him away from me. I don't like dogs."

That put a frown on Frank's face. He had a tendency not to trust people who didn't like dogs. On the other hand, he knew that Dog *did* look a lot like a wolf, and those sharp fangs of his could be frightening when he bared them in a snarl.

"He won't bother you," Frank told Stafford. "I'll see to that."

"Thank you." The lawyer paused. "Are you ready to go?"

"Soon as I saddle up."

Frank put his saddle on Goldy this time, since he had ridden Stormy out to the Montero ranch that morning. When he had agreed to take Goldy after the stallion's former owner had died trying to gun down Frank, he hadn't been sure about having two horses.

But being able to swap them had worked well so far, and kept both mounts from getting too played out. That meant it would be longer before Frank had to make the painful decision to put Stormy out to pasture.

Some people might say that *he* was getting old enough to be put out to pasture, Frank thought with a wry grin to himself as he tightened the cinches around Goldy's middle.

That likely wouldn't ever happen, he told himself as his expression grew more solemn. When the time came for him to be put out to pasture, it would be with a bullet or two—or half a dozen—in his carcass.

He rode out a short time later with Stafford rolling alongside him in the buggy. Goldy wanted to run, but Frank held him in so that they wouldn't outdistance the vehicle. The stallion didn't like it, but he cooperated.

As usual, Dog bounded on ahead, ran off to the sides of the trail, circled around, and generally had a fine old time flushing birds and small animals from the brush.

The small group made it through the pass over the Santa Monicas by dusk, and started down into the San Fernando Valley as night began to settle over the landscape. Frank knew they wouldn't have any trouble following the road even after it got dark.

Dots of yellow light were scattered through the canyons and across the broad floor of the valley like stars tumbled from heaven. They marked the locations of the oil rigs, Frank realized. Even with night falling, the drilling continued. It probably went on twenty-four hours a day, he thought.

Hundreds of feet below the earth, where the metal drill bits gouged deeper and deeper through dirt and rock, night and day had no meaning.

They were about a mile away from Salida del Sol, Frank estimated, when orange flame suddenly spurted from some rocks to the right of the road. At the same instant, a shot crashed out. Frank felt the hot wind of a bullet fanning his cheek.

The Colt on his hip seemed to spring into his hand of its own volition. As he leveled the gun on the spot where he'd seen the muzzle flash, he shouted at Stafford, "Go on, get out of here!"

Then the revolver in Frank's hand roared twice. He didn't think he would hit the bushwhacker unless it was by a stroke of luck, but he hoped to come close enough with the shots to make the varmint duck.

Stafford slashed at his team with the reins and sent the two horses lunging ahead. The buggy careened down the road after them.

Frank sent Goldy lunging around the rocks and called, "Dog! Hunt!"

The big cur was a gray streak in the gathering

gloom. He disappeared among the rocks as Frank circled them in an attempt to get behind the bush-whacker.

He had recognized the sound of the first shot as the whipcrack of a Winchester. A rifle wasn't the best weapon for close work, as the man would find out if Dog cornered him.

That seemed to be what was happening. Frank heard two more shots and then a man screamed. He pulled Goldy to a halt and swung down from the saddle before the stallion stopped moving. Gun in hand, Frank charged into the cluster of boulders, following the screams and Dog's ferocious snarls.

Dog let out an abrupt yelp of pain. Concern for his old friend surged through Frank. He didn't have long to worry, though, because the next second a dark shape loomed up in front of him. The faint red glow left in the western sky by the sunset glinted off the barrel of a Winchester as it swung toward him.

Both weapons roared at the same instant. Frank heard the wind-rip of a slug's passage beside his ear, then the high-pitched whine as it ricocheted off one of the boulders behind him.

The bushwhacker went over backward, driven off his feet by the impact of Frank's bullet. The rifle clattered among the rocks as it slipped out of the man's hands.

Frank hurried forward, intent on making sure the wounded man didn't try to pull a six-gun, but before he could reach the fallen bushwhacker, Dog appeared again, leaping at the man with fangs slash-ing and snapping. Frank was glad to see that the big cur was still alive, but he called him off anyway.

"Dog! Back!"

Dog backed away from the bushwhacker, who gurgled once and then lay still and silent. Even in the dim light, Frank could see the dark stain that had flooded down below the man's throat. He grimaced. Dog had finished off the bushwhacker, tearing out his throat.

Just to make sure, though, Frank fished a match out of his shirt pocket with his left hand while he kept the Colt ready in his right. He snapped the lucifer to life with his thumbnail, fully expecting that the yellow glow from the match would wash over the face of Jeff, the young cowboy from the Montero ranch.

Instead, the harsh glare revealed the hard, unshaven features of a man Frank had never seen before.

A frown creased Frank's forehead as he leaned closer and studied the bushwhacker's face. The varmint was dead, all right, no doubt about that. If Dog hadn't killed him, Frank's bullet would have, because there was a neat, black-rimmed hole in the man's breast pocket, right beside the hanging tag from his tobacco pouch. Frank had drilled him through the heart.

Straightening, Frank shook out the match and dropped it. He muttered to himself in disgust as he went over to Dog. If the dead man had turned out to be Jeff, Frank would have understood.

He wouldn't have liked it, because if he had killed Jeff as well as Lonnie, then there was no way anyone on Salida del Sol would ever trust him or cooperate with him. But he would have understood the motive behind the ambush.

Also, it made sense that Jeff could have found out

Frank was returning to the ranch this evening and lain in wait for him in these boulders beside the road. It was a spot ready-made for a bushwhack killing.

But the fact that a stranger had tried to gun him down made for a puzzle in Frank's mind—and he didn't like puzzles.

Kneeling next to Dog, Frank holstered his gun and ran his hands over the big cur, searching for wounds. All he found was a sticky lump on Dog's head, between the ears.

"Walloped you with that rifle butt, didn't he, old fella?" Frank asked. "He couldn't dent that thick skull of yours, but he knocked you silly for a minute. Then he practically ran right into me while he was trying to get away." Frank sighed. "And we can't even ask him who he was or why he tried to ventilate me."

Satisfied that Dog was all right, Frank stood up and went back to the body. It was possible the man was a member of Dolores Montero's crew that Frank hadn't seen on his earlier visit to the ranch, but the man didn't really look like a cowboy, he decided as he struck another match and took a look at the man's clothes.

The jeans and work shirt could have belonged to a ranch hand, but the lace-up boots on the man's feet looked like those of an oil driller. A battered Stetson lay on the ground next to him, though, where it had landed when the man fell.

Frank hadn't seen that many drillers in his life, but none of them had ever worn a hat like that, he thought. Having never seen the fella before and being unable to draw any firm conclusions from his clothes, Frank decided that the best thing to do would be to take the corpse to the meeting with him and see if anyone there recognized him.

That could open up a can of worms if the man worked for one of the other ranchers in the valley . . .

But if that was the case, why had the man tried to kill him? Frank hadn't even met any of the other ranchers yet.

He fetched his rope from his saddle, looped the lariat under the dead man's arms, and tied it to the saddle horn. Goldy backed away at Frank's command and dragged the man out of the rocks.

He was about to leave the corpse there for the moment and go see where Stafford had gotten off to, when he heard the clip-clop of hoofbeats and looked along the road to see the buggy rolling toward him.

"Mr. Morgan!" Stafford called. "Are you all right?"

"Fine," Frank said as the lawyer drove up and brought the team to a halt. "What are you doing back here?"

"Well, I . . . I heard all those shots, and I didn't know whether or not you'd been hurt, so I thought I should come back and find out."

Frank thumbed his hat back. "For all you knew, I was dead and that bushwhacker was waiting for you."

"Yes, I realize that, but we're working together. I couldn't just desert you." Stafford reached to the seat beside him. "I have a pistol. I'm not very good with it, mind you, but I would have tried to help you."

"I appreciate that, Counselor," Frank said with a nod. "There's one thing you can do for me."

"Of course. Whatever you need."

"I hope you don't mind sharing that buggy with a dead man," Frank said.

# Chapter 13

Frank got the feeling that Stafford minded, all right, but the lawyer didn't make any complaints as Frank dragged the corpse over to the buggy and hefted it into the space behind the seat. They set off toward the headquarters of the Montero ranch once again, but they hadn't gone very far when Frank heard the rumble of hoofbeats from a number of horses.

"Hold on," he told Stafford as he raised a hand in a signal for the lawyer to bring the buggy to a halt. He pulled his own Winchester from its saddle boot and levered a round into the chamber as he waited to see who the riders were and what they wanted.

The horsemen came into view, a dark mass in the shadows at first that resolved itself into individual riders as they galloped closer. Frank estimated their number at a dozen.

If they intended to kill him and Stafford, Frank would put up a fight, but he knew those odds would be overwhelming. In a nervous voice, Stafford asked from the buggy, "What do we do, Mr. Morgan?"

"Just sit steady, Counselor," Frank told him. "And it might be a good idea to keep your hand on that gun of yours until we find out who those hombres are. Don't start shooting, though, unless I give the word."

Frank heard Stafford swallow hard. "All right. But I wish I was back in a courtroom right now. I don't like all these guns in the night."

Neither did Frank, but he knew a fella had to play the hand he was dealt. The last cards in this one would be falling soon.

The riders reined their mounts in when they were about twenty yards from Frank and Stafford. They were well within range of Frank's rifle, but he wasn't going to start shooting until he knew who they were.

"Morgan?" a familiar voice called. "Is that you?"

Frank recognized the voice as Pete Linderman's. "It's me," he answered.

"Who's that with you in the buggy?"

"Mr. Stafford, Señora Montero's lawyer."

"Hello, Mr. Linderman," Stafford said with a tone of relief in his voice.

The foreman walked his mount closer while the other men stayed where they were. "We heard some shots," Linderman explained, "and the señora sent us to find out what was going on. She knew you were comin' back out here this evenin', Morgan, and she was afraid you had run into some trouble."

"We did, for a fact," Frank said. "Some varmint opened up on us from some big rocks back down the road a quarter of a mile or so."

Linderman had ridden close enough now so that Frank could see him nod. "Yeah, I know the place. Did you run the fella off?"

"Nope." Frank jerked the thumb of his left hand toward the buggy. "He's behind the seat there."

Linderman stiffened in the saddle. "Dead?"

"That's right. Come take a look at him. I'd like to know if you've ever seen him before."

Without hesitation, Linderman prodded his horse closer to the vehicle. Frank expected him to deny knowing the bushwhacker. Linderman would say that he had never seen the man before whether that was true . . . or whether he'd had something to do with the ambush.

Linderman struck a match and leaned over in his saddle to get a better look at the dead man. After a moment, he shook his head, just as Frank knew he would.

"No, I don't know him. He didn't ride for the señora, I can tell you that for damn sure. I don't recall ever seeing him around any of the other spreads in the valley either."

"All right," Frank said as Linderman shook out the match. "Maybe somebody else on your crew knows him."

Linderman grunted. "I wouldn't count on it. They can take a look when we get back to the hacienda. The señora's waitin' for you."

Stafford hitched his team into motion. Frank and Linderman fell in alongside the buggy after Linderman ordered the rest of the riders to return to the ranch.

"What about the other cattlemen who have spreads in the valley?" Frank asked. "Have they shown up for the meeting yet?"

"Some of them. Dave Guthrie and Ben Patterson

are there, and we passed Augusto Lopez as we rode out to check on those shots. Edwin Northam and Jorge Sandoval weren't there yet, but they both sent riders with word that they'd attend this meeting of yours, Morgan."

Frank nodded. "That'll account for all the big ranchers in the area, right?"

"Yeah. There are a few small spreads, but they don't amount to much. What we used to call greasy-sack outfits back in Texas."

"You're from Texas?" Frank asked. He had been born and raised in the Lone Star State.

"No, but I cowboyed there for a while, when I was a youngster. Never liked it much."

Frank let that go. He had more important things to do than get in an argument about the merits of his home state.

The rest of the men galloped on ahead to let Dolores Montero know that Frank and Stafford were all right. Frank and Linderman rode at a slower pace so as not to get ahead of the lawyer's buggy.

Even so, it didn't take them long to reach the ranch headquarters. The place was brightly lit. A number of lamps and lanterns were burning, including inside the barn where the gathering would take place.

Dolores hurried forward into the yard to meet them. She wasn't wearing the trousers and shirt and vest she had sported earlier in the day. She looked much more feminine now in a pale blue dress with a full skirt. The garment was cut low enough that just a hint of the valley between her breasts was visible.

Her lovely face was set in lines of concern. "Mr.

Morgan," she said. "And Mr. Stafford. You are both all right?"

"We're fine, Señora," Stafford assured her, "thanks to Mr. Morgan here."

"Somebody tried to bushwhack 'em on the way out here," Linderman said.

"Did the man get away?"

"No, he's in the back there, behind the seat," Linderman said with a nod toward the buggy. "You'd better not look at him, Señora. He ain't a pretty sight."

Dolores's chin came up defiantly in what was obviously an instinctive reaction at being told what to do, Frank thought. She stepped forward, saying, "Of course I'll look at him. I might recognize him." She turned her head and called for someone to bring a lantern.

One of the hands hustled forward with a light. He held it where Dolores could see the dead man's face, which was relatively unmarked despite the bloody mess Dog had made of his throat. Dolores stared at him, paling slightly, and murmured, "*Dios mio*. What happened to him?" She turned her head to look at Frank. "Your dog did this?"

"That's right," Frank said. "The varmint was already dying, though."

"Yes, I see the bullet hole in his shirt," Dolores said. She took a deep breath to steady herself, then went on. "I've never seen this man before. He doesn't work for me, if that's what you're thinking."

Frank believed her. She had no reason to lie to him. She had called a truce with him earlier in the day. Whether or not her crew would honor that truce was another matter, but Frank's gut told him that they would, with the possible exception of Jeff.

And so far this evening, Frank hadn't seen any sign of the young cowboy. He hadn't been among the group that had accompanied Linderman to check out the shooting, and he wasn't outside the bunkhouse or the barn.

"The rest of my men should look at him just to be sure," Dolores went on. "Mr. Morgan, Mr. Stafford, why don't we go on into the barn?"

"I'll see that your horses are tended to," Linderman offered.

Frank nodded, dismounted, and handed over Goldy's reins. "Maybe I'd better take Dog with me," he said.

"Probably a good idea," Linderman agreed. "After seein' what he did to that fella's throat, I don't reckon any of us would feel too comfortable havin' him around."

With the big cur padding at his side, Frank went into the barn with Dolores and Stafford. The large open area in the center of the cavernous building had been cleaned and swept, and a couple of bales of hay had been placed at the front of it.

"I thought you might want to have a place to stand while you're talking to everyone," Dolores said as she gestured with a slender, elegant hand toward the hay bales.

Frank wasn't real comfortable with the idea of being up there above everyone like a politician making a speech. He hadn't come here tonight to speechify. He just wanted information from the other ranchers, as well as a chance to size them up.

Three men stood talking near the hay bales, and a number of cowboys lounged around the outer walls of the barn. Frank pegged them as hands who had ridden over to Salida del Sol with the ranchers they worked for. That trio up front had to be the owners of the other spreads. Two were white, and the other was Mexican. All three were middle-aged and had the solid look of successful cattlemen.

They all wore worried frowns, though, as they talked to each other in low voices. The conversation came to an end as Frank walked up with Dolores and Stafford.

"This is Frank Morgan," Dolores said. She introduced him to Ben Patterson, Dave Guthrie, and Augusto Lopez. Frank shook hands with all three men. Guthrie hesitated a little before he took Frank's hand.

"I've heard about you, Morgan," he said. "If half of what I've heard is true, you probably don't even remember how many men you've killed."

Frank had encountered so many unfriendly receptions in his life that such thinly veiled hostility didn't really bother him anymore. He said, "I never shot anybody who wasn't trying to either kill me or hurt some innocent person, Guthrie. I'm not the enemy here. I came out to see what I can do to help you fellas."

Guthrie looked at Stafford. "You vouch for this gunfighter, Counselor?"

"I do," Stafford said without hesitation. "And so does my partner, Claudius Turnbuckle. I know you haven't met him, but I assure you, he's an excellent judge of character. If he says Mr. Morgan is all right, you can count on that."

Guthrie nodded. "All right. I'll give you the benefit of the doubt, Morgan. But I don't mind tellin' you, I'm not very fond of the idea of a gunslinger being here in the valley."

"Better he's on our side than working for Magnusson, Dave," Dolores pointed out. Guthrie shrugged in agreement.

Frank heard the sound of more horses coming up outside. A moment later, Linderman came into the barn, accompanied by a tall, handsome man in an expensive Spanish-cut suit. The newcomer's swarthy skin and raven-black hair, as well as his suit, testified to his Spanish heritage. He looked familiar, too, but Frank realized after a second that was because of his resemblance to Dolores.

Frank knew he was looking at Dolores's brother, Jorge Sandoval.

# Chapter 14

Smiling, Dolores went to Sandoval and hugged him. Frank couldn't tell which of them was older. They appeared to be about the same age, with probably not more than a year or so difference between them.

With her hand on her brother's arm, Dolores brought him over and introduced him to Frank. Sandoval gave Frank a cool nod as they shook hands.

"I have heard a great deal about you, Señor Morgan," he said. "You have quite a reputation. I won't ask you whether or not it was fairly earned."

"I appreciate that," Frank said as he returned the nod. "I get a mite tired of having to explain things to folks."

Sandoval turned back to his sister. "I'm not sure of the purpose of this meeting, but are we ready to begin?" he asked.

"Not quite," Dolores said. "Edwin Northam isn't here yet."

Sandoval grunted. "Why should we wait for him? He wants nothing to do with us."

"Perhaps not, but he has had trouble with Magnusson and the other oil drillers, just as we have. And Mr. Morgan wanted to speak with all the big ranchers in the valley."

Sandoval's words were the first hint Frank had had of possible friction between the Englishman Northam and the owners of the other spreads. He would have to keep that in mind, he told himself.

A scowl appeared on Sandoval's face. "I don't have the time to waste waiting around for Northam." He gave Frank a direct stare. "If you have something to say, Morgan, go ahead and say it."

Linderman spoke up before Frank could reply. "Hold on a minute," the foreman said as he held up a hand. "I think I hear more horses coming."

Sure enough, more hoofbeats rattled into the ranch yard, accompanied by the creak of wagon wheels. Frank and Linderman moved to the massive double doors that stood open and looked out.

A large wagon surrounded by riders was coming to a stop in front of the barn. Like all the other cowboys on the Montero ranch tonight, these newcomers were well armed, and from their hard-set expressions, they were ready for trouble.

Two men were on the wagon seat, both wearing dark suits and hats. The resemblance ended there, however. The one holding the reins was short and slender, with a face like a terrier and a short, bristly, grayish-brown mustache.

His companion probably weighed four times as much and loomed like a mountain over the driver. His face was as round and pale as a full moon, his thick lips as pouty as a baby's. Pudgy hands with short, sausagelike fingers rested on his knees.

The smaller man looped the reins around the brake lever and hopped down agilely from the wagon. He reached into the back and lifted out a set of two steps that had been hammered together out of thick planks. Despite his size, he had to be strong to handle the steps so easily.

He placed the steps next to the wagon so that his massive companion could use them, then stepped back and stood at attention. The big man heaved himself off the seat; then, using wrought-iron bars bolted to the wagon frame to support himself, he climbed down onto the steps and eventually to the ground.

Moving that much bulk took a while.

Even that much exertion was hard on the man, Frank noted. The fella's moonlike face had reddened, and his yard-wide chest rose and fell faster as he tried to catch his breath.

Frank leaned closer to Linderman and asked quietly, "Is that Northam?"

"Yep," the foreman replied.

Frank remembered what Stafford had told him about Northam being a British sailor who had left his ship and settled in southern California many years earlier. Northam must have changed a great deal since those days, because Frank couldn't imagine this behemoth of a man climbing around a ship's rigging. Northam seemed barely able to lift one leg and put it in front of the other.

His voice was deep, rich, and powerful, though, as he looked at Frank and said, "Good evening to you, sir. I assume that you are the notorious Frank Morgan I've heard so much about?"

"I'm Morgan," Frank said, not commenting on the "notorious" part.

The big man lifted a finger to the brim of the bowler hat he wore. "Edwin Northam, sir, at your service." As he lowered his arm, he gestured at the smaller man who had been on the wagon with him. "My manservant Bartholomew Fox."

Frank nodded to the man and said, "Howdy."

Fox's chin moved barely an inch in a perfunctory return nod; otherwise, he didn't acknowledge the greeting.

Wheezing slightly, Northam went on. "You should know, sir, that I seldom leave my home. I would not have done so this evening had it not been for the personal invitation extended to me by the very lovely Señora Montero. Is she here by the way?"

"Yes, I'm here, Edwin," Dolores said as she came forward to join Frank and Linderman in greeting the final member of the ranching community in the San Fernando Valley. "Thank you for coming."

Northam reached up and actually removed his hat this time, revealing a mostly bald head with a few stands of silver hair combed over the top of it. "For you, my dear, anything . . . as always."

Jorge Sandoval strode out of the barn as well and gave the Englishman a curt nod. "Northam," he said. Then he looked at Frank and continued. "Now can we get on with this?"

"I reckon we can, since we're all here," Frank said. He paused and spoke briefly to Pete Linderman as the others all started inside.

They went back into the barn with Edwin Northam lumbering along, followed by Bartholomew Fox. Frank couldn't help but notice the little man's military bearing, and he spotted a telltale bulge under Fox's left arm indicating that the servant was carrying a gun there in a shoulder holster.

Not many men in the West used a shoulder rig like that, but a few did. Frank recalled that Wes Hardin sometimes carried his gun that way. He didn't figure that Bartholomew Fox was as skilled as John Wesley Hardin when it came to gunplay, but he would have been willing to bet that Fox could handle himself all right in a fracas. He just had that look about him.

The six ranchers gathered in front of the hay bales. Frank noted that while Patterson, Guthrie, and Lopez all greeted Northam politely enough, they displayed the same sort of coolness toward the big man that Sandoval had. Clearly, Northam was something of an outsider here.

Still feeling a little odd about it, Frank stepped up onto the hay bales. The buzz of conversation in the barn died. With everyone's eyes on him, Frank said, "I want to thank all of you for coming tonight, and especially Señora Montero for agreeing to have this meeting here at her ranch. I reckon you all know who I am . . ."

Nods of agreement came from the ranchers.

"The reason I came here to the San Fernando Valley," Frank went on, "is because I wanted to lend a hand to Mr. John J. Stafford. Mr. Stafford's law partner, Claudius Turnbuckle, is a friend of mine."

He didn't mention that Turnbuckle and Stafford also represented some of his own business interests.

His connection to the Browning business empire wasn't widely known, and that's the way Frank wanted to keep it.

"I knew from Turnbuckle that Mr. Stafford was having some sort of trouble down here, and I thought maybe I could help," he went on. "Once I got here, it didn't take long to figure out what the trouble was."

Sandoval spoke up, saying, "It didn't take you long to kill one of my sister's ranch hands either, did it, Morgan?"

Frank's jaw tightened with anger for a second, but he suppressed the reaction. "That doesn't have anything to do with the problems you folks have been having."

"If it had been one of my men you gunned down, you never would have left my rancho alive," Sandoval snapped.

"Jorge, please," Dolores said as she put a hand on his arm. "Mr. Morgan and I have reached an understanding on that matter. Lonnie forced him into that gunfight."

Sandoval just snorted as if his sister's argument didn't mean anything to him, but he crossed his arms over his chest and shut up.

Frank tried to ignore the instinctive dislike he felt for the man and continued. "As I was saying, it's pretty obvious that you've got oil wells crowding in all around you. That's bad enough, what with the noise and the smell and the oil fouling your water supplies in places. What I want to hear about is the rustling and the bushwhacking that's been going on."

Several of the ranchers started to talk at once.

Feelings ran high, and Frank had to raise his arms and call for order to get them to settle down. Then, one at a time, he listened to their complaints.

It was the same story over and over: cattle disappearing, cowboys being shot at as they rode the range, barns set on fire. Typical range war tactics, Frank thought.

"The authorities haven't done anything to try to put a stop to this?" he asked. He knew what Stafford and Dolores had told him, but he wanted to hear from the others as well.

Dave Guthrie laughed humorlessly. "That blasted Magnusson flat out told me that the law was on his side. He's right, too. The sheriff claims he can't do anything without proof."

Ben Patterson said, "What more proof does anybody need besides missin' cows and shot-up punchers? I've got two men laid up with bullet holes in 'em right now! It's just pure luck that one or both of 'em ain't dead!"

The others joined in that chorus, with the exception of Edwin Northam. In fact, the big Englishman hadn't contributed anything to the meeting so far. Curious, Frank looked at him and said, "What about you, Mr. Northam? Have you been having the same sort of trouble as everybody else in the valley?"

Northam had caught his breath, although just standing seemed to be an effort for him. "Actually, no," he said. "I've lost a few head of stock to rustlers, but no more than usual." He moved a hand in a languid wave. "Any cattleman is going to have a cow taken now and then to feed a hungry family of farmers."

"This is not like that," Jorge Sandoval insisted. "This is organized, widespread rustling!"

"It is those oil drillers who are eating our beef!" Augusto Lopez put in. "And they who shoot at us when we ride on our land!"

"Nobody's ever spotted any of the bushwhackers, though, is that right?" Frank asked.

"Who else could it be except them?" Dolores said.

Frank turned back to Northam. "You haven't had any of your men shot?"

"No, sir, indeed not."

"You don't find that a mite suspicious?" Frank mused.

Mustache bristling, Bartholomew Fox stepped forward. "See here, sir!" he said in a high-pitched voice. "What are you insinuatin' about Mr. Northam, sir?"

Northam put out a hand. "No need to get upset, Fox. I'm sure that Mr. Morgan wasn't accusing me of anything." His silky voice hardened. "Are you, Mr. Morgan?"

"I don't have any reason to accuse anybody of anything . . . just yet," Frank said. "But I intend to find out what's going on here in the valley."

"Simply as a favor to your lawyer's partner?" Sandoval asked. "I find that hard to believe."

"Well, you can believe this, Señor," Frank said. "Somebody's taken potshots at me twice now, and I don't like it, not one bit. That makes it personal. That's why I intend to get to the bottom of things."

Sandoval sneered. "Surely, a man such as yourself has many enemies. You can't be sure that these attempts on your life are because you came here claiming to want to help us."

"Maybe not," Frank admitted. "Maybe one of you can shed some light on what happened."

He signaled to Linderman, who left the barn and came back a minute later accompanied by two cowboys carrying a blanket-wrapped shape. They brought it to the front of the barn and placed it in front of the hay bales.

Frank stepped down, bent and grasped the blanket, and straightened. The body of the dead bushwhacker rolled out onto the ground in front of the startled ranchers.

"Take a good look at him," Frank said to them. "Maybe he belongs to one of you."

# Chapter 15

Startled, angry exclamations came from all the ranchers except Dolores, who had seen the dead man earlier. Even so, she paled again at the grisly sight.

"Do you actually mean to say that you believe this man was working for one of us, Morgan?" Northam demanded.

"Was he?" Frank shot back at the Englishman. "Do you recognize him?" He swept his gaze over the other men. "Do any of you?"

"He's no ranch hand," Dave Guthrie said. "Look at those damned boots!"

Ben Patterson nodded in agreement. "No cowboy worth his salt'd be caught dead in a pair o' clodhoppers like those."

"It's obvious that he's one of the oil drillers," Sandoval snapped. "Magnusson sent him after you because he's afraid of you, Morgan."

That possibility had occurred to Frank, but he wasn't sold on it just yet. The attempt on his life in town had occurred *before* his run-in with Magnusson.

That first night in Los Angeles, the oilman shouldn't have known anything about Frank, let alone that he had come to southern California to help the ranchers. Frank had barely found out about it himself by that time.

Of course, he had no proof that the same man had been responsible for both ambushes, he reminded himself.

"Just take a good look at him," he told the ranchers. "Do any of you remember ever seeing him before?"

A couple of them groused about it, but they studied the dead man's face for several moments, then one by one they shook their heads and denied knowing him. All the denials sounded convincing . . . but Frank didn't know these men well enough to judge yet how good they were at lying.

"All right." Frank motioned to Linderman, who moved forward along with the two men who had carried the body into the barn. They rolled it up in the blanket once more and carried it out.

Frank turned to Dolores. "Linderman tells me you've got your own icehouse here, Señora. I'd like for you to keep the body here tonight and see that it gets taken into town in the morning."

"We can do that," she said with an uncertain nod. Clearly, she didn't like the idea of storing the corpse overnight, but that was the only practical solution.

"What are you going to do, Morgan?" Sandoval asked with a challenging glare. "Just how do you intend to get to the bottom of this, as you put it?"

"Those stolen cows have to be going somewhere," Frank said. "Maybe I can find out where, and if I do, that may tell me who's behind the rustling. Likewise, if there are any more shootings, I intend to track down the men responsible. If I can get my hands on some of them, they'll tell me who's been giving them their orders."

"You seem quite confident of that, sir," Northam said. "What do you intend to do, torture them?"

"Whatever it takes," Frank replied coolly, although in reality he didn't have any intention of torturing anybody. Usually, when he wanted information from someone who didn't want to give it, all he had to do was threaten to turn Dog loose on him.

"So you're gonna be like a regulator," Guthrie said.

"That's just another name for a hired killer," Patterson put in.

"More like a range detective," Frank said. "I don't plan on killing anybody . . . unless I have to."

The feeling of hostility was still thick in the air inside the barn. Northam turned to Dolores and said, "I'm not sure it's a good idea to give this man free rein, Señora. Despite his claims, he's known to be a killer. You may all wind up in trouble with the law for turning him loose on the valley. As for myself, I wash my hands of the matter."

"You would rather go it alone against Magnusson, Edwin?"

The Englishman smiled. "If you'd ever served on a schooner caught in a typhoon in the South China Sea, my dear, you'd understand why Magnusson fails to frighten me. If he causes trouble for me, I shall deal with it in my own fashion."

"All right," she said with a nod. "If that's the way you feel." She looked around at the others. "But it seems to me that having Mr. Morgan look into things is the best thing we can do."

Stafford stepped up, speaking for the first time in a while. "I agree, Señora. I'm sure you gentlemen aren't aware of it, but Mr. Morgan has served as a lawman himself in recent years. I know what sort of reputation he has, but it's not fully deserved."

Once, it had been, Frank thought. He had been a pretty cold-hearted son of a bitch at times in his life. Only in recent years, as Stafford said, had that begun to change.

And he wasn't sure that it ever would change completely. He didn't really like any of these people, with the possible exception of Dolores, and it would have been easier just to mount up and ride away, leaving them to their troubles. The Drifter could go on the drift again.

But he'd been shot at twice, he reminded himself, and until he was sure that the dead man had been responsible for both attempts, he hated to leave that question unanswered. He hated like hell being shot at.

"It's settled then," Dolores said firmly as she looked at the other ranchers. "Mr. Morgan will find the evidence we need to make the law stop Magnusson." She turned to Frank. "I know you said you didn't want us to pay you, but—"

He would have refused any offer she was about to make. Their money didn't mean anything to him.

But he didn't get a chance to, because at that moment guns began to roar outside. Frank's hand flashed instinctively to his Colt as he heard the slamming of six-guns interspersed with the sharper crack of rifles being fired.

Startled shouts and curses filled the air in the barn. Bullets thudded into the walls. "Everybody down!" Frank yelled. "Blow out those lanterns!"

Gun in hand, he ran toward the open doors. A slug whined through the air near his head. Somewhere in the barn, a man yelled in pain.

Frank glanced back and saw that Jorge Sandoval had grabbed his sister and forced Dolores down behind the hay bales. Sandoval crouched beside her, holding a gun. The other ranchers had scattered, hunting cover, except for Edwin Northam, who shuffled slowly toward the cover of an empty stall. Bartholomew Fox backed along beside his employer, also with a drawn gun. His head darted back and forth as he searched for something to shoot at.

Linderman dashed into the barn before Frank reached the doors. Frank grabbed the foreman's arm and jerked him to the side just as a hail of bullets scythed through the air where Linderman had been. They sprawled on the ground and rolled clear of the doorway as more slugs searched for them.

"What the hell's going on out there?" Frank demanded.

"Hell's the right word for it," Linderman gasped. "Must've been twenty or thirty men opened up on the place from the dark. Snuck up on us like a bunch of damned redskins! At least a dozen men went down in the first volley, some of 'em our boys, the rest hands who rode over here with the other ranchers."

Frank nodded as darkness began to fall inside the barn. His order to blow out the lanterns was finally being heeded. That didn't keep the hidden riflemen outside from continuing to pour lead into the building, though.

The cowboys who had been outside the barn were putting up a fight, but they had been riddled by the opening volley of the ambush. The firing from the defenders was sporadic and ineffective.

Linderman cursed bitterly. "Judgin' from the muzzle flashes I saw, they've got the place surrounded. That damn Magnusson must've brought every driller in the valley with him!"

Frank wasn't convinced that Magnusson was behind this attack, but at the moment it didn't matter. He had to figure out a way to turn the tables on the gunmen, or everybody in the barn might be wiped out.

"I'm going out there," he told Linderman through gritted teeth.

The foreman reached out in the darkness and gripped Frank's shoulder. "Don't be a damned fool! It's a hornet's nest out there. At least in here there's a little cover."

"Maybe so," Frank said, "but what'll we do if they kill all the men outside and then set fire to the barn?"

Linderman cursed again, then said, "You're right, Morgan. Let's go." His hand tightened on Frank's shoulder. "But let's go up, not out."

Frank smiled grimly as he realized what Linderman meant. The two men stood up. Linderman knew the barn like the back of his hand. In the flickering light of muzzle flashes from both inside and outside, the foreman led Frank to a ladder that took them up into the hayloft.

"There's a trapdoor onto the roof," Linderman explained. "If we can get up there without them seein' us, maybe we can pick off enough of them to make the others hightail it."

Frank nodded. That was their best chance, he knew. The defenders weren't necessarily outnumbered, but taken by surprise and pinned down like they were, their numbers didn't matter all that much.

Morgan and Linderman climbed rungs nailed to the wall to the trapdoor. Linderman unfastened it and pushed it up and out of the way. He and Frank crawled out onto the roof and hugged the sloping boards.

Using elbows and knees, they pulled themselves to the crest of the roof and peered over it. Muzzle flame bloomed like crimson flowers in the darkness around the barn. Frank focused his gaze on the spot where one of the flashes had appeared and waited for another one. As soon as he saw the jet of orange flame, he squeezed the trigger of his Colt.

It was impossible to tell if he'd hit the rifleman behind those muzzle flashes, but as a long moment passed, he didn't see any more from that spot. A few yards away, Linderman's gun blasted as he followed Frank's example.

Frank was already selecting another target. He waited patiently, saw the flash he was looking for, and fired. Again, no more flashes came from that spot.

"We can maybe whittle 'em down this way," Linderman called to him, "but if they ever figure out we're up here, we'll be sittin' ducks!"

The foreman wasn't telling Frank anything he didn't already know. Frank drew a bead, waited, fired again. He was convinced that he and Linderman were doing some damage . . .

But it was probably too little, too late. There were too many of the mysterious attackers. The odds had tilted too far for Frank and Linderman to tilt them back again.

And those odds were about to get a whole heap worse, Frank realized as he spotted an orange glare from the corner of his eye. He rolled onto his back in time to see the blazing torch that was arching through the air fall onto the barn roof. It rolled down a few feet, stopped, and continued burning fiercely. More torches followed, spinning through the air as they were thrown from below.

"Hell!" Linderman cried.

The foreman was right about that, Frank thought. If the barn started burning, it would be hell indeed.

And he and Linderman would be caught right on top of the inferno.

# Chapter 16

Frank leaped to his feet and jammed his gun back in its holster. "We've got to put those fires out!" he yelled as he ran awkwardly across the roof toward the spot where the first torch had landed.

He kicked the torch and sent it flying off the barn, then began stomping at the flames that had already started trying to take hold of the wooden shingles.

Linderman followed suit, scrambling desperately across the roof toward another torch. Frank knew that by doing this they were calling attention to themselves, but they had no choice. If the barn burned, they were doomed anyway, along with everybody inside it.

As soon as the fire started by the first torch was out, Frank hurried over to another one, bent down and grabbed it, and flung it off the roof. As he did so, a shot from down below whistled past his head.

With the muzzle flash still imprinted on his eyes, he palmed out his Colt and snapped off a shot. The rifle cracked again, but this time the flame from its barrel jetted straight up, telling Frank that the attacker had pulled the trigger as he was going over backward.

That was one of the bastards down anyway, Frank thought with grim satisfaction.

Gun still in hand, he kicked another torch off the roof. From the corner of his eye, he saw Linderman doing the same thing.

Suddenly, the foreman spun around and fell, obviously driven off his feet by a bullet. Frank wanted to check on him, but there was no time. He continued to dash back and forth, kicking some of the torches off the roof and tossing others, stomping out the flames that tried to flare up.

So far, although the shingles were charred in places, the roof wasn't actually on fire. He couldn't get rid of all the torches and dodge bullets at the same time, though, and now that the attackers knew he and Linderman were up here, they would concentrate on the barn roof with their shots. Frank knew he was quickly running out of time . . .

A fresh volley of gunfire blasted out, but these shots came from a different direction. Frank saw muzzle flame stabbing through the darkness and heard the pounding of hoofbeats over the roar of shots. A new group had entered the battle, galloping out of the night to take the fight to the attackers surrounding the barn.

That proved to be enough to finally tip the delicate balance. Tracking the battle by the muzzle flashes, Frank saw it streaming away from the barn as the attackers fled. Shots died away to be replaced by the frantic rataplan of hoofbeats. The killers had had enough.

Frank threw the last of the torches off the roof, then hurried over to Linderman and dropped to a knee beside the fallen foreman. Linderman was still conscious and struggling to sit up.

"What happened?" he asked through teeth gritted against the pain of his wound as his right hand clutched his bloody left arm. "What's goin' on down there?"

"Those bastards who opened fire on the barn are taking off for the tall and uncut," Frank told him. "We got some reinforcements from somewhere."

"I had a dozen men up at the northwest pasture where most of the herd's gathered. Been tryin' to keep extra guards where the cows are. They must've heard the shootin' and hustled down here to see what was goin' on."

Frank helped Linderman rise into a sitting position. "How bad are you hit?"

"Not bad. Feels like the slug just tore through my arm and missed the bone. I'll be fine."

Linderman's shirt sleeve was sodden and dark with blood. He wouldn't be fine if he lost too much more of the stuff, so Frank said, "Let's get you down off of here so that arm can be patched up."

He lifted the foreman to his feet. They went over to the trapdoor. Before they climbed down, Frank looked around the roof to make sure that none of the flames from the torches had taken hold.

Frank went down the ladder first so that he could help Linderman descend one-handed. It was a laborious process, but after a few minutes, they reached the ground in the barn.

Some of the lanterns had been lit again now that

the fighting was over. Dolores Montero spotted the wounded Linderman and ran toward the foreman.

"Pete!" she cried. "Are you all right?"

He jerked his head in a nod. "I'll be fine, ma'am," he told her as he gripped his wounded arm. "This is just a scratch . . ."

His eyes rolled up in his head. He slumped, and would have fallen if Frank hadn't been right beside him to grab him and hold him up.

"He's lost quite a bit of blood," he told Dolores. "He needs to get that arm cleaned up, then be put to bed so he can rest."

Dolores nodded. "I'll see to that," she declared. She called to a couple of her hands, who hurried forward to take Linderman from Frank. She told them, "Put him in one of the spare bedrooms in the house, and then someone needs to ride to town as fast as they can and bring back the doctor."

That was a good idea, Frank thought. Linderman wasn't the only one who needed medical attention. Quite a few of the men in the barn had been wounded. A couple of them lay motionless, and Frank figured there would be fatalities.

As the cowboys were helping Linderman to the house, John J. Stafford came over to Frank, hat in one hand and handkerchief in the other. Stafford used the handkerchief to mop sweat from his balding head.

"A man goes through his entire life never being shot at, and then twice in one night he almost gets killed!" the lawyer said. "I don't know how you stand it, Mr. Morgan."

"Never had much choice in the matter," Frank

said. "You either stand it or you give up, and that means giving up on life." He shook his head. "I've never been in the mood to do that. Are you all right, Counselor?"

"Thankfully, yes," Stafford said with a nod. "I got behind that water trough over there and stayed as low to the ground as I could." He used his hat to brush at the straw and dirt on his suit. "I heard a lot of bullets flying around, but none of them came too close to me."

That was a stroke of good luck, Frank thought. The thick sides of the water trough would have protected Stafford from a straight shot, but not from ricochets.

"What in the world was behind all this . . . this violence?" the lawyer asked.

"Think about it," Frank said. "All the big ranchers in the valley are here tonight. If they were all wiped out, Magnusson and the other oilmen would have a free hand. They could drill anywhere they wanted to."

Stafford's eyes widened. "My God, you're right! I suppose men who would stoop to rustling and bushwhacking wouldn't draw the line at a full-scale massacre! I know Señora Montero and her brother are all right because I talked to them, but we'd better see if any of the other ranchers are injured."

Frank and Stafford went around the barn, checking on the other cattlemen. Dave Guthrie had a bullet burn on his thigh, and Augusto Lopez had fallen and twisted a knee while he was running for cover, but those appeared to be the only injuries among the ranchers.

Edwin Northam was red-faced and puffing, though, and Frank had to wonder how much more the big man's heart could stand. Northam blustered, "If I ever needed any more proof that I shouldn't ally myself with the rest of you, this atrocity confirms it! Dash it all, I could have been killed! We all could have been killed!" He turned to Bartholomew Fox, who was also uninjured. "Let's get out of here, Fox, before something else happens!"

Frank didn't figure the attackers would be back, at least not tonight. He faced the ranchers and said, "This doesn't change anything. I'm still going to find out who's responsible for this and all the other troubles you've had. Fact is, I'm more determined to do that than ever."

Jorge Sandoval glared at him and snapped, "Forget it, Morgan. We don't want your help."

His sister clutched his arm and frowned at him in confusion. "Jorge, what do you mean?"

Sandoval pulled loose and jerked a hand toward Frank in a curt, angry gesture. "What has this man done since he came to the valley? Brought us here tonight so that Magnusson can kill all of us at the same time! Don't you see it, Dolores? He's working for Magnusson!"

That accusation took Frank so much by surprise that for a moment he was speechless. Then he shook his head and said, "You've got it all wrong, Sandoval. I didn't have anything to do with this attack."

Sandoval's jaw came out in a belligerent jut. "You expect us to take the word of a known gunfighter and hired killer?"

Ben Patterson said, "You know, Jorge might be

on to something there. Morgan's the one who wanted this meeting. Hell, he brought us here like lambs to the slaughter!"

Anger surged up inside Frank. He had come to southern California to help these people, and now they were starting to accuse him of being in league with their enemies. That was gratitude for you.

"And what is the first thing he did when he got here?" Augusto Lopez asked. "He killed one of Señora Montero's men."

"I've told you how that happened," Frank said, his voice cold and flat. "You can ask the señora about it if you want."

"You could lie to her as easily as you could lie to us," Sandoval said.

Stafford stepped forward and said, "Gentlemen, I assure you, Mr. Morgan is indeed on your side. Think about this logically. He was in as much danger during the attack as any of you. Quite likely, he was in more danger, because he climbed up onto the roof with Pete Linderman to try to pick off some of those gunmen. If not for his actions, the barn might have burned down with all of us inside it!"

"We don't know that," Ben Patterson said. "Maybe it was all an act, just to make us think that he's on our side. He ain't hurt, is he? Maybe those varmints outside didn't even aim at him any."

They were going to believe what they wanted to believe, Frank realized. There had been an element of distrust among them all along, brought on by his reputation and the unfortunate gunfight with Lonnie as soon as he'd arrived in Los Angeles. Even though he had thought that he was starting to win Dolores over, now he saw doubt in her eyes, too.

"This is insane—" Stafford began.

"No, it's just starting to make sense," Sandoval cut in. "How did Magnusson know that all of us would be here tonight unless Morgan told him? *I* certainly didn't tell him. Did any of you?"

He sent challenging looks around at the other ranchers, who all shook their heads in answer to the question. Sandoval gave Frank a triumphant sneer and went on. "It had to be you, Morgan. Everything is clear to us now."

Stafford mopped his forehead again. "Gentlemen . . . Señora Montero . . . I assure you that you're wrong. Mr. Morgan wants to help you—"

Dolores held up a hand to stop him. She said, "Maybe he fooled you, too, Mr. Stafford. You've been our attorney for a long time, and I know you would not double-cross us. But Morgan could lie to you, too."

Frank's pulse pounded angrily in his head. He hadn't expected the ugly turn that the aftermath of the battle had taken. He said, "You're wrong. I just want to help."

Dolores took a deep breath. "We don't want your help, Mr. Morgan. In fact, we don't want you in the valley."

The others all nodded, even Edwin Northam, who had lingered when Jorge Sandoval began making his accusations against Frank.

"We'll deal with the threat of Magnusson and the other oil men ourselves," Dolores went on. "We don't need someone who's supposed to be helping us betraying us instead."

Stafford tried again to reason with her. "You're making a terrible mistake, Señora—"

"I think you've said enough, Counselor," she cut in. "In fact, I think you and Mr. Morgan should return to Los Angeles now."

Stafford drew himself up. "You're discharging me as your attorney?"

"No," Dolores said with a shake of her head. "As I told you, I still trust you. But I believe Morgan has fooled you, too, and you need to think about what's happened here tonight."

Stafford looked like he was on the verge of losing his temper now. Frank took hold of his arm and said, "Forget it. They've got their minds made up. We might as well leave. Maybe you can talk some sense into their heads later."

After a moment, Stafford jerked his head in a nod. "Very well." He clapped his hat on. "I'm sorry you feel that way, Señora. I hope all of you don't have reason to regret this rash decision later on."

He and Frank turned toward the door of the barn. Dolores followed them out and called for someone to bring Frank's horse and Stafford's buggy. Dog was already trailing at Frank's heels.

The sound of horses coming made Frank reach for his gun, but these riders weren't in a hurry. A dozen men rode into the yard, among them Jeff, and Frank knew they were the Salida del Sol hands who had rushed in from the north pasture to drive off the mysterious attackers.

"Were you able to grab any of those varmints?"

Frank asked before Dolores had a chance to tell the men that he was no longer regarded as an ally on the Montero ranch.

One of the cowboys shook his head and said, "Nope, they gave us the slip in the foothills."

Frank turned to Dolores. "If your men had been able to capture any of them, maybe they would have told us who they're working for."

Sandoval had emerged from the barn as well. He said, "Or perhaps they would have identified you as a traitor, Morgan, so I'm sure you're glad they got away."

Frank just shook his head. It would be a waste of time, breath, and energy to argue any more tonight. Everybody was too upset to listen to reason . . . and after everything that had happened, he couldn't really blame them. The world they had worked hard for . . . the world that their families had worked for, in some cases for several generations . . . seemed to be falling apart around them, and there wasn't anything they could do to stop that destruction. .

Frank swung up into Goldy's saddle, and Stafford climbed into the buggy and took up the reins. They left the Montero hacienda and headed back toward the pass over the Santa Monica Mountains.

"I'm sorry about what happened back there, Mr. Morgan," Stafford said over the rattle of hooves and buggy wheels. "I never dreamed they would get such foolish notions in their heads. It's a shame they don't want your help anymore, but I'll tell Claudius that you tried."

"They may not want my help," Frank said, "but they're going to get it anyway."

Stafford drew the team to an abrupt halt. "What? But you heard what they said."

"I heard," Frank said with a grim, determined nod. "But this isn't over, Counselor. Fact of the matter is, I reckon it's just getting started."

# Chapter 17

Nobody took any shots at Frank and Stafford on their way back over the mountains to town, which was a relief considering how hectic this long day had already been. Stafford was curious about Frank's comment, but he didn't press for answers and Frank didn't volunteer any.

A number of things had happened that puzzled Frank, going all the way back to the attempt on his life the first night he was in Los Angeles. They formed a picture of sorts in his mind, but he needed a lot more information to fill in the missing pieces.

He had an idea how he might be able to get at least some of that information.

When they reached the Nadeau Hotel and Dog and the horses had been left at the livery stable, Stafford invited Frank to have a drink with him.

"No, thanks," Frank replied with a shake of his head. "I'm a mite tired. I think I'll go ahead and turn in."

"Suit yourself," Stafford said. "After everything

that happened tonight, I need something to steady my nerves a little. I'll see you in the morning?"

"Sure," Frank said.

He claimed his room key from the clerk and went upstairs, again deciding not to use the elevator. What would happen, he wondered, if the blasted thing got stuck between floors? Or if the cable that lifted it were to snap?

No, good old-fashioned stairs were plenty good enough for Frank Morgan, thank you very much, he thought with a smile.

When he reached his room on the third floor, he paused in front of the door and studied it for a moment. More than once in his life, somebody with a grudge against him had hidden in a hotel room, waiting for him to return so that they could shoot through the door at him.

That had gotten Frank in the habit of walking quietlike whenever he approached a hotel room. Not only that, but he had wedged a small piece of a broken matchstick between the door and the jamb, low, close to the floor, where it wouldn't be noticed easily. Nobody could open the door without dislodging the matchstick.

Frank's jaw tightened as he saw the matchstick was no longer where he'd left it. Instead, it lay on the floor, just in front of the door, where it had fallen when somebody went into his room.

Frank had a pretty good notion that whoever it was still lurked inside the room, probably holding a gun. He knew he hadn't made much noise as he approached the door, thanks to the thick carpet runner in the hallway. He moved on past the room, being careful to proceed even more quietly now.

The Nadeau didn't have balconies on its upper floors, but Frank had noticed a narrow ledge that ran below the windows of the rooms. He went to the end of the corridor and opened the window there. When he leaned out into the night air, he heard the clank and clatter of the drilling rigs and smelled the brimstone odor that went with them.

It looked like a long way down to the concrete sidewalk three stories below him, but Frank had ridden along narrow mountain trails with yawning drops of several hundred feet only inches away. Plus he had faced the guns of countless men who wanted to kill him. Steady nerves was one thing The Drifter had in abundance.

So he climbed out through the window, onto the ledge.

It was no more than six inches wide, but that was enough. Facing the wall, Frank began inching along the ledge. Most of his weight was on the balls of his booted feet, but the rough bricks provided a few handholds as well.

He didn't look down. No point in tempting fate. The tricky part came when he reached the corner of the hotel and had to navigate it. He got his right foot around the corner, planted his toe on the ledge, reached around with his right hand and dug his fingers into the small gap between the bricks, and took a deep breath.

Then he swung himself around the corner, holding on for a second with only one hand and one foot.

He planted his left foot on the ledge and found

a grip for his left hand, then paused for a moment to rest. Despite the steadiness of his nerves, his pulse was pounding a little harder than usual.

When it had calmed down, he started moving again. He had counted the rooms along the hallway, so he knew how many windows he had to pass before he came to the one that opened into his room.

Some of the windows along the way had gas lamps burning in them, and the curtains were open enough for Frank to see through them if he wanted to. He wasn't interested in prying into other folks' business, though, so he looked through the windows only enough to make sure nobody was standing right there to see him making his way past on the ledge. He didn't want to raise a ruckus, and he sure didn't want anybody throwing a window open right in front of him while he was so precariously balanced.

The minutes dragged past. His toes and fingers were getting tired from clinging to the ledge and the bricks. But he finally reached the window that opened into his room, stopping just short of it.

The room was dark, of course, since he hadn't been there to light the lamp when night fell and the interlopers wouldn't have wanted to call attention to themselves by lighting it.

Frank lowered himself into a crouch and reached for the window. He didn't recall if it had been locked when he left or not. On the third floor like this, with no balconies, there wouldn't be much of a reason to lock the window.

Not many people would be plumb loco enough to make their way along the ledge like he had done, he thought with a faint smile.

The window moved slightly when he exerted pressure on it. So it wasn't locked, he told himself. Now he could try to ease it up and hope that it wouldn't make any noise, or he could open it in a hurry and dive into the room to take the would-be killers by surprise.

He opted for stealth, raising the window a fraction of an inch at a time and then pausing to see if there was any reaction from inside. The air was still and heavy and humid tonight, with little if any breeze, so he didn't think the curtains would stir inside the room. They had been closed over the window when he left, he recalled, so whoever was in there wouldn't notice the glass slowly rising.

Over the years, Frank had been in many dangerous situations where patience was the only thing that saved him. So he was able to take his time raising the window until it was up far enough for him to bend over and slip through it into the room. Gun metal whispered against leather as he slid his Colt from its holster. That was the only sound he made.

The same wasn't true for whoever was in the room. He heard breathing, the rustle of clothes, the scrape of shoe leather on the floor. The varmint was getting tired of waiting for Frank to return.

As far as he could tell, the sounds he heard indicated that only one other person was in the room. That came as a small surprise. He had expected two or three. When he heard a tiny cough, Frank pointed the Colt at the sound, eared back the hammer, and said, "Don't move or I'll blow your head off, mister."

Someone gasped, and then there was a big surprise. A woman said, "Don't shoot. Please."

# Chapter 18

Frank was shocked that the intruder lurking in his hotel room was a woman, but he didn't let his guard down. A woman could pull a trigger as easily as a man.

She had sounded genuinely surprised and scared, though. He was about to tell her to light the lamp when he heard something rushing through the air at him.

Instinct made him jerk his head aside. Something hit the broad brim of his hat and knocked it off his head, then shattered against his shoulder, staggering him slightly.

He caught his balance and swung his left arm in a sweeping, backhanded blow. He didn't want to hurt the woman, but he wasn't going to just stand there and let her pound on him either.

His arm hit something soft. He heard the breath whoosh out of her lungs. That didn't stop her, though. A small but hard fist swung blindly in the dark collided with his jaw. Frank grunted. He reached out, trying to get hold of her.

His fingers tangled in long hair. Soft, thick hair . . . but that realization didn't stop him from grabbing hold and swinging her toward where he thought the bed was.

She cried out in pain, and a second later, he heard the bedsprings twang as she fell across the mattress. Frank holstered his gun and went after her, throwing himself on top of her and searching in the dark for her wrists.

The bedsprings squealed under his weight, too. If anybody in the adjacent rooms had an ear pressed to the wall, he knew what they had to be thinking right about now.

There was nothing sensuous about the struggle that was going on, though. The woman hit him again, this time with a stinging blow to the nose. Frank grabbed her wrist and pinned that arm to the bed. A second later, he found her other wrist and clamped fingers around it, too. He had her pinned down now, although she was still squirming underneath him.

Of course, having her body writhing against him like that *did* have a little effect on him. He was human after all. If he'd been younger, he probably would have gotten a mite hot and bothered by the situation, which might have given the woman an advantage.

As it was, he was able to tell her through gritted teeth, "Better just settle down, ma'am. You're not going anywhere until I find out who you are and what you're doing in my room."

Abruptly, she stopped fighting. "Your room?" she echoed. "You're Frank Morgan?"

"That's right."

"Well, get off me, you big stupid galoot! You're the man I came here to see."

Frank hesitated. The woman sounded mad, but not particularly threatening. He said, "Usually, when somebody wants to pay me a friendly visit, they knock on the door. They don't sneak in and wait in the dark."

"I didn't say anything about a friendly visit. I've got a business proposition for you."

Lying on top of a woman in bed, in a dark room, sometimes involved business, all right, Frank thought, but not the sort he took part in. That might not be what she was talking about, though, he reminded himself.

"If I let go of you, are you going to try to hit me again?" he asked. He wanted to get the lamp lit and find out what the hell was going on here.

"You're sure you're Frank Morgan?"

"Last time I checked," he said.

"Then what in blazes were you doing sneaking in the window like that? I thought you were some sort of assassin who'd come here to murder Morgan."

"Let's just say I had a hunch somebody was in here who wasn't supposed to be," he said. He didn't want to reveal the trick with the matchstick. "Somebody who was probably up to no good."

"So what did you do, climb all the way around the building on that little ledge under the windows?"

"Yep," Frank said.

"You're crazy! You could have fallen and broken your neck!"

"Could've walked right into both barrels of a

shotgun, too," he told her. "I'd rather choose the risks I want to run."

"You sound like Frank Morgan, all right." She sounded a little breathless, too. "Now, could you get off of me? You're sort of heavy."

"That depends."

"On what, blast it?"

"Who are you, and what do you want?"

"My name is Astrid Magnusson," the woman said.

That was the biggest surprise yet, and Frank couldn't stop his muscles from stiffening in response to it. If Victor Magnusson had been angry with him for that ruckus with the driller Hatch, Frank could imagine how the man would feel about him wrestling around on a bed with Magnusson's wife.

Unless . . .

"You're married to Victor Magnusson?" he asked.

"What? No. I'm his sister."

Well, that was a little better. Not much maybe, but a little.

"All right, Miss Magnusson," Frank said. "You still haven't told me what you're doing here, but I'm going to let you go anyway so I can light the lamp. You promise not to try to run away or wallop me again?"

"I promise," she said. "I want to talk to you as much as you want to talk to me."

She sounded like she was telling the truth, so Frank took a chance and released her wrists. He pushed himself off her and stood up next to the bed. The gas lamp was on the wall above the bedside table. He reached out and found it, then snapped a lucifer to life with his other hand and held it to the lamp.

As the glow brightened and filled the room,

Frank saw that Astrid Magnusson had sat up on the edge of the bed and was running her fingers through thick auburn hair. She was around thirty, Frank guessed, with brilliant green eyes. Mighty attractive, too, he thought, although at the moment she looked to be on the stern and angry side.

"You didn't have to try to yank my hair out of my head," she complained.

"I'm sorry," Frank said, "but right then I was just trying to grab hold of whatever I could."

"Yes, I noticed that you're rather free with your hands. You're not what I'd consider a gentleman, Mr. Morgan. But then, I wouldn't expect a hired gunman to be a gentleman, would I?"

Frank managed to keep the anger out of his voice as he said, "Ma'am, I wouldn't have any earthly idea what you'd expect or wouldn't expect. But I can promise you, I don't go out of my way to be rude to ladies."

She sniffed. "You could have fooled me."

"Yeah, well, I don't expect to find a lady waiting for me in a darkened hotel room either," he said pointedly.

A pink flush crept over the creamy skin of her face. "What are you insinuating?" she asked in an icy voice.

"I'm not insinuating anything. I'm saying it plain. If you don't want me to think you're a whore, then tell me why you're here."

She gasped again, just like when he had first spoken after climbing in through the window. He hoped that his blunt words would shock her into finally telling him why she was in his room.

It worked. She said, "If you must know, I came here to see about hiring you!"

"So that was the business proposition you mentioned?"

"That's right." Her voice was colder than ever. "My brother needs help, and I thought you might be able to provide it."

One more surprise in a day that had been full of 'em, Frank thought.

"The last time I saw your brother, he was mad as a hornet at me over a tussle I had with a driller of his named Hatch. He didn't look like a fella who'd be asking for my help before the day was over."

"He's not," Astrid said. "I am. And I heard about that fight you had with Hatch. The men who were with him on the wagon told Victor that you attacked them without provocation."

Something in her tone intrigued Frank, despite its chilliness.

"You sound like maybe you're not convinced of that," he said.

She shrugged. "I know Hatch. He has a reputation for getting into fights. If he thought you worked for that Montero woman, he's perfectly capable of coming after you."

"That's pretty much what happened," Frank said with a nod. He reached down, picked up his hat from the floor, and tossed it onto the table. "What did you hit me with anyway?"

"The chamber pot. Don't worry, it was empty."

"I'm always thankful for small favors," Frank said with a faint smile. He grew serious again as he went on. "Does your brother even know that you're here, Miss Magnusson?"

"Of course not. Victor would be furious. If I'd told him what I planned to do, he would have forbidden it." She paused. "He's a very proud man. Too proud for his own good, most of the time."

Having met Victor Magnusson, Frank didn't doubt what Astrid said.

"But when he told me about meeting you," she went on, "I remembered hearing your name. I asked around and confirmed what I remembered, that you're a gunfighter. I thought that if you really weren't working for Dolores Montero, as you claimed, then you might consider working for us."

"Us?" Frank repeated.

"Well, for Victor. He runs the drilling company. But I own a significant share in it."

"Why does Victor need to hire a gunfighter? I sure as blazes don't know anything about drilling for oil."

"Victor and his men can handle that part just fine. He needs you to keep those damned cowboys from sabotaging the wells and trying to kill the drillers!"

Frank recalled what the drillers had said that morning when he ran into them on the road to Salida del Sol. From the sound of it, they had been having the same sort of troubles as the ranchers in the San Fernando Valley.

And naturally, the drillers blamed the cowboys, just as the cowboys blamed the drillers.

Ever since the encounter with the drillers, Frank had been suspicious that a third party might be involved. What Astrid Magnusson had just said made his suspicions even stronger. But he needed more evidence before he made up his mind.

"The ranchers claim that the same sort of thing is going on directed at *them*. Their men have been shot at and their cattle rustled."

Astrid shook her head. "What else do you expect them to say? They're just trying to divert attention from what they've been doing. *Our* men have been shot at, derricks have been toppled, equipment ruined. They're trying to drive the wildcatters out so they can have all the oil for themselves!"

That was an interesting theory, but Frank didn't believe it for a second, having been there when Stafford suggested that the ranchers should drill for oil. Dolores and the other ranchers had no intention of doing such a thing. They were fighting to hold on to the way things had been before all the oil wells appeared on the range.

Frank didn't say that to Astrid, though, because an idea had come to him. Instead, he asked, "If you hired me, what would you expect me to do?"

"Put a stop to the violence directed at the drillers."

"How would I go about doing that?"

She crossed her arms over her breasts and gave him a haughty look. "I'm sure I don't have to tell a man like you how to handle trouble, Mr. Morgan."

"I'm not a hired killer." Frank stated that flatly.

"I'm not asking you to murder anyone," Astrid replied. "But if you were working for Victor, you'd defend your employer's interests, wouldn't you? You'd defend yourself if you were attacked?"

"I always have," Frank said.

"Then you guard our wells, and if anyone tries to

bother them, you deal with them, whatever it takes. Once those cowboys realize that the notorious Frank Morgan is on our side, maybe they'll quit trying to ruin us. Do we understand each other, Mr. Morgan?"

Frank nodded slowly. "I reckon we do." Astrid Magnusson wanted him to do exactly what Dolores Montero and the other ranchers suspected him of already doing. Once he took the job—if he took it—they would believe that they had been right about him all along.

He could deal with that, though. He was playing a deeper game now, he realized. The cattlemen didn't want anything to do with him, but by going to work for Magnusson, he'd have an excuse to stay in the area and try to ferret out whoever was really behind the trouble.

There was still one problem, though.

"You've forgotten something," he told Astrid.

"What's that?"

"You said that your brother doesn't know you're here. That means he doesn't know you asked me to work for him. He's still got to agree to that."

"We can take care of that right now. I can get Victor to listen to reason. We've rented a house here in town. Will you come with me and talk to him?"

"Now?" Frank said.

Her chin came up. "I don't believe in postponing things that need to be dealt with."

"I reckon I can see that." If Victor Magnusson had reminded him of a Viking from some old book, Astrid fit the same description. One of those fierce Viking women who stayed behind when their men-folk went to roving, but able to handle a sword and deal with threats on their own if need be. He could see Astrid in that role.

Problem was, it had been a damned long day already, packed with action and surprising developments. But as she had said, there was no point in postponing things.

"All right," he said. "Let's go see your brother."

For the first time, he saw a hint of a smile on her lips. "We'll make it well worth your while. You won't regret this, Mr. Morgan."

Frank hoped that turned out to be true.

# Chapter 19

Astrid had brought a buggy to the hotel from the house where she was staying with her brother, which was about a mile away. Frank suggested that they go downstairs together. He would fetch one of his horses from the stable and ride along with her.

She shook her head. "No offense, Mr. Morgan, but I'd just as soon not be seen going through the lobby with you and leaving the hotel with you at this time of night. I have a reputation to protect, you know."

"No, ma'am, I didn't know that, considering that I'd never heard of you before tonight." Frank shrugged. "But suit yourself. Tell me how to get to your house, and I'll meet you there."

She gave him directions, and then he asked one more thing that had been puzzling him.

"Why did you sneak in here and hide in the dark? Why didn't you just come up and knock on the door? For that matter, how'd you get in?"

"If you had refused to cooperate with me, I didn't see any reason why my brother ever had to know I'd been here. So I didn't want to walk in and just ask openly for you, because word of that would have gotten back to him. I came in the back and bribed one of the porters to let me into your room. Once I was there, I thought it might be better to leave the lamp unlit. You might have noticed the light in the window and summoned the police, thinking that a burglar was in your room. How would it have looked for the officers to come in and find me like that?"

"Sounds like you thought it through, all right," Frank said. "But you didn't stop to think that I might take you for a bushwhacker. What if I'd kicked the door open and come in shooting?"

"Well, that wouldn't have been very good for either of us, now would it?"

All Frank could do was chuckle and shake his head. She was right about that.

He opened the door and checked the hallway. Seeing that it was empty, he motioned her out of the room and told her, "I'll see you at your house in twenty minutes."

"Thank you, Mr. Morgan," she said. "Now comes the hard part: convincing my brother that you can help us."

They parted company then, Astrid heading for the rear stairs, Frank going down the main staircase to the lobby.

The clerk raised his eyebrows in surprise when he saw Frank. "Going out again, Mr. Morgan?" he asked.

Frank went out the door without looking back.

Astrid must have told the hostler at the stable to leave her buggy team hitched up, because she was gone by the time Frank walked the block around the hotel. The elderly man took his hat off and scratched his head at the sight of Frank.

"Don't you ever sleep, mister?" he asked. "You been goin' and comin' all day."

"I'm starting to wonder the same thing myself," Frank said.

He led Stormy out and saddled the rangy gray stallion.

"Stay here, Dog," he told the big cur. He didn't think he needed Dog to come along with him to the meeting with Victor Magnusson. That would just increase the tension that was already bound to be pretty thick.

Frank followed the directions Astrid had given him, thankful that they were pretty simple since Los Angeles had grown considerably since the last time he'd been here. He found the place without any trouble.

When Astrid had mentioned that she and her brother had rented a place to stay while they were in town, Frank had pictured some modest cottage.

Instead, the house in the hills just north of downtown was the next thing to a mansion, a sprawling, steep-roofed structure with a three-story tower at each end. It looked like the sort of place where a railroad baron or a silver king would live.

Frank rode through the gate and up a circular driveway to stop in front of a massive front door. He swung down from the saddle, looked for a place to tie Stormy's reins, and finally settled for looping them around one of the columns that supported an elaborate arched roof over the entrance.

A brass knocker was mounted on the door. Frank grasped it and rapped sharply several times.

Astrid ought to be back by now, he figured. If she wasn't, Victor Magnusson would be in for a surprise when he opened that door, assuming he opened it himself and didn't have some butler do it.

Instead, Astrid was the one who pulled the door back and motioned for Frank to come in. He pulled his hat off as he stepped into a fancy foyer. Astrid took it from him and hung it on a hat tree with a brass knob on the end of each curving projection.

"Did you tell your brother I was on my way over here?" he asked.

Before she could answer, Victor Magnusson called from somewhere down the hall, "Who in blazes is that at the door at this time of night?"

Astrid shrugged. "There wasn't time," she told Frank. "Anyway, it would have just meant starting the argument that much sooner."

He supposed she was right. He followed her down the hall as she said over her shoulder, "Victor is in the library."

"This is a fancier place than I expected."

"It belongs to a man who's a partner in a railroad. He's gone to Europe for a year with his family, though, so the house was just sitting here empty. His lawyer was glad to rent it to us at a reasonable price."

As they went along the hall, they passed several portraits of a grim-looking man and woman and some equally solemn children. Frank supposed they were the family that lived there. He hoped their trip to Europe cheered them up a mite. They all looked like their best friend had just died.

Astrid paused at a pair of double doors, one of which was partially open. Frank supposed that they led into the library. She looked back at him and summoned up a brave smile.

Then she pushed the door open the rest of the way and said, "We have a visitor, Victor."

Frank stepped into the library behind her as she entered. Astrid moved aside, giving Frank a good view of Victor Magnusson as the oilman sat behind a massive desk that was littered with papers.

Magnusson had a pencil in his hand, and obviously had been scrawling some sort of diagram on a piece of paper. Frank could see the drawing from where he was, but since he didn't know anything about drilling for oil, it didn't mean a blessed thing to him.

Magnusson had taken off his coat and rolled up his sleeves. His thatch of fiery hair was rumpled, as if he'd been dragging his fingers through it. He looked up as Frank and Astrid entered the room, and a second later, the pencil in his fingers snapped with a loud crack as that hand clenched into a fist.

"Morgan, by God!" he said as he surged to his feet. "What the hell are you doing here?" He threw the broken pencil aside and reached for one of the desk drawers. "I warn you, I've got a gun—"

"Victor, stop!" Astrid said. She cast a nervous glance at Frank, as if imploring him not to shoot her brother if he was foolish enough to drag a gun out of that desk drawer. "There's no need to be upset. I asked Mr. Morgan to come here tonight."

"After what I told you about the way he attacked Hatch and the other drillers? For God's sake, Astrid, what you were thinking?"

She met his angry stare with a determined one of her own. "I was thinking that he might be just the man to help us," she said. From the way she was standing up to him and not backing down, Frank got the feeling that this wasn't the first argument these siblings had had.

Magnusson made a contemptuous noise in his throat. "The day I need help from a gunfighter—" he began.

"That day has come, Victor," Astrid broke in. "You've been complaining for weeks about how the ranchers are trying to run you and the rest of the drillers out of the San Fernando Valley. You know it's only a matter of time until they hire gunmen of their own, if they haven't already. But maybe they won't if they know that Mr. Morgan is working for us. Maybe no one will want to face him." She glanced at Frank again. "I understand that he has quite a reputation with a gun."

"Yes, well, I'm still not convinced that he's not working for that Montero woman," Magnusson blustered. "They seemed rather close."

Astrid turned her head and gave Frank a cool glance. "Is that true, Mr. Morgan? I've seen Dolores Montero. She's a very attractive woman."

"I won't argue that point with you," Frank said, "but attractive or not, she doesn't have a bit of use for me. It's true that I rode out to her ranch today intending to ask her for a job, but once she found out who I am, she told me to get off her range."

He left out the meeting that was held at Salida del Sol this evening and everything that had happened there. Magnusson might hear about it later—if, of course, he didn't know about it already—but for the time being, Frank didn't see any need to go into those details.

And there was always the possibility that Frank would find out who was really responsible for all the trouble in the valley before word got around about the battle on the Montero ranch.

Magnusson pulled at his spade beard and frowned. "This is some sort of trick," he declared. But for the first time, Frank saw doubt in the man's eyes and heard it in his voice.

"It's not a trick," Astrid said. "In fact, it wasn't even Mr. Morgan's idea to come here tonight." Her chin came up defiantly. "I went to his hotel and asked him to come see you about a job, Victor."

Magnusson looked shocked for a second; then his expression turned into an angry glare.

"You went to a hotel . . . by yourself . . . to talk to this . . . this gunfighter? Good Lord, Astrid! Los Angeles may be growing, but it's still a small town at heart. Do you know what people are liable to say?"

"I don't care what people say," Astrid replied. "I care about you, Victor, and if things keep going like they have been, you're going to wind up either ruined—or dead!"

Then she surprised Frank by putting her hands over her face and starting to sob.

Looking flustered now, Magnusson came out from behind the desk and hurried to put his arms around her. He was a lot bigger than she was, and looked a little like a redheaded bear as he enveloped her in an embrace and awkwardly patted her on the back with one big paw.

"Blast it, Astrid," he said, his voice rough with emotion, "you know I can't stand it when you cry."

"I . . . I know," she sniffled. "I just can't bear the thought of you being shot down. It's no shame to ask for help, Vic, and who . . . who better to take on those gunmen than a man like . . . like Mr. Morgan?"

He put his hands on her shoulders and moved her back a step. "All right," he told her. "I'll at least talk to Morgan. Will that make you feel better?"

"I . . . I suppose so."

"You run along, then, and let Morgan and me talk in private."

"There won't be any trouble, will there?"

Magnusson turned his head and glared at Frank for a second before turning back to his sister.

"If there is, I won't be the one to start it," he declared. "You've got my word on that."

"All right then." Astrid pulled a fine lace handkerchief from somewhere in her dress and dabbed at her eyes. "Thank you, Victor. I know you won't regret this."

"I hope you're right," Magnusson said, but he still didn't sound completely convinced.

He went back behind the desk as Astrid turned to leave the library. While she was doing so, she caught Frank's eye, and suddenly one of her damp, red-rimmed eyes closed and then opened again in a conspiratorial wink that Magnusson couldn't see.

She had been acting the whole time, Frank realized, manipulating her brother with her tears. Frank didn't know whether to grin at her or frown at her.

He settled for doing neither, and kept his face carefully neutral as Astrid left the room. Magnusson had sat down behind the desk again, and he motioned for Frank to pull up one of the other comfortable arm-chairs in the room.

"You'll understand if I don't offer you a drink, Morgan," Magnusson said. "I'm not sure yet if we're going to be allies or not."

"That's fine," Frank replied as he sat down and faced Magnusson across the big desk. "I'm not sure I want to work for you. I'm here mostly as a favor to the lady."

Magnusson cleared his throat. "Astrid was out of line coming to your hotel like that."

"No harm done," Frank said with a shrug. "Why don't you tell me about the trouble you've been having out in the valley, and then we can decide what to do from there?"

Magnusson nodded and launched into the tale.

# Chapter 20

"People have been drilling for oil in the San Fernando Valley for nearly twenty years," Magnusson began, "but only on a limited basis. I came here to Los Angeles a couple of years ago and started drilling here in town when the boom hit. I did well enough I decided to expand to the valley."

Frank broke in to say, "Your sister told me the fella who owns this house is in Europe for a year with his family. If you've been out here for two years, where were you staying before you rented it?"

Magnusson waved a big hand. "Astrid wasn't with me then. I just had a room in a boardinghouse. The same place my drillers stay, in fact. But when she came west, I needed somewhere better for her, of course."

Frank nodded. "I reckon that makes sense. Mind if I ask what prompted her to join you?"

"Our mother passed away," Magnusson replied with that rough growl in his voice again. "Astrid had been taking care of her. But with her gone, there was no reason for Astrid to stay back in Minnesota."

"I'm sorry," Frank said.

Magnusson shook his·head as if to say that what was past was past. He went on. "When I decided to expand my drilling operation into the valley, I looked into the situation, of course, and found out the same thing other drillers had discovered. The title claims those ranchers have are pretty shaky legally, especially the Montero, Sandoval, and Lopez places. Those involve Spanish land grants, and some of the other drillers had already filed lawsuits seeking a ruling on them before I even got here."

"But you took advantage of the situation anyway, even if you didn't start it, didn't you?"

One of Magnusson's big fists thumped on the desk. "A man's got to grab hold of his chances where and when he finds them, damn it! If you were a businessman instead of a gunman, you'd know that, Morgan."

"Go on," Frank said, suppressing the irritation he felt at Magnusson's attitude.

Magnusson glowered across the desk for a second before he continued. "At first, I confined my drilling to areas that I either knew didn't belong to any of the ranchers, or property where clear title was in dispute. But my God, Morgan, there's so much oil down there! You don't know what it's like. To a man like me, knowing that oil's there is like a man who's dying of thirst knowing that there's a whole lake of cool, clear water right under the ground if he can just get to it."

"So you started setting up your rigs wherever you damned well pleased," Frank said.

"Yes, damn it, I did—but only after asking

Francisco Montero for permission. I would have paid him a good royalty on whatever I pumped out of his range." Magnusson shook his head. "But he turned me down flat, the old bastard."

"That's because he was a cattleman, not an oilman."

"No, it's because he was a damned fool . . . although he had sense enough to marry Dolores Sandoval, I'll give him that. She's a beautiful woman. Every bit as stubborn as her husband, though."

"Because she turned you down, too, when you asked for permission to drill on Salida del Sol range," Frank guessed.

"I could have made her a very rich woman."

"Maybe she's already got what she wants," Frank suggested. "Not everybody is interested in nothing but money."

With a faint sneer on his face, Magnusson asked, "What about you, Morgan? What are you interested in besides money?"

Frank shrugged and didn't answer. Despite everything he'd said, he knew that Magnusson still considered him a hired gun, available to the highest bidder. For now, it suited Frank's purposes to let the man believe that.

"Anyway," Magnusson went on after a moment, "I kept drilling, and a couple of months ago things started happening. My men were shot at. Equipment was damaged in the night. A wagonload of pipe was stolen from a drilling site. We found the wagon and the pipe at the bottom of a ravine. The bastards who took it had stampeded the team over the edge. It took us almost a week to recover all that pipe."

"And you think Señora Montero's men are responsible for all this?"

Magnusson's brawny shoulders rose and fell in a shrug. "I don't know it for a fact, but who else could be behind it? Other drillers have had the same sort of trouble, and it's happened on other ranches, too. I think the whole bunch of them have banded together to run us out. Then they'll bring in drillers of their own."

"It *is* their land," Frank pointed out.

"We haven't had the last word on that."

Frank let that dubious claim go and asked, "Have any of your men been wounded by the bush-whackers?"

Magnusson jerked his head in a nod. "Damn right they have. They've gotten busted arms and legs. A few have wound up in the hospital. I'd say that we've been mighty lucky no one's been killed so far."

The oilman's story sounded almost exactly like what Dolores Montero had told Frank earlier in the day. Frank didn't think that was a coincidence.

More than ever, he was becoming convinced that someone was trying to stir up trouble between the oil drillers and the ranchers in the San Fernando Valley.

And the best way to discover the identity of that troublemaker was to get right in the middle of the trouble. He could do that by pretending to go to work for Victor Magnusson against the cattlemen.

"If you hire me, what is it you want me to do?" Frank asked bluntly.

"Put a stop to the harassment, of course."

"How do you suggest I do that?"

Magnusson's voice hardened even more. "By whatever means necessary, of course."

"Including murder?"

Magnusson glared at him. "Damn it, my men are the ones who are getting shot at! Don't talk to me about murder."

"The ranchers claim the same thing is happening to them."

The oilman waved that off. "What else do you expect them to say?" he asked. "They're just trying to cover up for what they've been doing."

"Maybe so," Frank said.

"No maybe about it. I know who my enemies are. The question is, do you want to help me deal with them?"

Frank didn't believe for a second that Magnusson was right about Dolores and the other ranchers, but he nodded anyway. Astrid Magnusson coming to his hotel tonight had been a lucky break, and he intended to take advantage of it.

"Yeah, I'll sign on with you, Magnusson," he said.

"And you'll do whatever it takes to stop the trouble in the valley?"

"I will," Frank said, and that answer wasn't a lie. He might not proceed exactly as Magnusson expected him to, but his goal was definitely to put a stop to the trouble in the valley. Just so Magnusson wouldn't be suspicious, he added, "As long as I'm well paid."

"Oh, you will be," Magnusson said. Frank could sense the oilman's stiff-necked attitude loosening a little now that they had agreed to work together. "Maybe I'll offer you that drink now."

"And maybe I'll accept it."

Magnusson got up and went to a sideboard, where he splashed whiskey from a decanter into two glasses. He carried them over to Frank, who stood up to accept the glass that Magnusson offered him.

"To success," Magnusson said.

"To success," Frank echoed as he clinked his glass against the oilman's.

Of course, the two of them probably defined success in different ways, he thought wryly as he downed the drink. The whiskey was smooth, but it lit a fire in his belly.

Astrid must have lingered outside the library door. She came back in then, and Frank figured she had been eavesdropping and had heard the glasses clink together and taken that as a sign her brother and Frank were getting along now.

She said, "I take it you gentlemen have come to an agreement?"

"We have," Magnusson said with a curt nod. "I'll be honest with you, Morgan, I don't fully trust you yet, but I'm willing to give you a chance."

"That's all I've ever asked for," Frank said. "One thing concerns me. I'll have to be around your drillers quite a bit if I'm trying to find out who's been ambushing them. How are Hatch and the others going to react to having me around?"

"After you handed Hatch a beating, you mean?" A harsh laugh came from Magnusson. "Let me worry about the drillers. I'll pass the word that you're working for me now, and they'll leave you alone."

"I need more than to have them leave me alone. They're going to have to cooperate with me."

"Leave that to me," Magnusson snapped. "They all know better than to go against my orders."

Frank didn't doubt that. Magnusson was big enough to hold his own in a brawl with any of his men, and from the knobby-knuckled look of his hands, he had banged his fists against the faces of other men on numerous occasions in the past.

"If we're having a drink to celebrate this new alliance," Astrid said, "where's mine?"

Magnusson frowned at her. "You don't need a drink," he said. "Whiskey isn't ladylike."

Astrid smiled at Frank. "My brother has the usual protective attitude toward his little sister, Mr. Morgan. But I assure you, I'm all grown up."

She was more than grown up by several years, Frank thought, but of course it would have been impolite to say as much. So instead, he said, "To tell you the truth, I'm not much of a whiskey drinker myself, Miss Magnusson." He handed his empty glass to the oilman. "So I reckon that'll do me. It's been a long day, and I believe I'll be heading back to the hotel."

"We'll ride out to the valley together tomorrow," Magnusson suggested, "and I can show you where all my rigs are."

That sounded like a good idea to Frank. He nodded his agreement and said, "I'll meet you here after breakfast?"

"Fine. Astrid, fetch Mr. Morgan's hat."

"I'll show you out, too, Mr. Morgan," she said as she linked her arm with his.

That drew a disapproving frown from her brother, but Frank couldn't very well pull away from her. That would have been rude.

"Don't pay any attention to the way my brother barks and growls, Mr. Morgan," Astrid said as she and Frank went back along the hall toward the foyer and the front door. "That's just his way. He doesn't really mean anything by it. He's always taken good care of me."

"I imagine he has."

"He forgets sometimes, though, that I'm only a year younger than he is. I'm twenty-nine years old, Mr. Morgan . . . and I haven't spent those years in a nunnery."

She had tightened her arm around his so that her right breast pressed warmly against his left arm. Frank was well aware of that pressure, as well as the fact that he was almost old enough to be Astrid's father.

That didn't seem to bother her, though.

"I don't reckon we'll be seeing a lot of each other," he said as they reached the foyer and he extricated his arm from hers as discreetly as possible. "I'll be out in the valley a lot, trying to find out who's bothering those rigs of your brother's."

"You don't think it's the cowboys from those ranches?"

"It looks that way," Frank admitted. "But I intend to find out for sure."

"Well, I'm sure you'll be coming here from time to time. In fact, I intend to make certain of it by inviting you for dinner at least once a week."

"Your brother might have something to say about that."

Astrid's chin lifted in a gesture of defiance that was already becoming familiar to Frank. "Victor runs the oil field, I run the household. He knows better than to argue with me too much about such things."

*I'll bet a hat he does,* Frank thought.

She handed him his Stetson. "Good night, Frank. You don't mind if I call you Frank, do you?"

"Not at all," he said.

"And I'm Astrid."

"All right . . . Astrid." Frank put his hat on and nodded. "Good night."

For a second, he thought she was going to come up on her toes and kiss him. But she wasn't quite *that* forward, for which he was grateful.

He was already walking a thin enough line, pretending to work for Victor Magnusson when in reality he was just as much concerned with the welfare of the ranchers Magnusson considered his enemies. He didn't need the added complication of having Astrid pursuing him romantically.

Not that she wasn't a very attractive woman . . .

Frank pushed that thought out of his head as he rode back to the hotel. This had been one of the longest, most eventful days he had spent in quite some time, and he was ready for a good night's sleep.

# Chapter 21

After everything that had happened, some men might have found it difficult to relax and doze off. They might have lain in bed, stared at the darkened ceiling, and tried to sort through all the action-packed incidents of the past twenty-four hours.

Not Frank Morgan. Like most veteran frontiersmen, he had acquired the ability to rest whenever and wherever he got the chance, and he was asleep less than a minute after his head hit the pillow in his hotel room.

He was up early again the next morning as well, also a long-ingrained habit. He didn't know whether or not Victor Magnusson was an early riser, though, so he lingered over his breakfast.

The sun was up by the time Frank reined Goldy to a halt in front of the rented mansion where the Magnussons were staying. He wondered whether Astrid was awake yet.

Victor Magnusson was up and around and must have been watching for him. The oilman strode out the front door and gave Frank a nod.

"My horse is around back in the shed, but he's already saddled up. I'll be right back."

"You're the boss," Frank said.

"And don't you forget it," Magnusson snapped.

Frank didn't particularly like the man, and comments like that didn't make him any fonder of Magnusson. But mere dislike didn't mean that Magnusson was to blame for what had been happening in the valley.

While Magnusson was fetching his mount, Frank sat easily in his saddle and looked at the big house, which was even more impressive in the early morning light. He thought he saw a curtain move in one of the windows on the second floor, but he couldn't be sure about that.

Astrid, he thought. She was looking out at him.

The curtain fell closed quickly, though, if it had even moved to start with, as if she didn't want him to know that she was there in the window.

Magnusson came back a moment later riding a tall black gelding. He sat his saddle with ease and obviously was accustomed to riding.

The butt of a Winchester jutted up from the saddle boot on Magnusson's horse. He also wore a revolver in a cross-draw on his left hip, with a cavalry-style flap that snapped down over the gun.

Instead of the suit he had sported the day before, today he had on high-topped boots, whipcord trousers, and a plain work shirt. His hat was the same Stetson, though.

As they rode, Magnusson looked at Dog jogging along beside them and asked, "Is that animal part wolf?"

"I don't really know," Frank admitted. "He's never said one way or the other."

Magnusson grunted. "Well, keep him away from me. I don't like dogs."

Frank recalled that John J. Stafford had said pretty much the same thing. What was wrong with these people here in southern California that they didn't like perfectly good dogs?

He put that question out of his mind, figuring it would take too long to answer, and rode on with Magnusson. As they passed through the streets of Los Angeles, Frank looked at the dozens of oil wells dotting the landscape and shook his head in disbelief.

"It beats me why folks would want one of those things in their front yard."

"The answer to that is simple," Magnusson said. "Money. They get paid a royalty for every barrel that comes out of the ground. There are a lot more rich people in this town now than there were a few years ago, and they're only going to get richer."

"There are other things in life besides money," Frank pointed out.

Magnusson shrugged. "Sure there are. But it's a lot easier to appreciate and enjoy those things if you have plenty of money."

Frank couldn't argue with that, at least where most people were concerned.

But as for himself, he hadn't been any happier after he'd inherited half of the Browning financial empire. Less so actually, because the only reason those riches belonged to him was because Vivian Browning, one of the loves of his life and the mother of his child, was dead.

Frank would have traded all that wealth for Vivian's continued well-being without even a moment of hesitation.

That would mean changing the past, though, and it couldn't be done. All a fella could do was try to live with what had happened and go on the best he could.

"Some of these rigs are yours, you said?" he asked Magnusson.

The oilman nodded. "That's right. There hasn't been any trouble with the wells here in town, though. People here are happy for us to drill on their land. The only problems have been out in the valley, with those stubborn ranchers."

Magnusson thought of Dolores Montero and the other ranchers as being stubborn. To Frank, it just seemed like they were trying to preserve the way of life they had always known.

He understood that attitude. Over the decades, he had witnessed the West changing around him, in some ways for the better, but often not. He couldn't see how having a bunch of clanking, clattering, stinking oil wells all over the place was actually going to help anything.

But maybe the times were passing him by, too. In only a few more years, it would be a new century. The twentieth century.

Out with the old, in with the new. And Devil take the hindmost.

Frank and Magnusson followed the road through the pass over the Santa Monica Mountains, and by mid-morning found themselves in the San Fernando

Valley. Magnusson pointed out some of the oil drilling rigs they passed as belonging to him.

"Any trouble with these?" Frank asked.

"No, but we're not on Montero range yet. That's where most of the problems have been."

Frank spotted a haze of dust in the air some distance ahead of them. That much dust had to be caused by either a herd of cattle or a large group of riders moving fairly fast. He wondered which one it was.

A short time later, Frank reined in abruptly as he heard some popping sounds in the distance. Beside him, Magnusson brought his horse to a halt as well.

"What's wrong?" the oilman asked.

"Hear that?"

Magnusson frowned. "That's not a donkey engine backfiring, is it?"

"I'm afraid not," Frank replied with a shake of his head. "Those are gunshots."

"Damn it!" Magnusson burst out. "My men are being attacked again. Come on, Morgan!"

With that he jabbed his boot heels into his horse's flanks and sent the animal lunging ahead in a gallop. Grim-faced with concern, Frank leaned forward in the saddle and urged Goldy into a run as well.

Magnusson was racing blindly into trouble, Frank thought, and they had no idea what they would find when they reached the site of the battle. From what he had heard, though, before the pounding hoofbeats drowned out all other sound, quite a few guns were going off.

The road they were following wound through rolling hills and then cut straight across Montero range, Frank recalled from his visit to the valley the day before. Much of the landscape appeared flat at first glance, but that appearance was deceptive. It was cut through with gullies and shallow ridges and dotted with brushy, wooded knobs.

As Frank and Magnusson approached one such ridge, Frank spotted spurts of powder smoke coming from the guns of men firing from the top of it. The shots were aimed at a cluster of three drilling rigs on the other side of the road, with a large, circular wooden tank nearby. The drillers had taken cover behind storage sheds, as well as behind the derricks themselves, and were returning the fire.

"Those damned cowboys!" Magnusson yelled as he and Frank galloped toward the wells. "Somebody's gonna get killed this time!"

Frank thought that Magnusson might be right. This battle was a small-scale war, with a heap of powder being burned on both sides. Any time that much lead started flying around, the odds were that someone would die.

A bullet whipped past Frank's head as he and Magnusson approached the rigs. The riflemen on the ridge had noticed the two of them. They were targets now as well.

Magnusson headed for one of the sheds. Frank stayed with him. As they reached the shelter of the sturdy little building, they reined their mounts to skidding halts. Frank swung down from the saddle almost before Goldy had stopped moving. He hung on to the reins, keeping the stallion with him.

One of Magnusson's men, clad in oil-smeared overalls, crouched behind the shed with a rifle in his hand. When he turned to look at the newcomers, Frank recognized him as Rattigan, the man who'd been driving the wagon full of drillers he had encountered the previous morning.

Rattigan swung the rifle barrel toward Frank, crying, "Damn it, Boss, look out! He's one of them!"

Magnusson grabbed the Winchester's barrel and roughly forced it down. "Hold your fire, you idiot! Morgan works for me now!"

Rattigan's eyes widened in surprise. He looked like he could barely believe what he had just heard.

Frank nodded at Rattigan to confirm what Magnusson had said.

"That's right, Rattigan," he told the driller. "We're on the same side."

"Hatch isn't gonna like that," Rattigan muttered.

"I don't give a damn what Hatch likes," Magnusson snapped. "What's going on here?"

"Those cowboys started shooting at us from the top of the ridge. The bullets just came out of nowhere. They didn't give us any warning, just opened up on us."

"The hell you say!" Magnusson exploded angrily.

Frank asked, "How do you know they're ranch hands? Did you get a look at any of them?"

"How could we get a look at them?" Rattigan replied with a look of withering scorn. "They're a hundred yards away, in those trees on the ridge. Anyway, we were all too busy ducking bullets and running for cover to stand around gawking at the bastards!"

"Anybody been hurt so far?" Magnusson asked.

Rattigan gave him a bleak nod. "I saw a couple of

men go down. I don't know how bad they were hit. Some of the men dragged them behind cover."

Frank looked around the cluster of rigs, and saw the two men Rattigan referred to lying behind the base of one of the derricks. They weren't moving, which didn't bode well, and even from a distance Frank could see the bright crimson splashes of blood on their work clothes.

Magnusson jerked his rifle from its saddle sheath and roared, "This is the last straw! We'll wipe those damned cattlemen out if we have to!"

"Take it easy," Frank told him. "Flying off the handle's not going to help."

Magnusson swung toward him with a savage glare. "Whose side are you on, Morgan?" he demanded. "I knew I was a fool to trust you! My sister never should have roped you in on this deal!"

"I'm on your side, like I told Rattigan," Frank said, meeting the oilman's furious expression with a level stare of his own. "But wholesale slaughter's not going to solve anything."

"That's where you're wrong," Magnusson grated. "If we wipe out the Montero punchers, they can't ever ambush us like this again!"

That logic was indisputable, but Frank knew it wouldn't end there. In a war like Magnusson wanted to wage, one side seldom wiped out the other. What usually happened was that the enemies slugged away at each other until *both* sides were destroyed.

"Tell your men to hold their fire."

"What are you going to do?" Magnusson asked as Frank grasped the saddle horn and swung up onto Goldy's back.

"I'm going to circle around, get up on that ridge, and try to put a stop to this fight without anybody else getting hurt," Frank said.

Magnusson shook his head. "They saw you riding up with me. They won't hold their fire. They'll just gun you down like they're trying to do to us."

"They'll have to hit me first," Frank said with a humorless smile, "and Goldy and I don't intend to let that happen."

With that, he pulled the stallion around and heeled Goldy into a gallop again. They burst out from behind the shed and thundered back onto the road, heading away from the drilling rigs.

Frank leaned forward, low in the saddle, as bullets whined spitefully around them, searching for him like blazing messengers of death.

# Chapter 22

Frank headed back the way he and Magnusson had come. Slugs kicked up dust in the road around Goldy's flashing hooves.

None of the shots found either horse or rider. The stallion was moving so fast, it would have taken an extremely accurate shot to bring either of them down.

Once he was out of rifle range, Frank cut to the west, leaving the road and heading toward the spot where the ridge slanted down to the flatter ground.

The bushwhackers on the ridge might not see him coming right away because of one of the brushy knobs that jutted up and blocked their view, but they could be looking for him anyway. If they had recognized him, it was unlikely they would assume that the notorious Drifter would just cut and run. They would be expecting him to try something.

On the other hand, maybe they hadn't gotten a good enough look at him to realize who he was.

There was only one way to find out, Frank told himself. He knew he couldn't ride off and leave the drillers pinned down there to be picked off one by one, no matter how abrasive Victor Magnusson was.

He circled all the way around the ridge, then dropped off Goldy when he spotted a gully that ran all the way to the top of the slope. Dog crowded close beside him as Frank began making his way up the gully. Goldy would stay close at the bottom, waiting for Frank to either return or summon him with a shrill whistle.

Frank had his Colt in his hand, but he hoped he wouldn't have to use it, at least not to kill. He followed the sound of shots, making his way through the thick brush with a minimum of noise. He had a pantherlike grace about him that enabled him to approach one of the bushwhackers from the rear without even the faintest crackle of branches to warn the man.

A pang of disappointment went through Frank as he recognized one of the hands from the Montero ranch. He had been hoping that someone other than Dolores's crew was responsible for this attack on the drilling rigs, but clearly that wasn't the case.

When Frank was within arm's reach and the gunman still hadn't noticed him, he reversed the Colt, lifted it, and brought the butt of the heavy revolver crashing down on the man's head. The cowboy's Stetson absorbed some of the force of the blow, so that his skull didn't crack under the impact, but it was still enough to send him slumping senseless to the ground.

Frank pulled the man's belt off, pulled his arms behind his back, and used the belt to lash his wrists together. He took the man's bandanna off and crammed it into the cowboy's mouth. It would take the hombre a minute or two anyway to spit out the makeshift gag when he regained consciousness. Then Frank tossed the man's rifle and six-gun into the brush where they wouldn't be easy to find.

From the sound of the shots, he estimated that there were at least a dozen men up there on the ridge, firing down at the drillers. It was too much to hope for that he could sneak up on all of them and knock them out, Frank knew, but he intended to whittle down the odds as much as he could.

Luck was against him, though, because he suddenly came to a clearing where a couple of cowboys were holding the horses of the other men. The horses reacted to Dog's presence, rearing and neighing, and as the cowboys struggled to control them, one of the men spotted Frank.

"Morgan!" he howled. "Over here! It's Morgan!"

Frank recognized the man doing the yelling, too. It was the young cowboy called Jeff, who had carried a grudge against him since Frank's first day in Los Angeles. Jeff let go of the reins he was holding and clawed at the butt of the revolver on his hip instead.

That was a mistake, because the spooked horses he had just released bolted, and the shoulder of one of them slammed into Jeff as it went past, sending the young cowboy flying off his feet. The horses stampeded off, and it was all the other man could do to hang on to the ones he still had hold of.

Frank leveled the Colt at the man and ordered, "Let 'em go."

The puncher's eyes widened. "Mister, I can't! Then we'd all be afoot."

"That's the idea," Frank said. "Now let go of those reins, if you know what's good for you."

This was one of those times when having a reputation as a cold-blooded killer came in handy. The man's face paled under its tan, and his fingers spread out as he released the reins in both hands.

The horses took off. Some of them came between Frank and the second cowboy, though, and the man took advantage of the opportunity to snatch his gun out of its holster.

Before he could raise it and fire, though, Frank sprang across the clearing and slashed at the man's head with his Colt. The front sight raked across the cowboy's forehead, opening up a bloody gash.

The man stumbled back a step under the impact of the blow. Frank's left hand closed around the wrist of his gun hand and twisted hard. The puncher cried out in pain as he let go of his gun and it thudded to the ground.

Frank released the man's wrist and brought his left fist up in a short, hard blow to the jaw. That put the cowboy on the ground. He was stunned, and a quick kick to the head knocked him out cold.

Better to wake up with a headache than not wake up at all, Frank thought as he turned away from the man he had just knocked unconscious.

A gun roared behind him as he turned. He felt the heat of the bullet as it passed by his cheek.

Jeff had recovered from being knocked down by the horse and was on his knees, the gun in his hand thrust out in front of him. He froze that way, eyes widening, as he found himself staring down the barrel of Frank's Colt.

Frank almost fired. Only the tiniest fraction more pressure was needed to trip the big six-gun's trigger.

But he held off and said, "Drop it, Jeff. I don't want to kill you."

"You . . . you said that to Lonnie . . . and he's dead!"

Jeff was terrified—Frank could see that in the young man's eyes—but he wasn't willing to back down and lower his gun. He was too proud to do that.

Or too stupid, depending on how you looked at it.

But as Jeff hesitated with his own finger on the trigger, Frank heard running footsteps crashing through the brush toward him. Jeff's shouts and the eruption of handgun fire had drawn the attention of the other men on the ridge. Frank knew that if the rest of the Salida del Sol crew came up and saw him pointing his Colt at Jeff, they would open fire to save their young compadre.

So he did the only thing he could. He lowered his own weapon and said in a calm voice, "All right, son. You've got the drop on me."

Jeff's eyes widened even more, although that didn't seem possible, and for a second Frank thought the youngster was going to go ahead and shoot him. That was the calculated risk Frank was running.

But then Jeff's finger eased on the trigger. He wasn't a murderer, and that's what he would have been if he had gunned Frank down like this.

Slowly, Frank pouched his iron. He was standing there with his hands at his sides when several more men burst into the clearing and leveled rifles and six-guns at him. He was surrounded.

"Hold your fire!" a voice yelled behind him. Frank recognized it as belonging to Pete Linderman. Dolores Montero's foreman circled around Frank, covering him with a Winchester. Blood dripped from a bullet burn on Linderman's leathery cheek.

With a bitter note in his voice, Linderman went on. "Morgan. I didn't want to believe it was you. After fightin' side by side with you last night, I didn't figure you'd go over to the enemy this quick."

"How do you know I'm working for Magnusson?" Frank asked.

"He made us let go of the horses!" Jeff shouted as he struggled to his feet. He still seemed to be shaken up from having been knocked down by the horses.

He wasn't telling the story exactly as it had happened either. He had let go of the horses he was holding because he'd been surprised to see Frank again, not because he had been ordered at gunpoint to release them like the other cowboy.

Frank didn't think that any good would be served by pointing out that discrepancy, though, so he let it go.

"We're set afoot, Pete!" Jeff went on. "And those damn drillers are liable to come after us again!"

"We've got the high ground now," Linderman said curtly. "They won't get away with bushwhacking us again."

Frank found that comment mighty interesting, but having almost a dozen guns pointing at him wasn't a very good atmosphere for figuring things out. He said, "I didn't have anything to do with ambushing you, Linderman, and neither did those drillers down there."

"Bullshit!" Linderman shot back at him. "I saw you and Magnusson ridin' up with my own eyes,

Morgan. The señora wouldn't hire you, so you went and sold your gun to that bastard."

"It's true that I'm working for Magnusson," Frank admitted, "but what I'm really trying to do is find out who's causing trouble for both sides in the valley."

"I can tell you who's causin' the trouble, mister," one of the other punchers said around a chaw of tobacco that bulged out his cheek. "It's them greasy oil varmints."

Several of the other men nodded in grim agreement. All of them looked like they would welcome an excuse to fill Frank with lead.

He was careful not to give them one. "Tell me what happened," he suggested.

"The hell with that," Linderman snapped. "You probably know as well as we do. You and Magnusson probably planned the whole thing and then rode out here to see how it turned out. Well, it backfired on you, Morgan."

He used the barrel of his rifle to gesture to several of the others. "Somebody get his gun, and then tie him up. We're takin' him back to the hacienda."

"Hold on," Frank said quickly. He wasn't going to let them take his gun without a fight. He just wasn't made that way.

But in the end, the struggle probably wouldn't get him anything except a wallop over the head with a rifle barrel, and maybe a few kicks to the ribs for good measure. He went on. "If you don't want to explain it to me, then let *me* tell *you* what happened."

"Of course you'd know." Linderman shook his head. "Like I said, you and Magnusson must've planned the ambush."

"You and your men were riding the range not far from here." Frank pointed in the direction of the ranch headquarters and forged ahead as if Linderman had not spoken. "Somebody opened fire on you from the top of this ridge. Probably wounded a couple of you."

"Ed Matthews is more than wounded," Linderman said grimly. "He took a bullet right through the brisket. He's dead."

"I'm sorry to hear that," Frank said, and meant it. "For what it's worth, a couple of the drillers down there are wounded and maybe dead."

"They had it comin', the bushwhackin' sons o' bitches!" one of the cowboys shouted.

Frank shook his head. "The drillers aren't the ones who shot at you."

"What the hell are you talkin' about?" Linderman demanded. "Of course they are. We charged up here and ran 'em back down there to those rigs."

"Did you *see* any of them shooting at you?"

"Damn right we did! They're hidin' behind their sheds and those derricks—"

"No, I mean when the shooting first started," Frank cut in. "Did you see them up here on the ridge? Did you see them running back down to the wells?"

Linderman glared at him and didn't say anything for a moment, and the foreman's silence gave Frank the answer he expected. Frank had put together in his mind everything he had seen and heard earlier and had a pretty good idea how things had played out.

"That don't mean anything," Linderman finally

said. "It had to be them who shot at us. Who else could it have been?"

"That's the question we all need to answer," Frank said. "Here's the way I see it. The bushwhackers were up here on this ridge. They'd probably been following you to see which direction you were going, then circled around to set up their trap."

"On horseback, you mean?" Linderman asked with a frown.

"That's right. I saw the dust their horses raised a while ago. Some of them got on this side of the ridge, some on the other, and they opened fire on you fellas at the same time as they started shooting at those drillers on the other side of the ridge. All it would take was one volley each way. Then they lit a shuck out of here."

The foreman's frown deepened. "What the hell are you talkin' about?"

"You charged right up here, didn't you?" Frank asked. "And by that time, the drillers had gotten behind some cover and were shooting at the top of the ridge, because that's where they'd been ambushed from a minute earlier. You thought they'd taken those first shots at your bunch and then run down the hill, so you returned their fire." Frank shrugged. "It makes perfect sense."

One of the cowboys warned, "Don't listen to him, Pete! He's in with Magnusson. We saw it for ourselves!"

Linderman rubbed his jaw. "Hold on a minute. You're sayin' that somebody tricked us and those drillers into shootin' at each other by bushwhackin' *both* sides?"

"That's exactly what I'm saying," Frank replied with a nod. "There's already a wedge between the two bunches. Now that men have been badly wounded or killed on both sides, it'll just be driven in deeper . . . unless you and your men listen to reason, Linderman."

"What about them? What about Magnusson's bunch? They were shootin' at us, no doubt about that."

"Only because they believe you shot at them first."

"Damn it, this is makin' my head hurt." Linderman blew out a breath in disgust. "But I reckon things could've happened the way you're sayin' they did, Morgan. Wouldn't we have seen or heard the fellas ridin' off, though, if they did like you said?"

"What did you do when the first shots rang out?" Frank asked.

"Well, we were out in the open, so we picked up Ed and hustled into the cover of some trees. Once we figured out where the shots were coming from, we charged up here to flush the bastards out."

"So if they left a couple of men behind to keep you occupied for a few minutes and make you think there were more hombres up here than there really were, the others could've ridden along the ridge and dropped down off of it somewhere else."

"Maybe . . . but wouldn't those oil drillers have seen them if they did that?"

"Not if they stayed just on this side of the crest," Frank explained. "There are enough trees up there to screen them from view."

"You make a good case for it, Morgan, but where's the proof?"

Frank jerked a thumb over his shoulder in the direction of the oil rigs. "One of the drillers told me they were working down there when someone opened fire on them from the ridge. They just naturally assumed it was you fellas from Salida del Sol . . . and a couple of minutes later, it was."

"Yeah, that's fine," one of the other men said with a snort of contempt, "if you want to believe a bunch o' lyin' oilmen! As far as I'm concerned, they stink o' brimstone 'cause they come straight out o' Hell!"

"If you want proof," Frank suggested, "why don't you check for hoofprints and droppings somewhere along the ridge? Your horses were left on this side. If you find evidence of another group of riders being up here, you'll know that I'm right about what happened."

"That's not exactly proof," Linderman said with a shrug, "but I reckon we could take a look around."

He had lowered his rifle now and seemed to be giving serious consideration to Frank's theory, even though the rest of the cowboys were clearly reluctant to believe it.

"Why don't you let your men do that?" Frank said. "You and I will go talk to Magnusson and get the drillers' side of the story."

"Talk to Magnusson!" Linderman burst out. "I don't have anything to say to that skunk! Not unless it's over the barrel of a gun! I don't care what started it, they still shot at us."

"In what seemed to them like self-defense," Frank pointed out. "But I reckon if you're afraid that you'll find out I'm right . . ."

Linderman reacted just like Frank thought he would. The ramrod glared at him and snapped, "I'm not afraid of Magnusson or any other damn driller." He turned to his men. "Take a look for tracks and horse apples along the ridge. Morgan and I are gonna go talk to Magnusson."

With that, he stalked off. Frank walked beside him, hiding the grin he felt coming on at the way Linderman had played right into his hands.

# Chapter 23

The drillers' guns had fallen silent several minutes earlier, when the members of the Montero crew had stopped firing down at them from the ridge in order to surround Frank.

Now there was always the chance that they would open fire again when Frank and Linderman stepped out of the trees and into view. If that happened, they would be dead men.

But instead, Frank heard Victor Magnusson yell, "Hold your fire! Nobody shoot unless they start it!"

Beside Frank, Linderman grunted. "Sounds like Magnusson don't fully trust you either, Morgan."

"I'm sort of getting used to nobody around here trusting me," Frank said dryly. "I still don't like it."

"Reckon you'd be used to it, you bein' a hired gun and all."

Frank didn't waste any breath pointing out the obvious, that he wasn't the sort of gunfighter everyone around here seemed to take him for.

After the time he had spent being liked and respected in Buckskin, the suspicion that folks in southern California seemed to feel toward him wasn't very pleasant. It had been his choice to ride away from that Nevada settlement, though, so he had no one to blame but himself.

Magnusson and the drillers didn't emerge from cover. They stayed behind the sheds and derricks with the barrels of their rifles poking out, ready to open fire again.

When Frank and Linderman reached the road, Magnusson called, "That's far enough! What are you doing with that cowboy, Morgan? Switching sides already?"

Frank felt a surge of anger. He wasn't sure he had ever encountered such a level of distrust as the one that seemed to infect everybody in these parts. They were all mighty quick to jump to conclusions, especially where he was concerned.

"I'm calling a truce, Magnusson!" he replied. "Come on out here so you and Linderman can hash this out."

"There's nothing to hash out! They're a bunch of murdering, bushwhacking bastards! Both of my men who were wounded have died!"

Frank had been afraid of that. So there were casualties on both sides now. That would make them dig in their heels even deeper. The hatred they felt toward each other wouldn't go away, and neither would the violence.

Unless Frank could somehow talk sense into their heads.

"Señora Montero's men didn't attack you, Magnusson," Frank insisted.

"You're crazy!" the oilman shouted back. "That's her foreman Pete Linderman with you right there!"

"Come on out here and talk it over. I'll prove to you that you're wrong."

Magnusson couldn't resist that challenge. He stalked out from behind the shed where he had been crouched with Rattigan. His spade beard jutted forward as his jaw thrust out belligerently. He came toward Frank and Linderman with his rifle held slanted across his broad chest.

He came to a stop with the road still between him and the other two men. "All right," he snapped. "If you've got something to say, Morgan, go ahead and say it."

"Pay attention," Frank began. "I'm going to tell you what really happened here."

Quickly, he went over the same theory he had laid out for Linderman and the Salida del Sol ranch hands. Magnusson's bushy red eyebrows drew down in a puzzled frown as he listened.

"Wait a minute," he said when Frank was finished. He turned his head and called, "Rattigan! Come out here!"

The driller emerged from behind the shed with a nervous look on his oil-smeared face. At least Frank thought the man looked nervous; it was hard to tell for sure with all those dark smudges.

"What do you want, Mr. Magnusson?" Rattigan asked as he came forward.

"Did you see the men who were shooting at you from the ridge?"

"We sure did," Rattigan insisted. "We saw them jumping around from tree to tree and rock to rock up there while they were getting into position to massacre us."

Frank said, "No, before that, when you heard the first shots. Did you look up there and see anybody then?"

Rattigan glared at him. "No, we were too busy runnin' for cover. But we saw plenty of powder smoke from the top of the ridge. At least I did. I can't speak for all the other fellas."

Frank gave Magnusson a meaningful look. "You see, your men can't say for sure that it was Linderman and his pards shooting at them until *after* the fighting started."

"You really expect me to believe that somebody else was responsible for this bloodshed? That they tricked my men and the cowboys into shooting at each other?"

"That's exactly what I believe," Frank said with a firm nod.

Linderman spoke up. "You've got to admit, it could've happened the way Morgan says, Magnusson. I figured it was a loco idea at first, too, but now that I've thought about it, I reckon maybe he's right."

"I don't know," Magnusson said. "Who'd have a reason to do such a thing?"

"Now, that's what I haven't figured out just yet," Frank admitted. "But I'm going to."

Stubbornly, Magnusson shook his head. "I've got to have more proof than you've come up with so far, Morgan."

"Then give me a chance to get it," Frank responded without hesitation. "Keep this truce going for the time being while I look into the situation."

"I never agreed to any damn truce," Magnusson muttered.

"Neither did I," Linderman said. "But I'm willin' to tell my boys to steer clear of your rigs for now, Magnusson, if you'll promise not to cause any trouble for us."

"We haven't been," Magnusson snapped. "We just want to be left alone to drill for oil."

"To stink up the air and ruin the land for our cattle, you mean."

Frank held up his hands to forestall any renewal of the old argument that wasn't going to be settled today. He said, "How about it? Truce?"

For a long moment, neither of the other men said anything. Then Magnusson growled, "All right, damn it. Truce."

Linderman nodded. "Sure. I'll go along with that. You got to remember one thing, though, Morgan."

"What's that?"

"I don't speak for the señora. She may tell Magnusson to take his truce and stick it where the sun don't shine."

"It's not my truce," Magnusson said. "It's Morgan's."

"I don't care whose truce it is," Frank said, "as long as the two sides aren't shooting at each other."

Tension was still thick in the air as Frank and Linderman started back up the slope toward the top of the ridge. The drillers started slowly coming out from behind the sheds and the derricks, and some of the cowboys emerged from the trees, still holding their rifles in a threatening manner.

Frank had explained to Magnusson that he had to return to the top of the ridge to get Goldy and Dog. Also, he wanted to check and see if Linderman's men had found any sign of the riders he suspected of starting the battle.

Even if they hadn't, he intended to have a look for himself. Maybe he would see something that the others had missed.

Jeff came out of the trees to meet Frank and Linderman. The young cowboy wore a puzzled frown, which seemed to be his most common expression.

"Hey, Pete," Jeff said, "you'd better come have a look at this."

"What is it?" Linderman asked.

"Well . . ." Jeff glanced at Frank. "I hate to say it, but I think maybe Morgan was right."

Linderman grunted in surprise. "About there bein' another bunch of riders?" he asked.

"Yeah." Jeff led the two of them along the ridge for about twenty yards, then paused and waved a hand toward the ground. "Take a gander at those prints."

Linderman hunkered on his heels to study the faint hoof marks on the ground. After a moment he said grudgingly, "They look pretty fresh."

"And none of our horses were this far up the slope," Jeff said.

Linderman shook his head. "Just because another rider passed along here sometime today doesn't mean that Morgan's right."

One of the other cowboys stepped forward and held out his hand. Sunlight reflected off something that lay on his work-roughened palm.

"What about this, Pete?"

Linderman straightened and took the object from the man. Frank could tell now that it was a used shell from a rifle cartridge. When he saw the frown that creased Linderman's forehead as the foreman turned the shell over in his fingers, Frank asked, "Mind if I have a look?"

Linderman tossed it to him. Frank caught the shell. There was nothing unusual about it except . . .

"Thirty-thirty, isn't it?" Frank said.

"Yeah." Linderman grimaced. "And all of our Winchesters are forty-four-forties."

"You're saying that it didn't come from one of your rifles."

"I reckon not." Linderman took his hat off, ran his fingers through his hair in annoyance, then clapped the battered Stetson back on. "But damn it, how could they plan on gettin' away with a thing like that? Didn't they know we'd figure it out sooner or later?"

"Do you think you really would have?" Frank asked. "Would you have looked for hoofprints or shells from a different-caliber rifle?" He waved a hand toward the drilling rigs on the other side of the road. "Or would you and the drillers have just kept shooting at each other until one side or the other was wiped out?"

"It would've been them," one of the punchers muttered. "We had 'em pinned down good an' proper."

"That's right," Frank said. "And you would have killed them thinking that you were settling the score for Ed Matthews, when all you really would've been doing was the dirty work for whoever keeps stirring up all this trouble."

Linderman gave him a challenging stare. "Are you sayin' that *none* of what's been goin' on here in the valley was the doin' of those damn drillers?"

Frank shook his head and said, "I can't make that claim, but it wouldn't surprise me. And I'd bet a hat that Magnusson and his men didn't have anything to do with the attack on Salida del Sol last night."

"Well, what the hell do we do now?" Jeff wanted to know.

"If it was me," Frank said dryly, "I'd try to round up those horses that stampeded off a while ago. Otherwise, you boys are going to have a long, uncomfortable walk back to the bunkhouse."

That brought muttered agreement from some of the men. Like all cowboys everywhere, they didn't believe in walking anywhere that they could ride, no matter how close it was . . . and the ranch headquarters wasn't all that close.

"What about you?" Linderman asked. "What are you gonna do, Morgan?"

"I thought I'd see if I can follow the sign that the real bushwhackers left behind. They've got to be holed up somewhere here in the valley."

"They had to do something with all those cows they've rustled, too," Linderman pointed out. "We've tried to follow the trail before but always lost it up in the San Gabriels. You reckon you'll have better luck than we did?"

"I don't know," Frank said. "But I intend to try."

# Chapter 24

Linderman and the other Salida del Sol punchers went to find their horses. Frank didn't have to do that, because a whistle brought Goldy up the slope to him.

He swung up into the saddle and rode along the ridge with Dog trailing behind him. Eyes that were still keen despite the years spotted several more hoofprints, and as the trail led down the slope, Frank found even more sign.

Looked like fourteen or fifteen men, he estimated. A good-sized group. Whoever was out to raise hell in the valley had plenty of gunmen at his disposal.

That worried Frank. Things seemed to be escalating. Last night, the attack on the barn at Salida del Sol. Today, the attempt to trick the cowboys and the drillers into waging open war on each other.

Whoever was behind this must be getting impatient, Frank decided. Whether or not that had anything to do with his own arrival in the area, he couldn't say, but he thought it was possible.

Somebody wanted the conflict between the oilmen

and the cattlemen to explode into a bloody war before Frank had a chance to stop it.

Those thoughts led his mind down some intriguing paths, but he had more to do than just mull over everything that had happened. He had a trail to follow, too.

"Might as well earn your keep, Dog," he said to the big cur. "See if you can pick up the scent of those horses we're following."

Dog ranged ahead, nose to the ground. Frank had confidence in his own tracking ability, but Dog, with his extremely sensitive nose, was better.

The trail led down the western slope of the ridge and then paralleled it for more than a mile before the rugged, wooded height came to an end. At that point, the riders had turned and headed northeast, cutting across the valley toward the San Gabriel Mountains on the far side.

He was on Jorge Sandoval's range now, Frank recalled from the description Stafford had given him of the way the ranches were laid out in the valley. If Sandoval's plan had worked out and Dolores had agreed to the merger of their two ranches once she inherited Salida del Sol, then they would have controlled by far the largest amount of range in these parts.

Would Sandoval go so far as to try to ruin his own sister's ranch so that he could gobble it up? Frank couldn't answer that question. He didn't know the man well enough to say one way or the other what he was capable of.

But it was an intriguing thought, he told himself. When he got a chance to talk to Stafford again, he would suggest to the lawyer that he do some digging into Jorge Sandoval's background and financial situation.

Of course, there were other ranchers in the valley who might have designs on Salida del Sol, too. Edwin Northam had no close ties with any of the other cattlemen. In fact, he seemed to go out of his way to distance himself from them. He might not hesitate to try to get his hands on Dolores's ranch, by fair means or foul.

Nor could Frank forget that other oilmen had wells in the valley. Victor Magnusson wasn't the only wildcatter in the San Fernando, just the only one Frank had run into so far. He was never out of sight of at least one derrick as he rode across the valley, and usually he could see six or seven at a time as well as hear the racket that went with them. Magnusson could be telling the truth, and it could still be one of the oilmen behind the trouble.

All the questions might be answered if Frank could track the bushwhackers to their hideout. He was convinced that the gunmen were also the ones who had carried out the rustling. He just needed to get his hands on one of the varmints and make him talk.

Dog still had the scent, but he lost it when they came to a creek. Frank sighed as he watched the big cur loping back and forth along the opposite bank.

The men they were following weren't greenhorns. Just in case someone was following them, they had ridden one way or the other along the shallow creek to throw off any pursuit. Frank's only option was to choose a direction and hope that Dog could pick up the scent again.

And if the bushwhackers had doubled back, then even that might not do any good.

He was glad he had brought a couple of biscuits from the hotel dining room and slipped them into his saddlebags. This looked like it might be a long day, and he wouldn't be getting back to town for lunch.

Frank's prediction proved to be accurate. He and Goldy and Dog spent several hours riding up and down the creek, checking both sides in both directions for any sign left by the men they were after. It was well after noon before Dog suddenly put his nose to the ground and loped off toward the San Gabriels once again.

Frank heaved a sigh of relief and dug out one of the biscuits to snack on as he turned Goldy and followed his big, wolflike trail partner.

Once Dog had the scent again, he headed straight as an arrow toward the mountains. The bushwhackers must have thought that their jog through the creek had thrown off any pursuit, so they didn't waste time veering back and forth.

Frank was convinced that they were bound for their hideout, and with Dog on the trail, he had a feeling that he'd be able to find it.

By late afternoon, they were in the foothills of the San Gabriels, which were heavily wooded. The town of Pasadena was several miles to the east, Frank recalled, but over here the mountains were still wild and only lightly populated.

Not a bad place for a gang of rustlers and bushwhackers to hole up, in other words.

Frank scanned the sky over the foothills for smoke

from a campfire or stove, but didn't see any. "Slow down, Dog," he called to the big cur. "We don't want to ride right into the middle of that bunch without any warning."

Dog slowed down, but the glance he cast over his shoulder told Frank that he didn't like it. Once he was on the trail of varmints—either four-footed or human—Dog wasn't one to hold back.

They had long since left the old wagon road that cut across the San Fernando Valley, the trace that had been established by Remi Nadeau decades earlier. Frank began noticing signs that animals had been driven through here, though. A visible path had been beaten down by their hooves.

Those rustled cattle, he thought. His pulse quickened at this indication he was on the right trail.

The path led over a saddle in a long ridge, and then curved into a steep-sided canyon about a hundred yards wide. Frank reined Goldy to a halt just outside the canyon. Instinct told him that his quarry wasn't too far away.

"Stay here," he told Dog in a quiet voice as he dismounted. "I'm going ahead on foot."

He led Goldy into a clump of trees and looped the reins around a sapling so that it would be easy enough for the stallion to pull free if necessary. Then he pulled his Winchester from the saddle boot and started into the canyon.

Frank took it slow and careful, using every bit of cover he could find as he made his way through the canyon. It narrowed down to about fifty yards across.

If this was the entrance to the gang's hideout,

they were bound to have guards posted somewhere, keeping an eye on the place. Frank didn't want them to spot him.

He froze as a faint smell of tobacco smoke drifted to his nose. A moment later he heard a tiny clatter, like a pebble bouncing down a slope.

There was a sentry somewhere above and ahead of him, he realized. The man was smoking a quirly and moving around enough to have dislodged a rock. That was pretty careless of him, but Frank figured the guard wasn't really expecting trouble. The outlaws were probably confident that no one knew where their hideout was.

Frank knew, though. The trail had led here from the site of the battle between the cowboys and the drillers, a battle that had been provoked by the men who were hiding out in this canyon.

The stolen cattle might be somewhere up ahead, too. Their presence would be the last bit of evidence he needed to make the law take action. And once the outlaws were in custody, he had no doubt some of them would implicate whoever was behind this scheme to keep trouble stirred up in the valley.

Of course, the rustlers could have already disposed of the cows they had run off, selling them to some unscrupulous cattle buyer who didn't care what brands had been burned into their hides. That would complicate matters, but Frank still felt like he was on the verge of exposing the plotters.

He needed to get closer, though, to make sure of what the lawmen would find in the canyon when he led them back here.

Frank stayed where he was, motionless and silent,

until he heard the guard shifting around again. The man coughed. A match rasped on stone as he lit another quirly.

A faint smile touched Frank's grim mouth. The hombre might as well be shouting out loud to announce his presence. He was behind some rocks on a ledge, in a place where he could see anyone who came through the canyon.

Except someone who hugged the stone wall below him and could move quietly enough not to be heard.

Frank looked long and hard at the other side of the canyon to make sure no sentries were posted over there. There wasn't a good place for a guard to hide, he decided. The canyon wall was too steep and sheer. And as confident, even arrogant, as this gang seemed to be, they probably thought one sentry was enough.

Placing his booted feet carefully, Frank slipped along the rocky wall. He kept the Winchester in his right hand, well away from the rocks so that its barrel wouldn't bump against them and make a racket.

He had a bad moment when the butt of the sentry's cigarette fell right in front of his face to land at his feet. It took iron nerves for Frank not to react to the unexpected event, other than coming to a sudden stop. He knew the guard had just tossed the quirly off the ledge without thinking about where it would land. It didn't mean the man knew he was down here.

Good thing the cigarette butt with its glowing coal hadn't hit him on the back of the neck and gone down his shirt collar, he thought with a grin. That might have been harder not to react to.

He started off again, taking another careful step, then another and another. Soon the guard was behind him and he could move a little faster, although he was still careful to make as little noise as possible.

The canyon began to widen again. Within a few hundred yards, it had spread out until it was a quarter of a mile across. It was a box canyon, though, Frank realized, ending in a fifty-foot-tall stone wall that completely enclosed the large, parklike area.

He crouched in some brush to study the hideout. A couple of crude log cabins were next to the far wall, which thrust out enough so that its overhang created a cave of sorts underneath it.

That was where a large campfire was located. The rock ceiling deflected and dispersed the smoke from the fire, making the hideout even more difficult to find.

A pole corral for the gang's horses had been thrown up near the cabins. For water, a little stream trickled out of the rock wall, ran across the clearing for a couple of hundred yards, and ended in a small pond.

About fifty head of cattle grazed along the banks of the tiny creek. Those were the only cows Frank saw.

He knew that more than that had been rustled from the ranchers in the valley, so he figured the others had already been sold off. The little jag being held here now would be the spoils from the gang's most recent raid.

Frank tried to count the horses in the corral, but could only estimate them as being between thirty and forty. Even assuming that some of the men might have more than one mount, that meant the gang was pretty big.

Somebody had to be paying out a considerable amount of money to hire these hardcases. That meant the stakes they were playing for in the valley had to be high.

A few men were moving around the cabins. At this distance, Frank couldn't see them well enough to recognize any of them, but he knew their breed. Hard-bitten killers whose guns were for sale to the highest bidder . . . the sort of men that all too many people took *him* to be when all they knew about him was his unasked-for reputation.

He had what he needed—the location of the hideout and proof that these men were really the ones causing the trouble in the San Fernando Valley. The county sheriff might not want to accept Frank's word for it, but Stafford ought to be able to push the man into bringing a posse out here to see for himself, Frank thought.

It was time now to get back to Goldy and head for Los Angeles.

Frank cast a glance at the sky above the canyon and realized that the sun was no longer visible. It had dropped down below the walls of the canyon and shadows had already begun to gather.

Night would come on quickly now. Frank didn't mind because the gloom would help him get past the guard without being spotted. He turned to head in that direction.

Loud voices stopped him. More men were coming out of the cabins now, he saw as he swung back around. They headed for the corral and began cutting out and saddling horses.

Frank stiffened and crouched lower in the brush. The gang was about to pull out. Not for good obviously, because those rustled cattle were still here.

But the fact that they were saddling up to leave didn't bode well. They were probably headed out to raise more hell in the valley. Frank had already figured out from the violence of the past two days that things were starting to rush to a conclusion, possibly because his own presence had spooked the mastermind into speeding up the plan.

So even though the gang had already caused that ruckus between Magnusson's men and the Salida del Sol crew, now they were setting out on more deadly mischief.

And the only thing between them and whatever they had planned was The Drifter.

# Chapter 25

For a moment, Frank considered opening up on the men with his Winchester as they rode past him. Even in the fading light, he was confident that he could drop half a dozen of them before they knew what was going on.

But then the rest of the gang would charge him, and even though he knew he would be able to kill several more of them, the survivors would gun him down. He wouldn't be able to cut their numbers by more than half, if that much.

That wasn't worth trading his life for, even though it went against the grain for him to lay low and avoid trouble. He could do more good by biding his time and hoping to bring the whole gang to justice later.

The question now, he thought as approximately twenty-five men thundered past him on horseback, was whether any of them would spot Goldy and Dog near the entrance to the canyon. If they did, they were likely to realize that someone was scouting for their hideout, and they might just turn around, figuring that they had the interloper trapped in the box canyon.

Which, of course, was the truth. If that happened, Frank would have no choice but take as many of the bastards with him as he could.

But he had run head-on into trouble too many times in his life to go borrowing any extra. He stayed where he was in the brush, watching the hardcases ride by in the fading light.

It didn't take long. Frank heard someone call out a farewell to the sentry, who was evidently going to remain on duty in the canyon, as they went past that spot.

Then they reached the canyon mouth and disappeared as they veered away from the opening, leaving nothing behind but a slight haze of dust that blew away quickly in the twilight breeze.

Frank waited as the rumble of hoofbeats faded. Finally, he couldn't hear them anymore. That meant the gunmen hadn't spotted Goldy and grown suspicious.

The only obstacle Frank had to avoid now was the guard. He was sure he could handle one man if he needed to, but he didn't want anything to alert the gang that their hideout had been discovered. They would jump to that conclusion if they came back and found the guard missing or dead.

With the same sort of stealth that had carried him into the canyon, Frank catfooted his way back out. The guard was singing softly to himself this time as Frank crept along beneath him. Frank couldn't help but grin as he listened to the bawdy lyrics about a saloon girl and a camp full of miners. This fella was one of the worst sentries he'd ever run into.

At least some of the outlaws were tough and smart, though. Otherwise, they wouldn't have been able to get away with their deviltry for as long as they had.

Frank trotted out of the canyon a couple of minutes later, and headed toward the spot where he'd left Goldy. The big stallion nickered a soft greeting as Frank approached. Dog came out of the shadows, too, to nuzzle Frank's hand.

"You critters did a good job of staying out of sight," Frank told the animals as he slid the Winchester back into its sheath. He jerked the reins loose from the sapling and swung up into the saddle. "The night's work isn't over, though."

He wasn't sure where the outlaws had gone, and it was already too dark to trail them. Once the moon rose, there might be enough light to spot some tracks, but Frank didn't want to wait that long.

He rode through the foothills, and then headed straight across the valley instead, toward Salida del Sol. Most of the trouble seemed to revolve around Señora Montero's ranch, so Frank figured it was a good bet that would hold true tonight, too.

Leaning forward in the saddle, he urged Goldy into a run. Would the outlaws attack the ranch two nights in a row?

Anything was possible, but it seemed unlikely to Frank. After the raid the previous night, Pete Linderman and the rest of the crew would be alert for more trouble. The gunmen had to know that.

Maybe this time the strike would be directed at

Magnusson's oil wells. The gang probably wasn't aware yet that Frank had figured out what was going on and had persuaded the two sides to call a truce. If they attacked the wells on horseback, yelling and whooping, they would figure that Magnusson was likely to blame the ranchers.

That tactic had been working so far, but Frank was determined that it wouldn't again.

The last crimson vestiges of sunset had faded from the western sky by the time Frank reached Montero range. The stars were out, pinpricks of light against a sable backdrop, but the moon had not yet risen. Thick black shadows cloaked the landscape.

He reined Goldy to a halt and listened intently, searching the night for gunfire or any other sounds that were out of place. He heard the distant clank and clatter of drilling rigs, but that was all.

Moving at a slower pace and letting the sounds guide him, Frank rode toward the wells. He didn't know if he would find Magnusson at one of the rigs, or if the oilman had gone back to the rented mansion in Los Angeles. Either way, he intended to warn the drillers that they might be in for trouble tonight.

Frank figured he was still half a mile or so from the cluster of wells where the battle had taken place earlier in the day when he heard a sudden flurry of shots. He wasn't given to profanity, but he bit back a curse now.

The hired killers had had too big a lead on him. They had gotten here first and launched their attack, just as he had suspected they would.

Frank heeled Goldy into a run now that he knew where hell was a-poppin' tonight. He pulled his rifle from the saddle boot as he leaned forward in the leather.

As Goldy pounded around a curve in the trail, Frank spotted spurts of muzzle flame in the darkness up ahead. He pulled the stallion to a stop long enough to study the situation for a moment, trying to trace the movements of the outlaws by following the muzzle flashes from their guns.

It appeared that the gang had the wells, the sheds, and the oil storage tank surrounded. They were riding around the place like Indians ringing a circled wagon train, back in those savage days that didn't seem all that long ago to Frank. Guns roared as they poured lead in on the defenders.

Their marksmanship couldn't be that accurate, though, not with them firing from the backs of running horses in bad light. They were just trying to keep the drillers pinned down, Frank realized, while they worked their way close enough to do something else.

Frank didn't know what that something else might be, but he was sure of one thing.

It wouldn't be anything good.

"Dog, stay!" he snapped. He didn't want the big cur following him where he was going, right into that storm of lead. There was too great a chance that Dog would get hit by a stray bullet. Goldy would have to run the risk of that, as would Frank himself, because there was no way he could reach the wells otherwise.

He didn't know if one more defender would make a difference, but he intended to find out. He wanted to know if Magnusson was there, too.

And on the way in, he would do as much damage to the gang as he could.

As he rode closer, he picked out the muzzle flashes that came from the sheds and the derricks as the drillers tried to defend themselves. They were out-numbered and outgunned, though, and despite being bruisers who could handle themselves just fine in any sort of hand-to-hand brawl, they probably weren't any match for the deadly skill of gun-wolves like the men they faced tonight.

The Drifter was, though. This sort of fight was his meat.

Guiding Goldy with his knees, Frank charged into the fight. He snapped the Winchester to his shoulder and began firing as fast as he could work the repeater's lever. A couple of shadowy figures cried out in pain, threw up their arms, and toppled from the backs of their galloping horses as Frank raced by.

It didn't take long for some of the gunmen to re-alize what was going on. One of them shouted, "They've got reinforcements comin' in! Get those sons o' bitches!"

One man hardly qualifed as reinforcements, Frank thought, but he was firing so fast that the out-laws might think there were three or four of him. Colt flame licked out from gun muzzles as the men turned their fire on him, but Frank bent low in the saddle to make himself a smaller target, and Goldy leaped forward with blinding speed.

They broke through the ring of killers and thun-dered toward the wells. Now there was another problem for Frank to worry about—the defenders might easily take him for one of the bushwhackers and turn their guns on him.

"Hold your fire!" he shouted as loud as he could. "It's Morgan! Hold your fire!"

A bullet whistled past his head, and this one came from one of the derricks. Several more slugs screamed through the air around him before he heard Victor Magnusson bellowing, "Cease fire! That's Morgan!"

Grateful that now he only had twenty or more hardcases who wanted to fill his hide full of lead instead of the outlaws *and* the drillers, Frank rode around one of the sheds and dropped from the saddle. He slapped Goldy on the rump and sent the stallion racing off into the night. Goldy would get himself out of harm's way, but stay close enough to hear Frank's whistle if he was summoned.

Frank dropped to one knee, lifted the Winchester, and drew a bead on one of the racing gunmen. The rifle's sharp whipcrack was followed by the target pitching limply from the saddle as the steeljacketed .44-40 round bored through his body.

The sound of heavy footsteps beside him made Frank twist around and swing the Winchester toward a potential new threat.

But it was Magnusson who had run over to him, Frank realized as the oilman called, "Don't shoot, Morgan! It's me."

Frank levered the rifle. "Figured you'd have gone back to town."

"I wanted to know if you'd found anything, and I thought you might come back by here this evening." Magnusson had lost his hat somewhere, and his thatch of long, fiery hair was disheveled. "Then those bastards came out of nowhere and started shooting at us."

"Not nowhere," Frank said. "I found their hide-out."

"They're not Montero men?"

"Not hardly," Frank said, although in truth he couldn't be positive of that. He hadn't gotten a good look at any of them after all. But he couldn't imagine any of Dolores's punchers hiding out in that isolated canyon on the far side of the San Fernando Valley. They wouldn't have any reason to do that.

"Then who do they work for?" Magnusson demanded.

Frank ducked as a bullet smacked into the shed wall a foot or so above his head, chewing splinters from the wood.

"I don't know yet, and this isn't exactly a good time to be trying to figure it out," he told Magnusson. "I think they want to do more than just ride around and take potshots at us, though."

"What do you think they have in mind?"

"Don't know." Frank took another shot, but didn't know if he hit anything this time. "But I reckon we'll find out . . . if we live long enough."

In the back of his mind, he hoped that whoever was riding nighthawk for the Montero spread would hear the shooting and bring help from the ranch. That was a longshot, though, and Frank knew they couldn't count on it.

"How many men do you have here?" he asked Magnusson.

"There were sixteen men in the crew before the

two were killed this morning. I sent one man back to town with their bodies in a wagon, so that leaves thirteen." Magnusson's voice was grim as he added, "I don't know if any of them have been killed yet tonight."

So, thirteen defenders, Frank thought, plus Magnusson made fourteen and he was fifteen. Against maybe twenty hired killers, because the gang had suffered some losses, too. Those odds weren't terrible, but they weren't very good either.

"How many horses?"

"None but mine! I told you, I sent the wagon back to town. The crews come and go in it, not on horseback." Magnusson's voice hardened. "Anyway, I'm not going to cut and run, if that's what you're thinking, Morgan. These are my men and my wells, and by God, I'm not going to abandon them!"

"I was thinking more of trying to get a rider out to go for help to the Montero ranch," Frank said.

"I'd be glad for somebody to use my horse, but it won't be me."

Magnusson drew a bead and fired his Winchester past the corner of the shed, as if to punctuate his declaration.

"I doubt if anybody from the Montero place would come to help us anyway," Magnusson added, "even with that so-called truce in place."

Frank wasn't so sure about that, but a second later he realized that they didn't have time to send a rider for help. He spotted a sudden flare of light in the darkness, about a hundred yards away. It wasn't a muzzle flash this time. It burned steadily and grew brighter, and he realized after a moment that it was the leaping flame of a torch.

"Magnusson," he said, "I reckon that big wooden tank's got oil in it, doesn't it?"

"What? Of course it does. All three of these wells have come in and are steady producers. We store the oil there until it can be put in barrels and taken to the refinery. The tank's at least half full, maybe more."

"It'd probably be a good idea then," Frank said as he saw several more torches blaze into life, "if we kept those hombres away from it."

"Son of a bitch!" Magnusson yelled as he realized what Frank was talking about. "Stop them! Shoot them!"

The men carrying the torches were being covered, though, by the continued gunfire by the circling marauders. The drillers tried to shoot at them, only to be forced to dive back behind cover by a hail of lead.

Frank dared that fusillade and so did Magnusson. Both men stepped out into the open and leveled their rifles. Frank emptied the Winchester as bullets sang around him. He dropped the empty rifle and drew his Colt, began running forward to cut the range as he fired. Magnusson was beside him, also using a handgun now.

A couple of the torches went spinning through the air as the men holding them toppled from their saddles. The torches fell harmlessly to the ground and went out, well short of the oil storage tank.

A horse screamed shrilly as a bullet found it and its front legs folded up underneath it. The rider sailed over the head of the falling horse to crash into the ground, and his torch guttered out as it hit the earth, too.

That left one man, though, and he had almost reached the tank. He was close enough, in fact, that Frank could see him by the light of the torch as the man stood up in his stirrups and flung the burning brand high in the air.

The torch was still spinning through the night sky as the man who had thrown it yanked his mount around and rode hell-bent-for-leather away from there.

Frank watched the torch, which seemed to be moving in slow motion now as it climbed. It reached its zenith and then dropped down, down toward the waiting oil, thousands of gallons of the stuff.

Frank's revolver came up and roared twice as he attempted the almost impossible feat of shooting the torch out of the air, hoping that if he could hit it, his bullets would knock it clear of the tank.

That was too much to hope for, even for a phenomenal Coltman like The Drifter.

The torch dropped out of sight behind the circular wooden walls of the tank.

And the world exploded.

# Chapter 26

That's what it seemed like to Frank anyway as a huge ball of fire erupted where the storage tank had been an instant earlier and the concussive roar of the explosion slammed into him, knocking him off his feet.

He rolled over and snatched his hat from the ground where it had fallen. As he surged to his feet, he flung up his arm to shield his face as much as he could from the terrible heat of the fire.

That heat pounded at him like a fiery fist. As he staggered away from the searing assault, Frank looked around for Magnusson. He spotted the oil-man lying huddled on the ground a few yards away.

Frank clapped his hat on and hurried over to Magnusson's side. He realized that he still clutched his Colt in his right hand. The gun wouldn't do any good against the roaring fire, so he holstered it.

Then he bent and got both hands under Magnusson's arms. With a grunt of effort—Magnusson was a big man after all—Frank hauled him to his feet.

Magnusson shook his head groggily, the first sign

Frank had seen that the man was even still alive. He would have fallen, though, without Frank's strong grip holding him up.

Frank put his mouth close to Magnusson's ear and shouted, "We've got to get out of here!"

He knew that's what he was saying, but he couldn't hear the words even though he was the one who spoke them. He was deaf, he realized, and the roaring he heard wasn't from the fire. It was inside his own head.

Gripping Magnusson's shoulders, he shook the oilman. Magnusson's eyes began to focus again. He stood straighter, and Frank let go of him.

The explosion had probably deafened Magnusson, too. Frank gestured instead of yelling, indicating with his hands that they needed to get away from the blazing storage tank.

The tank wasn't the only thing that was on fire, Frank saw as he glanced around. Burning oil had been thrown all over the area by the blast. The sheds were burning, and so was one of the derricks.

That well went up suddenly with a huge, whooshing explosion. Frank felt it more than heard it, a massive thump that shook the ground under his feet and staggered him and Magnusson. A column of flame a hundred feet high shot into the air, followed by billowing clouds of black smoke.

The smoke rolled across the ground, choking the men who were caught in it. Frank gripped Magnusson's arm and stumbled blindly forward. The smoke would kill them if they didn't get clear of it.

But they also ran the risk of getting caught in the rapidly spreading flames. The other oil wells were liable to explode at any minute, too. The odds of anyone coming out of this holocaust alive kept climbing.

Added to that was the fact that the hardcases who had attacked the wells in the first place were still shooting into the conflagration. Frank couldn't see the muzzle flashes because of the smoke, or hear the blasts because he was still deaf from the explosion, but a couple of times he felt the lash of a slug through the air near his head.

He and Magnusson abruptly burst out into a clearing in the smoke that had been formed as the billowing clouds eddied around. Frank's eyes were stinging and watering so much, he still couldn't see very well. He blinked and looked around as best he could.

The sky was a bizarre orange-red dome lit by the hellish blaze. Frank spotted a couple of men on horseback galloping toward him and Magnusson. More flame spurted from the muzzles of their guns as they opened fire.

With that glare surrounding them and the smell of burning brimstone thick in the air, Frank thought for an instant that he and Magnusson must have already died and landed in Hell. Those gunmen were two of Satan's imps, trying to ride them down on devil horses.

But then he came back to reality as that awful moment passed. Those men weren't demons. They were just cold-blooded, hired killers. He dealt with them the way he always dealt with varmints like that.

He brought his Colt up and blew the sons of bitches out of their saddles.

The heavy revolver roared twice, and both of the

gunmen flew backward as if slapped from their horses by a giant hand. That emptied Frank's gun, though, and there was no time now to reload.

"Come on!" he shouted at Magnusson, and he was surprised to realize that he actually heard the words this time, though they were still faint.

He lunged toward the horses the killers had been riding and grabbed the dangling reins of one of them. Hauling the spooked animal's head down, Frank brought it under control and then shoved the reins into Magnusson's hands.

"Go! Get out of here!"

Magnusson's hearing had to be coming back, too, because he responded, "What about my men?"

"There's nothing you can do for them now! They'll either make it out or they won't!"

Frank didn't like having to take that fatalistic attitude, but the same thing could be said of him and Magnusson. Their fate was, to a large extent, out of their hands.

Magnusson hesitated, but only for a second. He grabbed the horn and swung up into the saddle. He waited, though, until Frank had caught the other horse's reins before he spurred away through the smoke.

Frank was right behind him, thundering through the black, choking clouds. The heat in the air seemed to sear his nose and throat and lungs. He bend forward over the horse's neck and held his hat down with one hand as he rode.

It would have been nice to be able to see what he was riding into, but that was impossible. The smoke had closed in again, and Frank was as blind as if someone had wrapped a thick woolen blanket around his head. Just about as hot and half suffocated, too.

Another massive explosion came from somewhere behind him. That would be the third well detonating, he thought. This oil field of Magnusson's was ruined.

There was no telling how long the wells would continue to burn either. Frank had no idea how anybody would even go about extinguishing such a terrible blaze.

Suddenly, he emerged from the smoke again. Blessedly clear air filled his lungs. He looked around for Magnusson or some of the drillers, eager to see if anyone else had escaped.

Instead of the oilman, Frank saw a group of riders about twenty yards away. They appeared to have been sitting there watching the towering columns of flame shoot up from the burning wells. They spotted Frank and hauled their mounts around to charge toward him.

His Colt was empty, but he saw the butt of a Winchester sticking up from a saddle boot strapped to the horse he had "borrowed" from one of the dead outlaws. He grabbed the rifle and jerked it from the boot.

Of course, he had no way of knowing whether or not it was loaded, he told himself as he brought the weapon up. He worked the lever, aimed at the hardcases attacking him, and squeezed the trigger.

With a welcome whipcrack of sound, the Winchester bucked against his shoulder. One of the gunmen slewed halfway around in his saddle and then slipped off his horse's back completely, crashing to the ground.

Even before that man hit the dirt, Frank had cranked another round into the rifle's firing chamber—at least he hoped that he had—and drew another bead. The Winchester blasted again. A second man fell, drilled by the steel-jacketed bullet.

That was enough for the gunmen. They peeled away, obviously unwilling to face any more of the deadly accurate fire from the rifle Frank had appropriated.

That was a stroke of luck, because when Frank tried to send a round after them to hurry them on their way, the Winchester's hammer clicked on empty.

He jammed the rifle back in the saddle boot and reached to the loops on his shell belt for fresh cartridges, which he quickly thumbed into the Colt's cylinder. When he had a full wheel, he holstered the gun and started looking for Magnusson again.

His ears were still ringing a little, but most of his hearing had come back. The sound of racking coughs led Frank to the oilman.

He found Magnusson in some trees across the road from where the wells had been. Magnusson lifted the reins and started to pull his horse away until Frank called, "Hold on, Magnusson! It's me, Morgan!"

"Morgan! You made it out of that hell alive?"

"Appears so," Frank said as he brought the outlaw's horse to a stop next to Magnusson's mount. "Are you hurt?"

Magnusson shook his head. "I'll be coughing up

smoke for a month," he said in a hoarse voice, "but that's all. We're both damned lucky." He laughed humorlessly. "If you can call it lucky to have thousands of dollars worth of oil go up in smoke."

"You're still drawing breath, even if it hurts," Frank pointed out. "I'd call that lucky, considering."

"Yeah. I guess you're right."

"Have you seen any more of those gunmen around?"

"No, but I heard some shooting a minute ago. Was that you?"

"I ran into a few of them right after I got out of the smoke and swapped a little lead with them. They lit a shuck after I dropped a couple of them."

"I wish you'd killed all the bastards!" Magnusson said with savage anger in his voice. "They may not have ruined me tonight, but they've come damned close!" He glared over at Frank. "Are you sure that bunch from the Montero ranch didn't have anything to do with this?"

"Positive," Frank said, but he didn't go into any details about how he had followed the gang here from their hideout in the San Gabriel Mountains, on the other side of the valley.

"Well, I'm sure Dolores Montero will be glad to hear about what's happened tonight anyway, whether it was her doing or not."

"I wouldn't be so sure about that. She just wants to be left alone to keep the ranch running the way her husband intended."

Magnusson shook his head. "She's not gonna be able to do that. Everybody knows there's oil down there now. If I'm not the one who goes and gets it, somebody else will."

Frank sighed. He knew that Magnusson was right. The same thing had happened here in California back in '49. Frank was a little too young to remember it firsthand, but he had talked to older men who'd joined the steady stream of Argonauts going west in search of gold.

The same thing had happened up in the Black Hills of Dakota Territory in '76 when gold was discovered there. Frank had been in the roaring boomtown of Deadwood, even though he'd had no real interest in prospecting. That just seemed to be where folks went back in those days.

And now it was happening all over again here in southern California, only it was black gold now that everyone sought. They didn't go after it with picks and shovels, but rather with drills and engines. Bubbling up from the ground it came, bringing with it the power to make men millionaires . . . or paupers if their luck was bad.

But either way, the search would go on. Magnusson was right about that.

It didn't have to be accompanied by violence, though. Magnusson and Dolores Montero would work out some sort of arrangement that would be tolerable to both of them, if Frank had to sit them down at a table at gunpoint and force them to negotiate.

That would have to come later, though. Right now, he still had to find out who was really behind the trouble that had culminated tonight in those massive explosions.

But the first step was to see if there were any survivors besides him and Magnusson.

The smoke was beginning to clear somewhat, although the flames still leaped high above the destroyed wells and storage tank. Frank couldn't even see the sheds anymore; they had burned to the ground.

All three derricks still stood, although they were aflame. As Frank and Magnusson watched, one of them collapsed in a shower of burning beams, sending a renewed burst of flames and sparks high in the air. The other two derricks followed suit a moment later, prompting Magnusson to shake his head sadly.

"Mr. Magnusson! Mr. Magnusson!"

The shouts came from the left. Frank and Magnusson turned their horses in that direction and saw half a dozen men hurrying toward them. A couple of the men limped, and one had to be helped along by his companions.

Frank recognized Rattigan as the men came up. He was glad to see that some of the drillers had made it out of that inferno.

"Rattigan," Magnusson said in a choked voice, "are you the only ones left?"

"As far as we know, Mr. Magnusson. I . . . I don't reckon the other fellas made it."

"God!" Magnusson burst out. "Seven men dead, and that doesn't even count the ones who were killed earlier! Somebody's going to pay for this!"

"You can bet a hat on it, Magnusson," Frank said.

The oilman turned toward him. "Five thousand dollars if you kill the man responsible for this, Morgan!"

"You don't have to put a bounty on his head. I'll see to it that justice catches up to him anyway."

"Well, just remember what I said, if it means anything to you."

It didn't, but Frank didn't bother arguing with the man. Instead, he just jerked his head in a curt nod, then hipped around in the saddle as he heard the swift rataplan of approaching hoofbeats.

Magnusson heard them, too. "Are they coming back to try to wipe us out for good?" he asked tensely.

"Don't know," Frank said as he drew his gun, "but I reckon we'll find out in a minute or two."

# Chapter 27

Magnusson and the surviving drillers had lost their weapons in their flight from the huge fire, so they were unarmed. Frank had six bullets in the Colt and a few more in the loops on his belt.

That wasn't much with which to hold off a gang of killers . . . but Frank intended to do the best he could.

Instead, as a group of a dozen riders came into view moving fast up the road toward the wells, he recognized Pete Linderman in the lead. The Salida del Sol foreman was backed by some of the Montero punchers.

The newcomers were bristling with guns, so they looked plenty threatening, but as Linderman spotted Frank, Magnusson, and the drillers, he held up a hand to slow his companions. They jogged on up to the group that had escaped from the fire and reined in.

"Good Lord!" Linderman exclaimed. "Even from the ranch house, it looked like the whole world was on fire over here, and that's just about right! I never saw such a thing in all my life. I'd just as soon never see it again."

"You and me both, Linderman," Magnusson said with a scowl. "You and me both."

"What did you do, accidentally set the whole she-bang ablaze?"

Frank said, "There was nothing accidental about it. The hombres who bushwhacked both sides earlier today came back and did this."

"We thought we heard some shootin' before all hell broke loose."

"They were trying to wipe me out," Magnusson said, "but they'll find out that I don't give up so easy!"

Linderman grunted. "Reckon I can vouch for that."

Magnusson glared at him, but Linderman ignored the oilman as he turned to Frank.

"Are you hurt, Morgan?"

Frank shook his head and said, "Just a little ringing in my ears from the explosions, that's all. But Magnusson lost another seven men, looks like."

"I'm sorry to hear that. Magnusson, why don't you and your men come on back to the ranch with us? You can get cleaned up and patch up your wounded."

"I don't think so," Magnusson snapped. "Morgan's convinced that Señora Montero didn't have anything to do with this, but I'm not so sure."

Linderman stiffened in his saddle, and for a second Frank thought the foreman was going to slap leather over that not-so-veiled insult to the lady.

But then Linderman forced himself to relax with a visible effort and said, "Go ahead and be a damned fool if you wänt to, mister. That's up to you. We were just tryin' to help."

"How about if you send a wagon over here?" Frank suggested. "That way Magnusson's men can get back to town."

Linderman considered the idea for a moment, then nodded. "I reckon we can do that."

"I'm obliged to you for any help you can give us," Magnusson said gruffly. Obviously, the idea of being in debt to Dolores Montero didn't sit well with him, but he had to do whatever he could for his men.

Linderman sent a couple of the cowboys back to the ranch headquarters to fetch the wagon, then turned to Frank and asked, "Did you manage to account for any of the varmints who did this?"

"We downed some of them," Frank said with a nod. "Let's have a look around and see if we can find any of the bodies."

Magnusson rode with them. The rest of the ranch hands and the surviving drillers stayed where they were, eyeing each other warily. None of them were ready to completely trust their former enemies.

Frank headed for the spot where he had shot two men out of the saddle. He was sure that both hombres had been either dead or badly wounded. They hadn't gotten up and walked off on their own.

But they were gone nonetheless.

"The rest of the bunch took the bodies with them," Frank said. "They're being mighty careful. They must be under orders not to leave anything behind that might let them be traced back to the man who hired them."

Linderman thumbed his hat back. "Who do you

reckon that might be, Morgan?" He glanced at the oilman. "We've spent so long thinkin' it was Magnusson here who was puttin' the burrs under our saddle, it's hard to figure on anybody else bein' to blame."

"Well, you know better now," Magnusson snapped. "If you're not responsible for this . . . this devastation"—and he wearily waved a hand toward the still-burning wells—"then it's obvious that there's a third party involved."

"I don't know yet who's to blame," Frank said in reply to Linderman's question. "I've got a few folks I'm wondering about, but no real proof to point to any of them yet."

"When you figure it out, let us know," Linderman said. "If the law won't do anything about it, I reckon the boys and me would be glad to form an unofficial posse and lend you a hand, Morgan."

Frank nodded. "I'll keep that in mind. We won't take the law in our own hands, though . . . unless we have to."

The three men rode around the area some more, just to make sure that none of the raiders who had been killed had been left behind. Their companions had been thorough, though. Even the horses the dead men had been riding were gone, except for the two Frank and Magnusson had used to escape from the blaze.

Looking for the outlaws' mounts reminded Frank of Goldy and Dog. He whistled, and sure enough, the stallion and the big cur came loping up a few moments later. Magnusson cast an unfriendly glance toward Dog, but didn't say anything.

Frank dismounted and handed the reins of the horse he'd been riding to Linderman.

"This horse belonged to one of the varmints," he told the foreman, "and so did the one Magnusson's riding. The brands probably won't tell us anything, but it might be a good idea to hang on to them anyway just in case."

"We can go through the saddlebags, too," Linderman suggested. "But like you said, it probably won't do any good. Those hombres are too smart to have left anything incriminatin' in 'em."

Magnusson turned to Frank and asked, "What are your plans now, Morgan?"

"Can't track those killers at night," Frank said, again not mentioning that he now knew the location of the gang's hideout. He had no particular reason for playing those cards close to his vest, other than being in the habit of doing so. "I reckon I'll go back to the hotel and try to get some rest."

"Why don't you come to the ranch with us?" Linderman suggested. "It's closer than town, and I'm sure the señora would be willin' to put you up for the night."

"Morgan works for me now," Magnusson snapped.

"I know that. And up until today, I reckon it would've been plenty of reason to be plumb inhospitable to him." Linderman shrugged. "But things are changin' here in the valley, at least a little. Not that we'll ever welcome those smelly, noisy contraptions of yours, Magnusson. But you're welcome to come to the ranch, too. You look like you been put through the wringer."

Frank could tell it took quite an effort on

Linderman's part for the foreman to unbend from his hostile stance enough to invite Magnusson to Salida del Sol.

Magnusson just shook his head curtly in response to the invitation. "I have to get back to town," he said. "My sister will worry about me if I don't show up at all tonight. I'll just stay here with my men until your men get back with that wagon."

"Shouldn't be too much longer. We'll wait, too." Linderman nodded toward the burning wells. "Anything we can do to help with those blazes?"

"Just see that they don't spread to the rest of your range. They'll have to burn themselves out."

"How long will that take?"

Magnusson shook his head. "There's no way of knowing. The fire where the storage tank was will go out as soon as all the oil that was in there is burned up. The well fires will probably die down some overnight, but it'll be days, maybe even weeks, before they go out entirely."

Linderman's face was grim as he asked, "You mean we'll maybe have to keep an eye on those fires for weeks?"

"That's right."

Linderman leaned over in the saddle and spat on the ground next to his horse. "One more reason we don't want any more of those damned wells on Montero range," he said.

Magnusson's face darkened with anger, and for a moment Frank thought the two men were going to start arguing again.

But then Magnusson turned away. "I'm too tired to get into that right now, Linderman. Anyway, it's not up to you, is it? Señora Montero makes the important decisions on Salida del Sol, doesn't she? And she probably wouldn't like it if she knew you'd invited me to spend the night there."

"I stand by what I said," Linderman declared stubbornly. "If the señora don't like it, that's between her and me."

The oilman made a slashing motion with his hand. "It doesn't matter. Like I told you, I'm staying right here with my men until that wagon comes to take them back to town, and then I'm going with them."

"Well, it shouldn't be much longer now." Linderman left the *good riddance* part unsaid, but Frank heard it plain enough and suspected that Magnusson did, too.

Several more minutes passed. Magnusson shifted impatiently in the saddle and asked, "Shouldn't your men have been here with that wagon?"

"Hold your horses," Linderman snapped. "I'm sure it took 'em a little while to get a team hitched up, and you can't move all that fast in a wagon, even an empty one. They'll be along directly."

But as the minutes dragged by, Linderman began to frown worriedly. Frank understood the feeling. He thought the wagon should have arrived already from the ranch headquarters, too.

The surviving drillers had sat down on the ground to rest with their shoulders slumped in exhaustion. Several of the Montero punchers looked at each other, then dismounted and walked over to the drillers. One of them reached for the tobacco pouch in his breast pocket and asked, "Want to borrow the makin's?"

Rattigan looked up at the cowboy with a resentful expression on his face at first, but then his grimy features smoothed out and he shrugged.

"Don't mind if I do. Thanks."

"Welcome," the puncher said as he handed over the pouch. "Pass it around to the rest o' you fellas if you want."

That was a good start toward mending the fences between these two bunches, Frank thought. He was glad to see it, but it didn't ease his worry about the wagon.

That worry got a lot worse in a hurry when the sound of distant shots came drifting through the night air.

Linderman had dismounted. He jerked around toward the shots and exclaimed, "That sounds like it's comin' from the ranch!"

Frank's jaw tightened. He had done some damage to the gang during his three encounters with them, but there were still at least twenty of the hired killers roaming around the valley raising hell.

He had thought that after the destruction of the oil wells, they would head back to their hideout, but maybe they had gone to Salida del Sol instead, to attack the ranch for the second night in a row.

"Son of a bitch!" Linderman went on as he fairly leaped into the saddle. "We got to go see what that's about!"

"I'm coming with you," Frank said as he swung up onto Goldy's back.

"I'm not leaving my men," Magnusson declared. "This could be some sort of trick."

"Nobody asked you to," Linderman said. He

pulled his horse's head around and spurred the animal into a run.

Frank was right beside him, and the other punchers from Salida del Sol hurriedly mounted up and galloped after them. Linderman probably knew this range like the back of his hand, Frank thought, so he let the foreman take the lead.

The shooting had stopped by the time the group of hard-riding men approached the ranch headquarters. An orange glow similar to the one that had lit up the sky above the burning oil wells, but smaller, could be seen up ahead.

"Somethin's on fire, damn it!" Linderman said as he hauled his horse around a bend in the trail. "Looks like one of the barns!"

That was what it was, all right, Frank saw a moment later. Flames leaped from the roof of the big structure. Men ran around it, flinging buckets of water onto the blaze without much noticeable effect. They could probably keep the fire from spreading that way, but they wouldn't be able to save the barn.

Linderman flung himself out of the saddle before his mount stopped moving, and grabbed one of the ranch hands as the man went by with a bucket of water.

"What the hell happened here?" Linderman shouted over the crackling roar of the burning barn.

"It was some of those damned drillers!" the man replied, sending a shock through Frank. "They snuck in and set the barn on fire, then started shootin' at us when we came a-runnin' out o' the bunkhouse!"

Frank dismounted as well and confronted the

man, studying his face in the garish light of the burning barn. "Are you sure about that?" he demanded. "You know it was Magnusson's men?"

"We got a good look at 'em, damn it!" the man replied angrily. "They sure as hell weren't cowboys!" He turned back to Linderman. "A couple o' the fellas who went with you rode back in just as hell started poppin', Pete, and they got gunned down right away!"

That was why the men hadn't come back with the wagon, Frank thought.

The shocks weren't through coming yet. "That ain't the worst of it!" the grizzled old cowboy went on. "Some of 'em got in the house."

Linderman's face twisted with fear. "The señora—!"

"They took her, Pete! Carried her outta the house kickin' and screamin', threw her on a horse with one o' the bastards, and rode off into the night with her!"

# Chapter 28

Linderman looked like he'd just been walloped over the head with a sledgehammer. Once again, Frank got the impression that there was more to the relationship between Dolores and Linderman than that of ranch owner and foreman.

But that didn't matter at the moment. Other things were much more important.

"Was she hurt?" Frank asked the cowboy who had just broken the shocking news to them.

"Not so's you could see. Like I said, she was fightin' like a wildcat."

"Well, damn it, didn't you try to *stop* 'em?" Linderman burst out.

"Of course we tried! Run right into a hail o' lead from those skalleyhooters, though. There's two boys a-layin' dead in the bunkhouse right now from tryin' to stop 'em!"

"Sorry," Linderman muttered. "I know you wouldn't just let anybody take the señora without puttin' up a fight. I just can't believe those blasted drillers would do such a thing!"

"They didn't," Frank said.

Linderman and the cowpoke turned to glare at him.

"You heard what Sammy told us," Linderman said. "They saw the drillers."

"Yeah, and they was mighty hard to miss in them oily clothes!" Sammy put in.

Frank shook his head. "You saw men *dressed* like drillers." He turned to Linderman. "I'd bet a hat they were really the same men who set fire to Magnusson's wells earlier tonight."

Linderman rubbed his jaw and frowned in thought. After a moment, he said, "Yeah, I reckon it could've been at that."

"Don't listen to this no-account gunfighter, Pete!" Sammy urged. "You heard him say yourself that he's workin' for Magnusson now. Of course he's gonna claim Magnusson didn't have nothin' to do with kidnappin' Señora Montero!"

"I don't know," Linderman said slowly. "Somebody blew the hell outta three of Magnusson's wells tonight, as well as a big storage tank full of oil, and it wasn't us. I think Morgan's right. Somebody else is tryin' to keep trouble stirred up between us and those drillers." He looked at Frank. "But what do they hope to gain by carryin' off the señora?"

Frank had to think about that question for a moment. Finally, he said, "They don't know that we're on to them. They think each side is still blaming the other for what's going on. That's why they were dressed like cowboys when they attacked Magnusson's wells, and that explains why they changed in drillers' outfits before raiding the ranch."

"I reckon that makes sense," Linderman allowed. "They figured by kidnappin' the señora, it'd finally push us into tryin' to wipe out Magnusson's bunch once and for all."

"No, what they really want is for both sides to wipe each other out. It's what they've been after all along."

Linderman's eyes widened as understanding sunk in on him. "With Magnusson and the señora both out of the way, somebody could come in here and grab up the best ranch *and* the biggest oil drillin' operation in the valley!"

"That's the way it looks to me," Frank agreed with a nod.

"Then they're gonna kill Dolores!"

The fear that Linderman felt made him slip and forget to refer to her as the señora as he usually did, Frank noted, but again, he didn't care whether or not Linderman had romantic feelings toward Dolores Montero.

"They won't hurt her, at least not right away," Frank said. "They're smart enough to know that they may need her for leverage. Anyway, if their plan is to blame Magnusson for the kidnapping, you're liable to get a phony ransom note with some clues pointing back to him, just to cinch the deal."

"But if they realize that you've figured out what's goin' on, they're liable to get rid of her just so she can't ever testify against them."

Frank nodded again, this time with a grim expression on his weathered face. "That could happen all right," he admitted. "That's why I've got to get her away from them as quick as I can."

"You mean, why we have to go after her," Linderman corrected.

Frank shook his head this time. "This is a one-man job, Pete, and since I'm the one who's got a pretty good idea where they took her, it looks like I'm elected."

Linderman and Sammy stared at Frank for a long moment before Linderman turned to the puncher and said, "Go throw that water on the fire."

Sammy looked like he didn't want to leave, but the boss had given him an order. He hurried off to carry it out.

Linderman said to Frank in a low voice, "You know where their hideout is, don't you?"

"I figured you'd tumble to that, but there was no way around it. Yeah, I trailed them there earlier today. Or rather, Dog did. I probably couldn't have done it without that educated nose of his."

"Damn it, tell me where it is," the foreman demanded. "I'll get every man on the ranch and we'll ride in there and wipe those bastards out!"

"That's the *last* thing you need to be thinking about doing," Frank said. "For one thing, you'd lose at least half your men getting into the hideout, and for another, the first thing those varmints would do if you attacked the place is kill Señora Montero. You don't want that."

Linderman grimaced. "No, I sure as hell don't. But you can't be serious about goin' in after her by yourself."

"Sometimes a job is cut out more for one man than an army," Frank pointed out. "This is one of those times."

Linderman regarded him with an intent stare for a few seconds, then said, "What about two men?"

"Meaning you and me?"

"Damn straight."

Frank pondered the suggestion for a long moment, then slowly nodded.

"Two men might be able to get in where they'll be taking the señora. I'm not sure it would be a good idea to tell the crew where we're going, though. They might not be able to resist the temptation to come after us."

"And that could ruin everything if the situation's as dangerous as you make it out to be, Morgan. I don't like the idea of nobody else knowin' where the hideout is, though. What if you and I don't come back?"

"That's a good point," Frank agreed. "If you've got a man you can trust, I'll write down the directions and seal them up, with orders that the note should be turned over to Stafford if you and I don't come back by tomorrow morning." He shrugged. "If we're not back by then, it'll probably be too late for Señora Montero anyway, so the sheriff can take a posse in and clean out that rat's nest."

"And if the sheriff won't do it, I know a bunch of cowpunchers tough as whang leather who will." Linderman nodded to show he was willing to go along with Frank's plan. "I'll give the note to Jeff for safekeeping."

That brought a slight frown to Frank's face. "That young hothead?"

"You've got him all wrong, Morgan. He was upset

about Lonnie, sure, but he's a top hand, and he knows how to do what he's told."

"I've wondered if he bushwhacked me my first night in Los Angeles. Somebody sure did."

"It wouldn't have been Jeff," Linderman insisted with an emphatic shake of his head. "That boy's no murderer."

"You sound like you know him pretty well."

"I ought to. He's my nephew. I've known him since he was knee-high."

Frank hadn't been aware of that. If he trusted Linderman's judgment, then it raised even more questions in Frank's mind. Something was missing from the picture when he thought back over everything that had happened since his arrival in southern California. He had overlooked something, or just didn't yet know something, that would have made the whole thing make sense.

However, he could ponder that later. For now, he was more concerned with getting Dolores Montero out of the hands of those hired killers.

"All right. If you've got pen and paper in the house, I'll write out the directions to where we're going. And then we'd better get started."

Linderman nodded. "The sooner the better." His voice caught a little as he added, "If those bastards have hurt one hair on that lady's head . . ."

"Don't think about that," Frank said.

But the same thoughts were going through his brain, despite the advice he had given Linderman, and they made a chill go down his back, too.

\* \* \*

Frank wished he had Stormy with him so he could switch horses. Goldy had already done plenty today.

But Stormy was back in Los Angeles, Goldy was young and strong, and Frank decided that he'd rather have the stallion under him than borrow a horse from the Montero remuda. At least, Goldy had gotten to rest a spell while Frank and Linderman were talking and while Frank wrote the note to leave with Jeff.

Linderman called the young puncher into the hacienda and handed him the sealed envelope.

"What's this?" Jeff asked.

"Never you mind what it is. All you got to know is that if Morgan and I ain't back here at the ranch by sunup tomorrow, you light a shuck for town and give that envelope to Lawyer Stafford at the Nadeau Hotel."

Jeff's eyes widened. "You and the gunslinger are goin' after the señora!"

"You just don't worry about where we're goin'," Linderman said.

"Take me with you! I swear, Pete, I'll do whatever you tell me, just let me come along and help. I got a powerful hankerin' to shoot some of those drillers!"

"Dad-gum it, just do what I told you!" Linderman roared. He started for the doorway, then stopped. "One more thing. You didn't try to ambush Morgan three nights ago in town, did you?"

Jeff looked utterly confused. "What? You mean after . . . after Lonnie got himself killed?" He shook his head. "No, you know I didn't do anything like that, Pete. I just brought Lonnie's body back out here to the ranch."

Linderman looked at Frank. "You believe me now, Morgan?"

Frank nodded and said, "I believe I do." He clapped a hand on Jeff's shoulder. "We're counting on you, son. Don't let that envelope out of your sight, and take it to Mr. Stafford if we don't come back."

Jeff nodded, his eyes still wide. "All right, Mr. Morgan. I'll do it. But I still wish you and Pete would let me come with you."

"Maybe another time," Frank said.

They left the big ranch house. The barn roof had collapsed by now and the walls had fallen in as well. That had made the fire burn larger and brighter for a while, but it was dying down now. The hands continued to throw buckets of water on the rubble. It would smolder for days, Frank knew, an all-too-vivid reminder of the wanton destruction that had struck at Salida del Sol.

Frank was looking forward to settling the score with the men who had done this, but that would have to wait. First, he and Linderman had to rescue Dolores. Once she was safe, then would come the showdown that had been building up for months in the San Fernando Valley.

It had taken his arrival to make things blow up, Frank thought as he swung up into the saddle on Goldy's back. Once again, he asked himself just how that had come about. He was starting to have an inkling, but he would have to find out more information before he could be sure.

The two men rode out, taking an extra saddled horse with them. Dog loped behind them. Linderman looked back at the big cur and said, "That brute's got some wolf in him, don't he?"

"More than likely, but I wouldn't know for sure."

Frank was waiting for the rest of the comment he'd been getting from folks lately, about how they didn't like dogs, but Linderman just nodded and said, "Looks like a fine dog."

That nudged the foreman up a notch in Frank's estimation.

As they rode, Frank went ahead and told Linderman where they were going. He described the box canyon in the San Gabriels and added, "That's why I said a whole bunch of men couldn't do this job. They'd be picked off going through that notch leading into the canyon."

"I've been around those mountains some, but I don't recall ever seeing a place like that," Linderman said. "The forest is so thick over there, you could poke around for days and never find what you were lookin' for if you didn't know right where it was."

"I probably wouldn't have found the place if not for Dog. He can follow a trail better than any human tracker."

"I don't doubt it." Linderman paused, then said, "You know, Morgan, you're not a bad sort of fella . . . for a gunslinger. It beats me why you'd go to work for a man like Magnusson. Maybe he's not the one who's behind all the rustlin' and killin', but he still wants to ruin the valley with his damned oil wells."

"He doesn't see it as ruining anything. I think he believes he's actually doing a good thing by pumping that oil out of the ground. Folks can get enough use out of it to make drilling for it worthwhile."

Linderman shook his head. "Maybe so, but I sure don't see it. Seems like a waste of time to me. I know he can make money from it, but Lord, what a way to get rich!"

"I'm afraid we may have to get used to it," Frank said. "If you carry any weight with the señora, Pete, it might be a good idea to try to convince her to come to an agreement with Magnusson."

"Go into business with that skunk! Good Lord, Morgan! I thought a man like you who's lived his whole life in the West would have more sense than that."

"You ever try to stand in the middle of a river when it's flooding, Pete?"

"What? Hell, no."

"Well, you'd have just about as much luck doing that," Frank said, "as you would trying to stand up to time and progress without getting swept away."

"Progress." Linderman said the word like it tasted bitter in his mouth.

"I know what you mean, amigo. I surely do."

They rode on in silence then. Frank hoped that Linderman would at least give some consideration to what he had said. Once all this ruckus was settled, the conflict at the heart of it would still remain. Each side would have to learn to adjust to the needs of the other, or sooner or later violence would break out again.

Frank estimated it was around midnight by the time the thickly wooded mountains loomed dark and sinister above them. Even though the moon had risen and gave some light, Frank had to take it slow to make sure he and Linderman were headed in the right direction.

He soon found the saddle in the ridge that led to the canyon, though, and held up a hand in a signal for Linderman to halt. He reined Goldy in as well. The two men dismounted, and Frank whispered, "We'll leave the horses here and go in on foot, like I did this afternoon. Be as quiet about it as you can. They're liable to have extra sentries out tonight, just in case somebody trailed them back here after all the hell they raised."

"I know how to be quiet," Linderman said. "Don't worry about me."

"I'm not worried about you, so much as I am about Señora Montero. Her life may be riding on us, Pete."

"Don't I know it," Linderman muttered. "Lead the way, Morgan. I'll be right behind you."

Winchesters in hand, the two men started into the canyon.

# Chapter 29

Dog padded along behind them, and this time Frank didn't make him stay with Goldy. Having the big cur with them might come in handy before the night was over, and Dog could move as quietly as— or more quietly than—any human could.

Frank knew he was putting a lot of confidence in Pete Linderman. The ranch foreman was a good man and plenty tough, but he wasn't a professional fighting man. He had handled himself all right during the attack on Salida del Sol the night before, but this was a different situation that required stealth as well as guts.

So far, though, Linderman was doing all right, Frank thought as they crept deeper and deeper into the canyon. He thought they were nearing the spot where the sentry had been posted earlier in the day when he heard a soft voice call, "Everything all right over there, Chet?"

"Yeah, quiet as can be," the reply came back, confirming two things for Frank—he was right about where he and Linderman were the canyon, and the assumption that the gang would have extra guards posted tonight was correct, too.

He and Linderman had frozen in their tracks when the first sentry called out. With a man on the other side of the canyon, they couldn't rely on silence alone to get them into the hideout safely, as Frank had earlier in the day.

If the man on the far side was watching the canyon floor over here, he might see them slipping along. They would have to use every patch of shadow they could to conceal themselves. Luckily, the moon was low enough in the sky by now so that it wasn't shining directly into the canyon.

Frank leaned closer to Linderman and with hand motions communicated to the foreman that he was to follow exactly in his footsteps. Frank knew he could count on Dog to stay in the shadows. The big cur was like a phantom in the night, unseen and unheard until it was too late for his quarry.

Frank suspected that the men posted on the walls of the canyon wouldn't be the only guards. The faint orange wink of a cigarette glowing up ahead told him that he was right.

The sentry should have known better than to smoke while on duty, but the members of the gang still believed that no one knew where their hideout was. That belief led to the carelessness that Frank was counting on to help get him and Linderman in there.

Frank couldn't see the quirly glowing anymore, but he could still smell it. He let that guide him to the guard. Keen eyes finally spotted the man lounging in some scrubby trees that grew along the base of the canyon wall, cupping the cigarette in his hand now to keep it from showing.

A shot now would ruin everything. Frank touched Linderman on the arm and then motioned for him to stay put. He slid his Colt from its holster and moved forward inch by inch, taking great care each time he put a foot down.

Unfortunately, when he entered the shadows under the trees, it was impossible to move without pine needles crunching underfoot, but by that time Frank was close enough to strike. As the guard realized someone was there and started to turn, saying, "Who—?" Frank lunged forward and lashed out with the butt of the revolver.

It landed against the guard's head with a solid thud and crunch of bone. The man folded up without making another sound. Frank knelt beside him and checked for a pulse. The one he found was fast and thready and fluttered to a stop after a moment.

The fractured skull had been enough to kill the guard. That was one more man whittled from the odds against him and Linderman, Frank thought.

Considering all the hell these hired killers had been raising, as well as the fact that they had kidnapped Dolores Montero, Frank knew he wouldn't lose one second of sleep over this dead man.

Linderman jumped a little when Frank reached out of the darkness to touch his shoulder, but the foreman didn't make a sound. Barely visible in the murky gloom, even though only inches separated them, Frank pointed out the way he was going and Linderman followed.

The canyon began to widen out again. Frank

sensed as much as saw the dimensions growing larger. That meant they were reaching the area where the cabins were and where the rustled cattle were kept until they could be driven out and sold to unscrupulous beef buyers.

He suspected that Dolores would be kept in one of the cabins, but as he knelt and studied the layout, he saw that he was wrong about that.

She was under the overhang of the bulging bluff that formed the rear wall of the canyon, sitting with her back against a rock not far from the fire. Her hands appeared to be tied together in front of her.

Three of the hardcases stood near the fire, smoking and passing a bottle back and forth. They had been posted there to keep an eye on Dolores, Frank decided. Her legs weren't tied, so she could get up and run if she took it into her head to do such a thing.

But where would she go? She couldn't get out of the canyon without the guards seeing her. Chances are, she wouldn't even make it that far.

One of the men called something to Dolores. Frank couldn't make out the words, but from the way she turned her head away and pointedly ignored him, he figured it was probably something lewd.

Pete Linderman must have come to the same conclusion, because he stiffened at Frank's side and a muttered curse came from him.

"Take it easy," Frank whispered.

"But—"

"It doesn't matter what they say to her. All that's important is that we get her out of here."

"How are we gonna do that? That fire's big enough

it lights up that whole area under the bluff. We can't even get close to her without them seein' us."

Frank had already realized the same thing, and he was already searching for an answer to the problem. After a moment, he thought he might have found one.

"The fire's far enough back under the overhang that it doesn't shine on the bluff up above," he pointed out, still whispering so that his voice couldn't be heard more than a foot or two away.

"What good does that do us?"

"That's the way we'll come down. We'll be on top of those varmints before they know we're there. If we can take care of them without a lot of racket, we can slip the señora out of here before the rest of the bunch realizes what's going on."

For a long moment, Linderman didn't say anything. Finally, though, he whispered, "That's crazy! The face of that bluff's too sheer. Nobody could climb down it, and the señora sure as hell couldn't climb back up."

Linderman was right about the second part of his statement. Frank said, "We'll take her out the front door of this place. If we move fast enough, they won't have a chance to stop us. As for getting down there, I got a good look at that bluff during the day, and it's not as smooth as it looks. There are enough crevices and rough spots so that we can find some handholds and footholds."

Again, Linderman was silent for a moment as he mulled over what Frank had said. Then, not sounding all that convinced, he replied, "I reckon it's worth a try. Lord knows we can't just waltz in any other way."

"That's right," Frank agreed. "When all the other routes are blocked, you take whatever path is left."

"That don't explain how we're gonna get up there in the first place."

Frank smiled a little in the darkness. "We'll have to climb up before we get there and work our way around."

Linderman breathed a curse and then said, "That's gonna take forever!"

"I don't have anywhere else I have to be right now, do you?"

"You know damn well that I don't."

"I reckon we'd better get started then. We'll get as close as we can before we head up."

Staying next to the canyon wall, they catfooted their way toward the fire. The guards' laughter became louder as Frank and Linderman approached. Frank could understand some of what they were saying now, and as he had thought, they were talking about what they were going to do to Dolores as soon as they got the chance.

He knew that Linderman had to be hearing those things, too, and hoped that the foreman would be able to control the rage he felt. It would be satisfying as all get-out to walk into the firelight with gun in hand and blast the hell out of those varmints, but that wouldn't help Dolores in the long run.

Finally, Frank judged that they were close enough to begin their ascent. Any closer and they ran the risk of being spotted as they climbed. He touched Linderman's shoulder in a signal to halt. They had already discussed how they were going to proceed from there.

Linderman carried pigging strings in his pocket, as most cowboys were in the habit of doing in case they had to bulldog a calf. The two men took their boots off, used the pigging strings to tie each pair together, and slung the boots around their necks. Clambering around on the rocky walls of the canyon would be a lot easier in stocking feet.

Then Frank knelt beside Dog, ruffled the cur's thick coat, and told him to wait there. Frank knew that Dog would do just that, unless and until he was summoned.

The little whine that Dog let out told Frank that he didn't like being left behind, though. "Believe me, I'd take you with us if I could, big fella," Frank whispered. "You'd have to be part mountain goat instead of wolf, though, to go where we're going."

He wouldn't have minded being part mountain goat himself right now, he thought as he regarded the dark canyon wall looming over their heads.

Then he reached up, felt around until he found a good handhold, and dug the toes of his right foot into a small crevice. He pulled himself up and reached above him to search for another handhold. A few feet away, Pete Linderman did the same thing.

They maintained their silence as they climbed, except for the occasional faint grunt of effort. Frank's fingers and toes began to ache from supporting his weight, and he knew that Linderman had to be going through the same thing.

It was so dark Frank found it difficult to judge how high he was when he looked back over his shoulder. He figured they needed to be at least twenty feet off the ground as they worked their way above the overhang where Dolores was being held prisoner next to the fire.

When he decided that they had to be high enough, he began angling to his right. That would take him above the cavelike area. The light that spilled out from the fire would be his guide. Linderman followed.

One slip, one rock that pulled loose, one wrong move would doom them—and Dolores.

Because Frank was convinced that he and Linderman represented her only chance to get out of here alive. Even if Jeff delivered the note to Stafford and the lawyer managed to get a posse up here, the pack of gun-wolves that held Dolores would never let her go.

So far, so good, though. No one had raised an alarm down below, so Frank knew he and Linderman hadn't been seen. And they were almost where they needed to be. He could tell that from the glow given off by the fire.

He reached for the next handhold, but couldn't find one. The face of the bluff wasn't perpendicular; it leaned inward slightly. That was the only thing that allowed Frank and Linderman to make their way across it like human flies as they had been doing.

But there was a limit to how long they could hold on. Frank stretched a little farther, running his fingers over the rough rock. Finally, the tips of them slipped into a narrow opening. He wished it was deeper, but there was nothing he could do about that.

He swung out, searching with his toes. They slipped on the rock for a second, which meant that all of Frank's weight was hanging from his fingertips. He gritted his teeth against the strain on his hands, arms, and shoulders.

Then his toes found some purchase and eased that terrible strain. He leaned against the rock for a moment to rest and catch his breath. A couple more feet and they could start down, he thought.

Two feet away, Linderman's hand scrabbled at the rock as he started to slip. Frank let go with his left hand, which shot out and clamped around Linderman's wrist. Again, his jaw tightened as he strained to hold on to the foreman and keep Linderman from toppling off the bluff.

After a couple of seconds that seemed much longer, Linderman got his fingers in a crack in the rock. He nodded to let Frank know that he was all right. Frank let go of him and continued edging on toward their goal.

They had come far enough, he decided a moment later. When he had both feet and one hand in secure holds, he used the other hand to point downward. Linderman nodded again in understanding.

Before they could begin their descent, though, one of the guards who were now almost directly below them said, "Here comes that little runt. Wonder what he wants."

Frank twisted his head and saw that the door into one of the cabins had opened. Two figures strode toward the fire. Frank couldn't make out any details at first, but as the men came closer he saw that one was short, slender, and dressed in a brown tweed suit and derby hat. The other wore the rough range clothes of one of the gunmen.

Frank had never seen the dude before. He was sure of that. But it was more important that the dude not see him now. So far neither of the newcomers had looked up as they walked toward the guards.

But if they did, there was a good chance they would spot the two men splayed out against the rocky face of the bluff.

If that happened, those hired killers could stand down there and just about take target practice. They wouldn't need more than a minute or two to shoot Frank and Linderman plumb full of holes.

# Chapter 30

So far, though, the two men hadn't looked up. The dude's attention was on the three guards, and the man with him was following his lead.

"Damn it, Warner, what did I tell you about getting drunk?" the dude asked angrily as he strode up to the cavelike area under the bluff.

"Sorry, Mr. Mitchell," one of the guards replied. "We're not drunk, though, I can promise you that. Just takin' a little nip ever' now and then to help us stay awake."

Mitchell snorted as if to demonstrate how ridiculous that sounded to him.

"Anyway," one of the other guards put in, "you can see for yourself that Meskin bitch ain't gone nowhere. She's right there."

"And lookin' mighty fine, too," the gunman called Warner added. "When can we start takin' turns gettin' to know her better, Boss?"

"I've told you, I'm not the boss," Mitchell snapped. "But I speak for him and he's given firm orders that

Señora Montero is not to be harmed unless and until he says so. Is that understood?"

"Sure, sure," Warner answered sullenly. "You can't expect a fella not to notice how pretty a woman is, though."

"You can notice all you want. Just keep your hands off her."

"Fine."

After a second of silence, the dude called Mitchell spoke again. "Señora, I apologize for this ordeal you're having to go through. You should have cooperated when Mr. Magnusson first approached you."

"So you work for that bastard Magnusson, you little weasel," Dolores said. "That doesn't surprise me. I never trusted him."

Up above, though, Frank wasn't so quick to accept Mitchell's words at face value. Mitchell and the other members of the gang would still be maintaining their pose of working for Magnusson while they were around Dolores, just in case she managed to get away somehow, no matter how unlikely that seemed.

If she did escape, though, she would blame Magnusson for her kidnapping instead of the man who was really behind it.

"What do you want?" Dolores went on. "Do you want me to sign some sort of agreement with Magnusson that will let him drill for oil on my range?"

"I'm afraid it's too late for that. You'll have to relinquish all claim to Salida del Sol."

"Relinquish all—" A burst of rapid, furious Spanish came from Dolores. "You're loco!" she said in English. "Magnusson's loco! Give him my ranch? Never!"

"We'll see," Mitchell said calmly. "Perhaps you'll regard things differently by tomorrow. I'll bid you good night and let you think it over. I warn you, though, Señora, your time is limited."

"It doesn't matter how long you give me to think it over! I'll never give up my ranch!"

Mitchell just gave an infuriating chuckle, then turned and walked off, accompanied by the hardcase who had brought him out here to talk to Dolores. Neither man looked back.

Frank didn't heave a sigh of relief until Mitchell had mounted one of the horses tied near the cabins and ridden off toward the canyon entrance. He was going back to wherever he had come from, probably Los Angeles. The outfit he wore was a town suit if Frank had ever seen one.

The other man went back into the cabin and shut the door. Then and only then did Frank glance over at Linderman and nod. They began edging their way down the rock face.

All the cabins were dark except the one from which Mitchell and his companion had emerged earlier. The yellow glow of lamplight was still visible in its window. Most of the members of the gang had turned in for the night, though.

If Frank and Linderman could dispose of Dolores's guards without firing any shots, they stood at least a chance of being able to hustle her out of the canyon before the rest of the gunmen knew what was happening.

Then, if they could reach the horses, they would head for Salida del Sol and hope to outrun any pursuit.

The glow from the fire grew brighter around the two men as they climbed down the bluff. The ceiling of that cavelike area underneath the overhang was about eight feet high, Frank had estimated when he was studying it from a distance. When he and Linderman were no more than ten feet off the ground, he paused, slipped his gun out of its holster, looked over at Linderman, and nodded.

The foreman drew his own revolver and returned Frank's grim nod.

Then both men pushed off from the wall and dropped through empty air toward the sandy ground, their hats flying off as they fell.

The second that it took them to land seemed longer to Frank. But then his feet smacked the ground and he staggered to catch his balance.

Directly in front of him, no more than two feet away, one of the gunmen gaped at him in openmouthed amazement. Frank lashed out with the gun on his hand, smashing it into the man's face. He heard and felt the hardcase's jaw shatter. The man went down without a sound.

Linderman had gone to one knee when he landed, unable to stay upright. From that position, he launched himself forward in a diving tackle aimed at one of the other guards. His arms went around the man's waist and the impact of the collision bore the guard over backward.

Frank went after the third and final guard, who opened his mouth to yell as he clawed at the gun on his hip. Frank could have shot him down, but that would have defeated the purpose. Instead, he grabbed the man's gun wrist with his left hand and slashed at his head with the Colt in his right hand.

The man threw his left arm up and blocked the blow. The shout welling up in his throat was about to emerge when Frank lowered his head and butted the man in the face with it. Blood spurted as the guard's nose pulped under the impact.

That shut him up, but only for the moment. He was big and brawny and strong, and Frank had his hands full wrestling with him. He hoped that Linderman was taking care of his man, but he couldn't check to see how the foreman was doing. At least, there hadn't been any shots or yells yet.

Frank thrust a foot between the man's ankles, throwing him off balance. But at the same time, the guard clamped his free hand on Frank's throat, so that when he fell, The Drifter was pulled to the ground, too.

The two men rolled over and over on the sand. The hardcase tried to drive his knee into Frank's groin. Frank twisted at the hips to take the blow on his thigh. He couldn't get any air past the brutal grip on his throat, and a red haze was beginning to descend over his eyes.

He jabbed a short punch to the other man's throat. That made the man gag as his eyes widened in pain. When he continued to choke and his face started to turn red, Frank knew he must have damaged the man's windpipe.

That injury just made the hired killer fight all the more desperately. He knocked Frank's gun aside. The Colt slipped out of Frank's fingers and slid away over the sand.

With both hands now free, Frank cupped them and slammed them against his opponent's ears. That did some damage, too, but again it seemed to infuriate the man and rouse him to greater heights of frenzy. He started slamming punches at Frank's head.

Frank rolled away from the attack and kicked the hombre in the side. A rib broke with a sharp snap. Frank laced his fingers together as he came up on his knees. Clublike, he swung both hands and drove them into the guard's face as the man tried to struggle up.

The hardcase went over backward, twitched a couple of times, and then lay still. Blood oozed from his mouth, nose, and ears. A strangled sigh came from him as well, and then his chest ceased rising and falling. The injury to his throat had finally choked him to death.

Frank was a mite out of breath himself as he pushed to his feet and looked around. A few yards away, Linderman was getting up as well. The man he had been struggling with lay there unconscious.

As soon as Linderman was on his feet, he ran over to Dolores and dropped to a knee beside her. She hadn't said anything so far, but she was looking at Frank and Linderman like they were guardian angels that had dropped down unexpectedly from heaven.

That must have been what it seemed like when they suddenly appeared, Frank knew . . . although nobody had ever accused him of actually being angelic, he thought wryly.

"Are you all right, Señora?" Linderman asked Dolores while Frank picked up his gun and checked the man whose jaw he had broken. The varmint was out cold.

"I . . . I'm fine, I guess," Dolores answered. "Pete, is . . . is it really you?"

"It's me, all right," Linderman told her. He pulled a clasp knife from his pocket and opened it. "Let's get those ropes off of you."

Frank looked in the barrel of his Colt to make sure it hadn't gotten any sand in it when he dropped it. Satisfied that the weapon was all right, at least for now, he pouched it and said, "We've come to get you out of here, Señora. We've got some horses outside the canyon. You feel up to doing some riding?"

Dolores tossed aside the bonds that Linderman had cut from her wrists and began rubbing her hands together to improve the circulation in them. "Just stand back and watch me ride, Mr. Morgan," she said. "Unless you have an extra gun for me, in which case I think we should go teach those bastards who kidnapped me a lesson."

"There's too many of 'em for that, Señora," Linderman said. "We need to get you outta here while we've got a chance."

"Of course. Did the two of you come alone, or is the rest of the crew waiting outside the canyon?"

"It's just us, ma'am."

Frank and Linderman pulled their boots on; then the three of them started along the canyon wall, moving fast but not making any more noise than they had to.

Dolores whispered, "What happened at the ranch? How many of the men were hurt?"

"I don't know for sure about that," Linderman told her, "but the barn burned down."

"We can build another barn. I'm worried about the men. Magnusson will pay for this."

"Magnusson's not to blame for it," Frank said.

"What?" Dolores paused and turned to look at him. "Of course he is. That little bookkeeper or whatever he is said so!"

Frank shook his head and said, "We'd better keep moving, señora. I'll try to explain as we go along."

Keeping his voice low, he laid out the theory he had formed about a third party hiring the gunmen to provoke open warfare between Salida del Sol and the oil drillers. "Magnusson lost three of his wells tonight," he told her, "and then the same bunch raided your ranch and carried you off."

"You have to be mistaken," Dolores insisted. "Who else but Magnusson would benefit from ruining me and my ranch?"

"Somebody who wants the ranch and Magnusson's drilling operation both," Frank said. "That's the big boss Mitchell is really working for."

"What Morgan says makes sense, Señora," Linderman put in. "I didn't want to believe it at first either, but I reckon he's probably got it right."

"I don't know . . . I've been blaming Magnusson for everything for so long . . ."

"That's exactly what the fella behind this was counting on," Frank said. "As well as Magnusson feeling the same way about you."

"All right, maybe it's true," she admitted grudgingly. "What do we do now?"

"Get you back to the ranch where you'll be safe,

or at least safer. Then I want to see if I can find Mitchell. I've got a hunch he'll talk if I can ever lay hands on him."

With an angry toss of her head, Dolores said, "If he won't, let me ask him the questions for a while. He'll talk."

The savagery in her tone was a reminder that she came from a long line of proud people who could be ruthless when they needed to be. The old Californios had been plenty tough.

Right now, though, the first objective was to get out of the canyon before anyone discovered that Dolores was missing. When they found that she was gone and saw what sort of shape the three guards were in, they would know she'd had help getting away. She couldn't have handled those hardcases like that by herself.

They had to worry about the sentries posted along the canyon walls, too. Frank thought they were getting close to the spot where the lookouts had been earlier when he and Linderman were sneaking in. From here on, they would have to be as silent as possible, which he indicated to his two companions with gestures.

But the need for stealth disappeared suddenly, heralded by an outbreak of gunshots from behind them and a bellowing voice. "The woman's gettin' away! Stop her!"

"Move!" Frank said as he grabbed Dolores's shoulder and propelled her toward the canyon mouth. "Run straight out and then turn to the right. You'll find the horses in some trees about a hundred yards in that direction!"

"But what about you and Pete?" she gasped.

"Don't worry about us, Señora!" Linderman said as he drew his gun. "Just do like Morgan says and get out of here! We'll be right behind you!"

Dolores nodded and broke into a run. Frank and Linderman spread out to either side of her to cover her escape. The canyon mouth loomed not far ahead of them . . .

But then dark shapes ran out to block their escape, and a harsh voice yelled, "Hold it!" When they didn't slow down, muzzle flame blossomed in the shadows like crimson flowers, and Frank heard the sinister song of a bullet whistling past his ear.

# Chapter 31

Frank's gun was already in his hand. It came up with blinding speed, roaring and bucking against his palm. He aimed above and to the right of the muzzle flash, and his instincts were true. The sentry yelled in pain as Frank's slug bored through his body.

More shots came from the left. Linderman returned that fire. He grunted and stumbled, and Frank knew that he'd been hit.

Dolores realized that, too, and cried, "Pete!" She slowed and started to turn back toward him.

"Go on!" Linderman told her. "I'm fine!"

"You're hurt—"

"Damn it, Dolores!" Linderman roared. "Get out of here!"

She still hesitated, but only for a second before picking up speed again.

Frank veered toward Linderman and grabbed the foreman's arm with his left hand to steady him as they ran. "You elected?" he asked.

"Just . . . nominated," Linderman replied through

clenched teeth. "Slug knocked a chunk of meat out of my leg, but feels like it missed the bone. I can keep movin' as long as my boot don't fill up with blood."

A Winchester cracked and another bullet whined between Frank's head and Linderman's. Both of them fired at once, and saw the shadowy figure of a guard go spinning off his feet as their slugs tore into him. They hurried past the bullet-riddled hombre.

Frank thought they were past the sentries now, but the rest of the gang would be coming after them in a hurry. They had to reach the horses and start putting some distance between themselves and the canyon.

Up ahead, Dolores ran through the canyon mouth and turned right, as Frank had told her. Frank and Linderman were about twenty yards behind her. As they made the turn, more rifles opened up behind them, but the gunmen were a long way back and were probably firing blindly. Some of the bullets chipped rock splinters off the canyon wall as Frank and Linderman hustled past.

Then they were out in the open again and headed for the horses. Frank saw that Dolores was already mounted and had the reins of Goldy and Linderman's horse in her hand. She hurried to meet the two men with their mounts.

"That dog of yours almost scared me to death when I came up, Mr. Morgan," she said as she handed down the reins. "I thought he was a wolf!"

"A lot of people make that mistake," Frank said. He gave Linderman a hand getting into the saddle, then swung up onto Goldy's back. "Come on!"

They turned their mounts and kicked them into a run. Goldy was the biggest and fastest of the three horses, and even though he had been ridden the hardest today, his competitive instincts made him want to pull out in front. Frank held the stallion back so that he could bring up the rear and fight a delaying action to protect Dolores and Linderman if he had to.

He knew it wouldn't take long for the gunmen to throw their saddles on their horses and come after him and his companions. They would want to recapture Dolores, or failing that, kill her. As far as they knew, her death would send the cowboys from Salida del Sol off on a vengeance quest against Magnusson's men and finally set off the bloody war they had been trying to provoke for weeks now.

Maybe the tables could be turned on them, though. Frank thought for a second, and then edged Goldy up alongside Linderman's horse.

"I'll take the señora back to the ranch," he told the wounded foreman, raising his voice so he could be heard over the pounding hoofbeats. "You find Magnusson and tell him to round up as many of his men as he can and get over there, too."

"What the hell for?"

"We're going to catch those varmints between us," Frank explained. "They need to be wiped out once and for all."

"I suppose it could work," Linderman said. "But I'll stay with the señora. You fetch Magnusson."

"That's a better job for you, Pete. You're hurt."

"Damn it, Morgan—"

"You know I'm right," Frank broke in. "Don't worry. I'll see to it that the señora's all right."

"You'd damned well better," Linderman said. "All right. You reckon he's still at those burned-out oil wells?"

"That's the first place I'd look for him," Frank said.

Linderman nodded and veered his horse to the left. Dolores saw him angling away from them and called, "Pete!" When Linderman didn't answer, she turned to Frank and asked, "Where's he going?"

"To fetch help," Frank explained. "Keep heading for the ranch, Señora."

"But he's hurt! What if something happens to him?"

From the worry that was evident in Dolores's voice, the feelings Linderman had for her might be returned. They might even develop into something more in time.

Frank hoped that both of them lived through the night and had that chance.

He and Dolores headed straight across the San Fernando Valley toward Salida del Sol. Frank looked back over his shoulder from time to time to see how close the pursuers were. At first, he couldn't make out anything, and he hoped for a second that the gang wasn't coming after them.

That was a doomed hope, though, and he knew it. So he wasn't surprised a few minutes later when he saw the flicker of muzzle flashes. He couldn't hear the shots, but he knew that the hired killers were throwing lead at them.

It would take a mighty lucky shot at this range to find its target, especially considering that the gunmen were firing from the backs of galloping horses. But stranger things had been known to happen, so Frank leaned forward over Goldy's neck and urged the stallion on to greater speed. Goldy drew even with Dolores's horse.

"Lean over like this," Frank told her. "Make yourself a smaller target!"

She did as he told her. Her horse was fairly fresh, and Linderman had chosen a good mount for her. It seemed to have plenty of speed and sand.

Goldy had to be wearing down, though, and in fact Frank could feel the stallion's pace slowing slightly.

"Keep going," he told Dolores. "Don't slow down and don't look back. Just make it to the ranch!"

"What about you, Mr. Morgan?"

Frank put a grin on his face. "Don't worry about me!"

But she was worried, and he could tell it. He had to wave her on a couple of times before he let her horse have its head and started to draw away.

Goldy's sides were heaving. Frank patted him on the shoulder and said, "You've run a mighty good race, big fella. Nobody could ask for more than you've given me."

Goldy continued to slow down. Frank let him set his own pace now. The hardcases were still at least a hundred yards behind him, but they were cutting the gap now. Their guns continued to flash in the night.

Frank knew he was outnumbered by twenty to one, if not more. The odds of him surviving the next few minutes were mighty slim. But at least Dolores continued to pull away, and Linderman had disappeared in the darkness several minutes earlier as he went to find Magnusson. They would have a chance to get away.

He could increase their chances by delaying the pursuit. Hauling back on the reins, he pulled Goldy in a wide circle that ended with him facing the on-rushing gunmen.

Frank opened his Colt and thumbed fresh cartridges into the expended chambers. He slid it back in the holster and then pulled the Winchester from the saddle boot. The rifle was fully loaded with fifteen rounds. With the six in the Colt, that gave him twenty-one shots.

One bullet for every varmint, he thought with a grin. Simple enough.

He looped the reins around the saddle horn to keep them out of the way and pressed his knees into the stallion's flanks. Then he lifted the Winchester to his shoulder and called in a ringing voice, "Trail, Goldy, trail!"

Together, man and horse charged straight into the faces of their enemies.

# Chapter 32

The way the hired killers were bunched together, all Frank had to do was fire in their general direction to have a good chance of hitting something. He swung the Winchester from left to right, spraying lead as fast as he could work the rifle's lever and pull the trigger.

Bullets continued ripping through the air around his head as the gap between him and the gunmen closed in a matter of heartbeats. Suddenly, he was among them, just as the Winchester's hammer clicked on empty.

If he had taken the time to think about it, Frank would have been amazed that he was still alive after that reckless, headlong charge. He had fully expected some of the owlhoot bullets to find him.

But since he was alive, he continued to fight. As Goldy crashed into one of the horses, Frank swung the empty rifle like a club, smashing it across the head of one of the gunmen. The stock shattered, and so did the man's skull.

Frank twisted in the saddle and drove the jagged

end of the broken stock into the face of another man, who screamed and clapped his hands over his eyes as he was blinded. Frank dropped the rifle and palmed out his Colt as he whirled Goldy around.

The big stallion's momentum had carried them right through the line of gunmen. Frank charged the men again. As long as he kept them busy, they weren't chasing Dolores anymore.

The heavy revolver bucked in his hand. Powder smoke stung his eyes and nose. It was hard to see anything in the flickering light of muzzle flashes, but he knew the killers were all around him.

Suddenly, Goldy went down. Frank felt the stallion falling, and kicked his feet out of the stirrups in time to avoid being pinned. He was thrown through the air and crashed to the ground. As he rolled over, he was heartsick that Goldy was probably dead now.

But he was convinced that he would follow the valiant stallion within seconds.

As he surged to his feet, still gripping his gun, a horse loomed up close beside him. Frank tried to get out of the animal's way, but its shoulder clipped him and knocked him down again. He had to throw himself aside to avoid being trampled by another horse.

He scrambled up again and tried to lift his gun, unsure whether or not there were still any bullets in it, but determined to go down fighting. One of the riders kicked it out of his hand, though. He waited for the heavy impact of bullets slamming into his body.

That impact didn't come, because a familiar

voice suddenly called, "Hold your fire! Have you got him?"

"We've got him, Boss!" one of the men replied. Frank was ringed by guns now, and if the killers decided to start shooting again, he would be riddled with slugs in an instant.

"Who is it? Who helped Dolores escape?"

The knot of gunmen parted slightly to allow another man on horseback through.

"It's that bastard Morgan."

"I should have known." The newcomer edged his mount through the ring of killers. Frank had felt a moment of surprise as he recognized the man's voice, but he didn't show it now as he finally confronted the mastermind behind all the trouble in the San Fernando Valley.

"Howdy, Sandoval," he said. "I'm sure sorry Dolores is going to have to find out what a no-good son of a bitch her own brother is."

Jorge Sandoval glared down at Frank. "Dolores has no idea what's going on around here. Once I'm through with her, she'll be so broken she'll have no choice but to turn to me. Then I'll have the ranch I was supposed to have all along, the largest ranch in the valley!"

"Never got over the fact that she didn't just turn everything over to you after her husband died, did you?" Frank was surprised to still be alive, but as long as he was, he was going to find out as much as he could. "That was your plan all along when you pushed her into marrying him, wasn't it? You didn't figure she'd decide to hang on to Salida del Sol."

"She is a woman!" Sandoval blazed. "She has

no business running a ranch! And she clings to Francisco's foolish notions about not cashing in on the oil underneath her range!"

"She's your own sister," Frank said coldly. "How can you try to ruin her this way?"

"I don't want her hurt, if it can be avoided. But I'll do whatever I have to, Morgan. Once I own both ranches—and the oil—any legal disputes over the ownership of all this range will be resolved in my favor." Sandoval laughed. "You know the richest man always wins in court."

"Who's Mitchell?" Frank asked, hoping to catch Sandoval off balance with the abrupt question. Not that it mattered, of course. He couldn't have much longer to live.

Sandoval laughed again. "You don't need to know everything, Morgan. You can die with questions unanswered."

The guns in the hands of the killers started to come up.

"But not yet," Sandoval went on. "Bring him with us." A sneer distorted his handsome face. "I want him to see us wipe out the rest of my sister's crew, so she has no choice but to give up."

So the gang was going to raid Salida del Sol yet again, Frank thought, for the third time in two nights. Sandoval was really going for the knockout blow now.

And so was one of the men who followed Sandoval's gestured command, leaning down from his saddle and slamming the butt of his gun against Frank's head. Frank was driven to his knees by the blow and felt consciousness slipping away from him. He tried to hang on to it . . .

But he failed, and a darkness deeper than the night around them claimed him.

The ache that filled Frank's head when he woke up made him sick to his stomach for a moment before he forced the feeling down. A stroke of luck—and arrogance on the part of Jorge Sandoval—had given him another chance at life, and Frank didn't intend to waste it.

Gradually, he became aware that he was slumped forward in a saddle with his hands tied to the horn. The horse underneath him was still, other than a little nervous shifting around every now and then. He heard other horses stamping nearby and figured they belonged to the gunmen.

A man's harsh voice said, "Any time you're ready, Boss, just give the word."

Frank expected Sandoval to reply, but instead another familiar voice spoke up—a woman's voice.

"Are you sure you want to go through with this, Jorge? Your sister might be hurt."

"And what about your brother?" Sandoval shot back. "You didn't try to stop us when we went after him."

"That overbearing son of a bitch deserves whatever he gets," Astrid Magnusson said.

When Frank first heard her voice, he had almost reacted from the shock he felt, but he'd managed to control the impulse. He hadn't been all that surprised by Jorge Sandoval's betrayal of his sister;

Sandoval had been one of the strongest suspects when Frank put together his theory of a third party orchestrating all the trouble in the valley.

But he had never dreamed that Astrid might be in on it with Sandoval. The two of them had gotten together somehow and decided to double-cross their siblings. It made sense, in a way. Between the two of them, they always knew what both sides in the conflict were thinking and planning.

This discovery of their dual villainy didn't answer quite all of Frank's questions, but those other little matters could wait. Right now, he had to figure out a way to get loose from his bonds and turn the tables somehow on those two.

"Every minute we wait gives them more time to get ready for us down there, Boss," the gravelly voice warned. Frank assumed it belonged to the man in charge of the hired killers.

"I know that," Sandoval snapped. "Wake up Morgan. I want him to see what's happening before I put a bullet in his brain."

Frank had pretended to still be unconscious so he could find out what was going on around him, but the need for that ruse was over. He stirred and lifted his head slowly as if coming to naturally, before any of Sandoval's men could do anything.

"Ah, I see you're awake, Morgan," Sandoval said in a gloating tone.

"Yeah," Frank rasped, "but nothing's changed. You're still as big a polecat as ever."

Sandoval spurred his horse over next to Frank's and slashed a backhanded blow across his face with the quirt he held. The pain of the cut on his cheek chased away the last of the cobwebs in Frank's brain.

"Jorge!" Astrid said. "That's not necessary."

Frank looked past Sandoval and saw her sitting in a buggy with the reins in her hands. "Miss Magnusson," he said.

He couldn't see her face well enough to read her expression, but the stiff way she held her body was telling. She was upset, but she wasn't backing down.

"I'm sorry things have to be like this, Mr. Morgan. I enjoyed making your acquaintance. If I thought you could be trusted, I might have offered to let you in on what was really going on."

Sandoval's disgusted snort made it clear that he would have shot down that notion.

"Why did you try to get me to work for your brother anyway?" Frank asked her.

"Jorge sent word to me that your meeting with all the ranchers failed to rally them together and that you weren't going to work for his sister. I thought that if Victor could hire you, it would infuriate the Montero faction even more."

"And you had to keep both sides stirred up so they'd wipe each other out for you and Sandoval here."

"It's still going to work," Astrid insisted. "Once Dolores turns her ranch over to Jorge—"

"You'll have your brother killed," Frank interrupted to finish for her. "That way you can inherit his company."

"I wouldn't have put it so bluntly, but . . . yes, that's what's going to happen."

Sandoval said, "All you've done is make a nuisance of yourself, Morgan. I don't know how you managed to get Dolores away from my men by yourself tonight, but that will be the last time you interfere with my affairs."

Frank felt his pulse quicken. Sandoval didn't realize that Pete Linderman had been with him when he rescued Dolores! The guard Linderman had knocked out must have either died or not regained consciousness when the pursuit started. The man whose jaw Frank had broken had never seen Linderman.

And during the brief shootout with the sentries as they fought their way out of the canyon, everything had been dark and confused, so that Sandoval's hardcases hadn't realized there were two men helping Dolores escape, not just one.

That was another stroke of luck, because it meant that Sandoval didn't know Linderman had gone to find Magnusson either. Neither he nor Astrid were aware of the truce that had been called between the two sides. Their plans were already ruined; they just didn't know it yet.

But that wouldn't save the cowboys from the Montero ranch. Once this pack of gun-wolves swept down on Salida del Sol, they would be wiped out.

"All right," Sandoval said to the man in charge of the gang. "Kill them all. Burn the place to the ground."

"What about your sister?"

"Spare her life if you can. If you can't . . ." Sandoval shrugged. "Well, either way, Salida del Sol will be mine, won't it?"

The outlaw gave Sandoval a curt nod, then turned

his horse, waved his arm over his head, and called, "Let's go!"

The gunmen thundered down the hill where they had paused at the top of the slope. The lights of the hacienda were visible down below. Guns began to roar from attackers and defenders both as the hired killers began their assault.

Sandoval drew his gun, brought his horse closer to Frank's, and said with vicious satisfaction, "Now for you, Morgan."

# Chapter 33

Frank had been working unobtrusively on his bonds, twisting and pulling at them in an effort to loosen them. But he hadn't made much progress yet and his wrists were still held tightly to the saddle horn.

Since his feet were free, his only chance was to try to kick the gun out of Sandoval's hand and gallop off into the darkness before Sandoval could recover the weapon.

However, as if realizing that, Sandoval grinned, pulled his horse back a little, just enough to be out of Frank's reach, and raised the gun.

"*Adios*, Señor Morgan," he said.

But before he could pull the trigger, a gray shape came flying out of the night and crashed into Sandoval, knocking him out of the saddle. Sandoval cried out in surprise, and the gun in his hand went off as he fell. The bullet arced high and harmlessly into the air. Dog was on top of Sandoval the instant the man hit the ground.

Frank had lost track of the big cur during the

escape from the gang's hideout canyon, but he had figured Dog was still around somewhere and would follow his scent until he caught up. Dog had gotten there just in time to save Frank's life, not for the first time.

Sandoval screamed as he thrashed around on the ground and tried to ward off the slashing teeth of the shaggy, wolflike animal. In the buggy, Astrid cried out in horror and stood up as she reached in her bag. Starlight winked on the gun in her hand as she jerked it out of the bag.

Frank didn't know if she intended to shoot him or Dog or both, but he didn't figure to give her a chance at either of them. He jabbed his boot heels in the flanks of the horse and sent the animal leaping toward the two horses hitched to the buggy.

Frank's mount collided with one of the buggy horses, spooking both of them. The team lunged forward, jerking the buggy into motion as they bolted. With a shrill cry, Astrid was knocked off her feet and fell over backward. The little pistol in her hand popped.

She had let go of the reins as she stood up to fumble for her gun, and now they dangled loose on the floorboard, Frank saw as the vehicle flashed past him. Astrid had fallen into the space behind the seat and was struggling to get up.

She probably wouldn't be able to bring the runaway horses under control, Frank thought as he kicked his mount into a run and took off after the buggy. With his hands tied to the saddle horn, he couldn't reach over and grab the harness to bring the horses to a stop, but he thought maybe he could get in front of them and crowd them into a turn that would eventually bring the buggy to a halt, as cowboys turned stampeding cattle to make them mill instead of run.

He heard Astrid's frightened cries as the buggy bounced and careened over the rough ground. Frank drew up behind the vehicle, then swung his horse to one side to gallop past it.

As he came even with the buggy, orange flame jetted from the gun that Astrid still held. She must have thought he was chasing her with the intention of hurting her, rather than helping her.

"Hold your fire!" he shouted. "I'll try to stop the team!"

But if she heard him, she didn't believe him. The pistol cracked again, twice, and Frank leaned forward in the saddle as he felt the wind-rip of a bullet past his ear.

A glance ahead of them filled him with sudden horror. One of the gullies that cut across the valley loomed no more than a hundred yards away. He had to stop the team before the buggy reached that slash in the earth. He urged his mount ahead and angled it toward the madly running horses hitched to the buggy.

Astrid fired three more times, emptying her gun. None of the bullets found Frank, but one of them burned across the neck of his horse and made the animal scream in pain as it gave a leap and then started to sunfish. Frank clamped his knees to the horse's side as hard as he could, knowing that if he was thrown, the horse would probably bolt like the others and he would be dragged to his death by his hands lashed to the saddle horn.

It took him several seconds to bring the horse under control again, and in that time the buggy raced away from him. There was nothing he could do now except hope that the runaway team would see the gully and turn away from it in time.

The horses spotted the gash in the earth all right, but not until they were almost on top of it. They shied away from the gully in a sharp turn, so sharp that the buggy swung out wide behind them. Frank heard Astrid's terrified scream. Then the vehicle disappeared as it hurtled into the gully, snapping the harness traces, and landed with a huge, splintering crash.

With grim lines etched onto his face, Frank galloped toward the scene of the wreck.

When he came to the edge of the gully, he peered down into the shadows gathered there. It was about twelve feet deep. He could see one of the buggy wheels sticking up, still spinning.

"Astrid!" he called. "Astrid, can you hear me?"

No reply came back.

Grimacing, Frank tugged angrily at the rawhide thongs holding his wrists to the saddle horn. He felt them scraping and tearing at his flesh, and blood began to flow and make the bonds slicker. Still, it was going to take him a while to get free, and the knowledge that Astrid might still be alive and need help gnawed at him.

Despite the fact that she had thrown in with Jorge Sandoval and had even planned to murder her own brother, Frank couldn't bring himself to just let her die if there was anything he could do to save her. If she survived this crash, the law could deal with her.

The horse shied underneath him, and he looked around to see what had caused the reaction. Dog trotted up, tongue lolling from his mouth.

He must have been finished with Sandoval.

"Dog, come here!" Frank called. He clamped his knees tight on the horse's flanks again to hold it steady even though it wanted to get away from the big cur, which it no doubt regarded instinctively as a predator. Frank went on. "Dog, chew!"

Dog hesitated, then reared up on his hind legs and placed his front paws on Frank's thigh. That brought him up high enough to reach the saddle horn. He went to work with his sharp teeth, gnawing and tugging on the rawhide thongs.

Those teeth grazed Frank's flesh more than once, and Dog wanted to pull away. Frank urged him to keep going, though, and he twisted and pulled on the bindings himself.

After a few moments, they loosened enough for Dog to get his mouth around them, and he chewed through one of the thongs. Frank was able to slip a hand out then and untie his other wrist. Free again at last, he slipped out of the saddle and ran to the edge of the gully.

Half-sliding, half-falling, he went down the bank and then hurried over to the wrecked buggy. "Astrid!" he called again. "Astrid!"

The only reply was the squeaking of the wheel as it continued to turn slower and slower.

Ignoring the pain in his wrists and the blood that

coated them, Frank reached into his pocket and found a match. Snapping the lucifer to life with his thumbnail, he leaned forward into the buggy and held the match up so that its flickering light washed over the pale, still face of Astrid Magnusson.

She lay crumpled between the buggy and the gully's far bank, with the lower half of her body underneath what was left of the vehicle. Frank didn't have to be able to see it to know that her legs and pelvis had to be crushed.

But she hadn't been forced to suffer the pain of that awful injury. The odd angle at which her head sat on her shoulders told him that much.

Her neck was broken. She must have died instantly.

He backed out of the wrecked buggy, dropped the match, ground it out under his boot heel. A long sigh of regret came from him . . . regret at the fate that had claimed Astrid, regret at the demons within her that had led her to betray her brother and ally herself with a vicious bastard like Jorge Sandoval.

Thinking of Sandoval reminded him that the Montero ranch was still under attack. He could hear the guns in the night, still blasting out their murderous melody.

Dolores must have reached Salida del Sol safely, Frank thought. Otherwise, the ranch hands wouldn't have known that Sandoval's hired killers were on their way and wouldn't have been ready for them. He didn't know how many men Dolores could muster after the battles of the past few days, but he hoped there would be enough to hold off the attack until Magnusson arrived with help.

Assuming, of course, that Pete Linderman had been able to find the oilman and convince him to come to the aid of his former enemy.

Since there was nothing he could do here, Frank scrambled up out of the gully and ran back to the horse, which had wandered off a short distance to get away from Dog. He swung up into the saddle and rode toward the spot where Sandoval had fallen. He intended to get the man's gun and take a hand in the fight going on around the Montero hacienda.

The only problem with that was that Sandoval was gone.

Dark splashes of blood on the grass showed where he had been. Either someone had come along and taken his body, or he hadn't been dead when Dog left him to come after Frank. Sandoval's horse was still there, however, so Frank rode over to it and pulled the Winchester from the saddle boot strapped to the animal.

He hoped the rifle was fully loaded, because he still had work to do. The sort of work he did best.

Gun work.

# Chapter 34

Deciding that Sandoval had probably crawled off somewhere to die from the injuries Dog had inflicted on him, Frank figured he could find the man later. Right now, he galloped toward the ranch house, Winchester in hand.

As he headed down the hill, he watched the muzzle flashes and read the story they told. Sandoval's men had surrounded the hacienda. The bunkhouse was on fire, and the defenders seemed to have forted up inside the main house.

Using whatever cover they could, the killers were working their way closer and closer. The thick adobe walls of the hacienda would stop their bullets, but sooner or later the raiders would force their way inside, and then the defenders—including Dolores Montero—would be wiped out in a bloody slaughter.

Frank didn't know if he could turn the tide of this battle by himself, but he damn sure intended to try.

Before he could reach the ranch headquarters, though, a couple of riders suddenly loomed up out of the night to his left, followed by a wagon packed full of men. He veered toward them, knowing they could only be Linderman and Magnusson with reinforcements. All of Sandoval's men were already down there around the ranch.

"Pete!" Frank shouted as he approached the newcomers, who appeared to be about a dozen strong. "Pete!"

"Morgan! Is that you?" Linderman galloped up to him and reined his mount to a sliding halt. "Where's the señora?"

"Down there," Frank replied with a jerk of his head toward the hacienda. "She got away, but then Sandoval's men surrounded the ranch."

"Sandoval!" That startled exclamation came from Victor Magnusson, who had ridden up with Linderman. "What the hell are you talking about, Morgan?"

"Jorge Sandoval was behind all the trouble," Frank said, not mentioning Astrid's involvement for the moment, or the wreck that had taken her life. "It's a long story, but he wanted both Salida del Sol and your oil drilling operation, Magnusson."

"Where is he?" Linderman raged. "Where is the son of a bitch?"

"Dead, more than likely," Frank replied. "He tangled with Dog a few minutes ago. But his men don't know that, and they'll keep shooting until everybody down there is dead—unless we stop them."

"Then what the hell are we waiting for?" Magnusson said. He used the rifle in his hand to wave on the men he had brought with him. "Let's go!"

Those men were oil drillers, not cowboys. But they were tough and well armed, and that was all that mattered. In grim silence except for the swift, thundering rataplan of hoofbeats, they swept down toward the hacienda.

They held their fire until they were practically on top of Sandoval's hired killers, who must not have heard the horses approaching over the continual boom of the guns . . . at least, not until it was too late. Suddenly, the drillers were among them, rifles cracking, muzzle flame spurting. Men leaped from the wagon and grappled hand to hand with the killers. Powder smoke clogged the air.

Frank was in the thick of it, the Winchester bucking in his hands. He didn't bother to count his shots. He just fired until it was empty as he swept past the burning bunkhouse and plunged right into a group of gunmen who had been using some wagons as cover as they fired toward the house.

He kicked his feet out of the stirrups and leaped from the saddle, landing in the middle of a couple of gunnies. He slammed the butt of the rifle's stock into one man's head, rammed the barrel into the belly of another, and then brought it down on the back of the man's neck when he doubled over in pain.

It was a brutal, close-quarters fight. A bullet burned along the side of Frank's neck. A second later, he smashed the rifle butt into the mouth of the man who had fired that near-fatal shot, shattering teeth and sending the man sprawling into unconsciousness.

From the corner of his eye, he saw Pete Linderman. The foreman had both hands filled with Colts that he had gotten somewhere. The guns roared and bucked as his bullets slashed at the killers.

That looked like a pretty good idea to Frank. He

stooped and picked up the revolver dropped by the man he had just knocked out, then looked around for another one. He snagged a Colt from the holster of a dead gunnie who had been using a Winchester, then started toward Linderman just as several of the hired killers charged the foreman.

Frank reached Linderman's side just as Victor Magnusson also loomed up out of the powder smoke carrying a rifle. Linderman dropped to one knee as Frank and Magnusson flanked him. Frank and Linderman blazed away with the pistols, while Magnusson jacked the Winchester's lever and spewed lead from its barrel. The four men who had thought to jump Linderman were driven off their feet, their bodies shredded by the hail of bullets they ran into.

The three men lowered their weapons slowly as they realized that the shooting was dying away to nothing. The eerie silence that always followed the end of a battle settled over the hacienda and the area around it.

By the light of the burning bunkhouse, Frank looked around and saw that the cowboys who had been holed up inside the house had charged out once they realized reinforcements had arrived. Linderman got to his feet and called, "Jeff!" as he spotted his nephew.

The young puncher limped over to them, grinning despite the blood that dripped down his face from a bullet scratch on his cheek. The left leg of his trousers was stained with blood, too.

"One hell of a fight, wasn't it, Pete?" he asked.

"Where's Dolores? Is she all right?"

"You mean the señora? She was in the house the

last time I saw her, but yeah, she was okay. She had a rifle and was taking potshots at those bastards along with the rest of us."

Linderman turned toward the house, evidently about to go look for Dolores, but before he could start, she came running out of the hacienda, calling, "Pete! Are you all right?"

He dropped the empty six-guns and looked like he was about to lift his arms and step forward to meet her and draw her into an embrace.

But then he stopped, the natural deference of a foreman for his boss cropping up, Frank thought as he looked at Linderman's smoke-grimed, weary face.

"I reckon if anyone's earned it, Pete, you have," he said softly.

Linderman glanced at him as Dolores slowed, unsure what to do. After a second, Linderman nodded to Frank and said, "Yeah, I reckon so."

He turned back to Dolores, grinned, and reached for her.

A bloody apparition came out of the darkness behind her just then, looped an arm around her neck, and jerked her back as the grisly figure's other hand pressed a gun to her head.

"Stay back!" Jorge Sandoval cried hoarsely. "My sister's coming with me!"

"Jorge!" Dolores gasped, barely able to get the name out past the arm he had clamped brutally around her throat. "Jorge, no! These are . . . our friends . . ."

"You've got that wrong, Señora," Frank told her as he stood there, taut and watchful. He had guns in his hands, and he didn't need much room to make a shot . . . "I hate to tell you this, but none of us are friends with your brother. Not any more. Because he was the mastermind behind all the trouble."

Dolores's eyes widened with shock and disbelief. She tried to shake her head.

"It's true, Señora," Linderman said. "He wanted the whole shebang for himself. Both ranches and Magnusson's oil wells. And he was willing to kill anybody, even you, to get 'em."

Sandoval began backing away, dragging Dolores with him. His face was covered with blood from the numerous gashes Dog's teeth had left on it, and his clothes were dark with blood as well. He must have had the presence of mind to play dead during the big cur's attack, and despite the wounds he had suffered, he'd been strong enough to get away and slip down here to the ranch.

Frank didn't know what Sandoval hoped to gain by threatening Dolores. From the look in the man's eyes, he was more than half loco with hatred.

"I'm going to kill you, Morgan," Sandoval grated. "Then I'm getting out of here, and no one's coming after me."

"That's where you're wrong, mister," Linderman said. "If you hurt Dolores, I'll hunt you down and kill you myself. I'll do it anyway for all the hell you've put her through."

"I don't think so," Sandoval replied with a laugh that bordered on hysteria. "Step up here, Morgan. Take what you've got coming to you."

"The thing of it is," Frank said slowly, "the second you take that gun away from your sister's head, you're a dead man. You may get me, but I'll get lead in you, too. Or you can drop the gun and take your chances with the law."

"Go to Hell!" Sandoval had continued to back away from Frank, Linderman, Magnusson, and Jeff. Now he was within reach of one of the loose horses milling around. "Maybe I'll just kill her first!"

"No!" Linderman shouted. He leaped forward, his fear for Dolores making him stop thinking for a second. Suddenly, he was in the line of fire, blocking any shot by Frank.

Sandoval jerked the gun away from Dolores's head and fired at Linderman, who grunted and staggered as the bullet tore into him. Then, Sandoval gave his sister a hard shove and sent her crashing into Linderman. Their legs tangled and both of them went down, nearly knocking Frank and Magnusson down in the process.

That gave Sandoval time to leap onto the horse, whose reins he grabbed. Frank got around Dolores and Linderman in time to snap a shot at the fleeing man, but Sandoval jabbed his spurs into the horse's flanks, and the animal's frantic leap in response made Frank's bullet miss.

Magnusson and Jeff shot at Sandoval, too, but he kept going, bent low over the horse's neck. Magnusson said, "He's getting away!"

Frank grabbed the reins of another riderless horse and grunted, "Not hardly."

A second later he was in the saddle, pounding through the night after Sandoval.

Frank saw the muzzle flashes as Sandoval twisted around and fired back at him. Sandoval was taking the road toward the pass through the Santa Monica Mountains. Maybe he thought he could stay ahead of Frank all the way to Los Angeles and give him the slip once he got to town. Frank didn't intend to let that happen.

But the horse underneath him seemed pretty played out, he realized, and Sandoval was gradually pulling away. Frank didn't know if Magnusson or anyone else had followed them from Salida del Sol. He wasn't going to count on any help. He wanted to settle the score with Sandoval himself.

That might not happen, though, he realized as the lights of the ranch headquarters fell behind them. It was a desperate, two-man race through the night now as the trail curved and twisted into the foothills and Frank's mount continued to struggle.

He had to do something to slow down Sandoval, or the man might get away. As one of Magnusson's drilling rigs loomed to the right of the trail up ahead, silent and abandoned at the moment because Magnusson had taken its crew with him to Salida del Sol, Frank lifted the Colt in his hand and drew a bead on Sandoval's horse.

It would be one hell of a shot if he made it, he thought as he squeezed the trigger.

Sandoval's horse broke stride and then went down, its legs crumpling underneath it. Sandoval flew out of the saddle, crashed to the ground, and rolled over several times before he came up running.

That fall should have been enough to knock him out, Frank thought. But Sandoval was being fueled by his insane hatred, and he kept going, heading straight for the derrick. Frank angled the horse after him.

Sandoval turned and fired, but Frank kept coming. Where Sandoval was headed, though, the horse couldn't go.

As he reached the derrick, Sandoval began climbing up the wooden framework.

Frank grimaced. Sandoval had to be plumb loco now. Once he was up on that derrick, there was nowhere else for him to go.

But maybe he didn't plan to go anywhere. Instead, he held on to a crossbeam with one hand and twisted around to fire down at Frank with the other hand. The bullet whined past Frank's ear. He brought the Colt up and squeezed off a shot.

Nothing but a click as the hammer hit an empty chamber.

Frank reined in and reached to the loops on his shell belt. They were empty as well, he discovered. The hardcases had taken all his bullets while he was their prisoner.

He flung himself out of the saddle as Sandoval fired again. Frank ran around to the other side of the derrick to put its wooden structure between him and Sandoval. That wouldn't give him much cover, but it was better than nothing.

"Give it up, Sandoval," he called. "Magnusson and the others will be here in a minute or two. There's nowhere for you to go."

Sandoval didn't answer. He just kept climbing.

Frank sighed. The smart thing to do would be to wait for help to arrive. Somebody else could shoot down Sandoval from the derrick if need be.

But something inside Frank stirred, and he knew he couldn't do that. Because of Jorge Sandoval, life had nearly been ruined here in the valley. A lot of good men were dead—and so was Astrid Magnusson. Pete Linderman might be, too, and Frank hadn't forgotten what had happened to Goldy.

He started to climb, too. If he could work his way around to Sandoval, he might be able to disarm the man and take him down to face justice . . .

Sandoval fired again, the slug chewing splinters from one of the beams near Frank's head. But then as Sandoval jerked the trigger for another shot, the hammer clicked on an empty chamber just like it had with Frank's gun a few moments earlier. Sandoval screamed a curse, drew back his arm, and flung the gun as Frank came around onto the same side of the derrick.

Sandoval was about twenty feet off the ground, Frank maybe ten or twelve. Even if the empty gun had hit him and knocked him off, he probably wouldn't have been hurt too bad.

But he ducked and let it sail past him, then resumed his climb after Sandoval, who now seemed to be scrambling for the top of the derrick.

Frank took his time about it. There was only so far Sandoval could go. The derrick was only about fifty feet tall.

Sandoval reached the top while Frank was still ten feet below him. Hearing hoofbeats, Frank paused and looked over his shoulder. He saw riders galloping down the road toward the derrick. That would be Magnusson and the others, he thought.

"Time to call it quits, Sandoval," he said. "We can wait for you all night, if that's what it takes."

Sandoval clutched the square framework at the top of the derrick and laughed. "Now *you're* wrong, Morgan. If I'm going to hell, you're going with me!" He fumbled inside his shirt. Frank heard paper crinkling, then the rasp of a match. Flame flared up. "I'm going to blow this well up with both of us on it!"

He dropped the burning ball of paper down the center of the derrick.

Frank watched it fall, hit some of the drilling equipment, bounce off, and come to a stop against one of the derrick's legs.

"Too bad you don't know much about drilling for oil, Sandoval," he said. "I don't either, but I know this well hasn't come in. There's no oil down there to burn."

Sandoval screamed a curse as he glared down crazily at Frank. His grandiose, last-ditch play had failed.

So he dived at Frank instead.

That took Frank by surprise. He barely had time to swing himself out of the way before Sandoval's plummeting body could slam into him and knock both of them off the derrick. As it was, Sandoval hit Frank's shoulder and jolted one hand and both feet loose. He hung for a second by that hand as he swung his feet back onto a crossbeam.

Sandoval was just below him, hung by one foot that had caught in the angle between a diagonal support and a crossbeam. Frank thought he had heard a sharp crack, and he figured Sandoval's ankle was broken. Sandoval didn't seem to notice, though, as he grabbed the crossbeam and levered himself back up. He used his hands to pull himself upright and lurched toward Frank, reaching out in an attempt to grab his enemy by the neck and choke the life out of him.

Frank warded off Sandoval's arms and slammed a punch to the man's blood-smeared face. Sandoval grabbed a support with one hand and slugged with the other. Forty feet above the ground, the two men traded punches for a long, desperate moment.

Then Sandoval slung a looping right at Frank that The Drifter ducked under. Frank hooked a left to Sandoval's midsection, then let go with his right and drove it into the man's jaw. Sandoval went backward off the crossbeam, shrieking as he fell down the center of the derrick. He tried to catch hold of one of the cables that supported the drill bit, but his hand slipped off it.

A second later, with a grotesque crunching sound, he landed on top of the drilling rig at the bottom.

Frank leaned on the derrick for a long moment to catch his breath as Magnusson and the other riders galloped up. Magnusson dismounted hurriedly and ran over to stomp out the small fire that had been ignited by Sandoval's futile attempt to blow up the derrick. Then he tilted his head back and called, "Are you all right, Morgan?"

"Yeah," Frank replied. "I'll be down in a minute."

"No hurry," Magnusson said. "Sandoval's not going anywhere. He's dead."

No, Frank thought, Sandoval wasn't going anywhere. He had already crossed the divide, and right about now he was probably shaking hands with the Devil.

There were a few unfinished bits of business, but for now, Frank was content to rest there on the derrick and look up at the stars, a mite closer to heaven than he normally was.

# Chapter 35

When they got back to Salida del Sol, Frank was glad to discover that Pete Linderman was still alive. Sandoval's bullet had put a deep crease in his side, but that was all. However, Linderman had lost enough blood from his various wounds so that he was going to be pretty weak for a while.

Frank figured that Dolores Montero would be more than happy to nurse him back to health.

Now he had to break the bad news to Victor Magnusson. There was no way of getting around it.

"You'd better brace yourself, Magnusson," Frank said as the two of them stood in the hacienda's courtyard. "I found your sister's buggy in a gully on the other side of the ridge. It looked like the team had run away from her."

"Astrid!" Magnusson cried in horror. "Was she with the buggy? Is she all right?"

"I'm sorry." Frank shook his head. "As best I could tell, the crash broke her neck. I don't reckon she suffered much, if any."

"Oh, my God." Magnusson covered his face with

his hands and sobbed, a big, brawny roughneck brought to tears by something more powerful than any drilling rig—love and sorrow. "What . . . what was she doing out here anyway?"

Frank took a deep breath. "I reckon she was looking for you. I guess she brought the buggy out when you didn't come back to town. Maybe she ran into Sandoval's men and they tried to capture her. I reckon they might have thought they could use her for leverage against you."

"The bastards! I'm glad they're all dead, but even that's more merciful than they deserve!"

Mercy came in all forms, Frank thought. And he didn't see any reason why he shouldn't show some of it to Victor Magnusson by keeping the true details of Astrid's death to himself. It sure as hell wouldn't change anything for Magnusson to know the truth now.

With that unpleasant chore taken care of, Frank borrowed a horse from the Montero remuda and headed back to town. Dog trailed along behind him, head down, as if he were already missing Goldy, too.


When John J. Stafford opened the door of his hotel room in response to Frank's knock, the lawyer was wearing a dressing gown, but he didn't appear to have gone to bed yet. He stared in shock at Frank's battered appearance and exclaimed, "My God, Mr. Morgan, what happened to you?"

"Plenty," Frank said. "But the important thing is that the trouble in the valley is over."

"Over?" Stafford repeated. "But . . . but how?"

"Why don't I come in and tell you all about it?"

"Of course, of course," Stafford said as he moved back and swung the door open wider. "I was just dictating some notes to my clerk—"

He turned as he was speaking and started to gesture toward the man who sat at a desk on the other side of the room, then stopped abruptly as he saw the gun that had appeared in the man's hand.

"Howdy, Mitchell," Frank drawled.

The little man he had seen in the hideout bolted up out of the chair and fired. Frank was already moving. His left hand shot out and shoved Stafford out of the line of fire. His right dipped to the Colt on his hip and drew it in a flicker of motion too fast for the eye to follow.

The heavy revolver roared. Mitchell was slammed back against the chair by the impact of the bullet as it shattered his shoulder. The chair overturned and Mitchell toppled over it to land groaning in the floor.

"Oh, my Lord," a wide-eyed Stafford whispered. "What . . . what . . ."

Frank moved across the room to kick the fallen gun well out of Mitchell's reach . . . not that the wounded man had any fight left in him. In fact, he appeared to have passed out from the shock of his wound.

"I thought for a while that you were double-crossing me, Stafford," Frank said to the lawyer, "because somebody tried to kill me the same night I got here to Los Angeles, and I figured you were the only one who knew I was coming."

He lowered the gun but didn't holster it, just in

case Mitchell was shamming and had some trick up his sleeve.

"But then I remembered that your partner Turnbuckle has a law clerk who travels with him on cases, and I figured you might, too."

"Yes, of course," the shocked attorney managed to say. "Mitchell came down here with me from San Francisco."

"And proceeded to sell you out and pass along information to Jorge Sandoval."

"Sandoval! You mean, Señora Montero's brother?"

"Like I said, it's a long story." Frank heard rapid footsteps in the hall. "And I reckon that'll be the police coming to check on those shots, so I think I'll wait and just tell it once, if that's all right with you."

He was surprised to find Pete Linderman up and around when he rode Stormy out to Salida del Sol the next day. The men were busy cleaning up after the battle the night before, and Linderman was supervising, leaning on a cane on one side with Dolores on his other side ready to help him if need be.

"There's a lot of work to be done around here," Linderman said when Frank commented about expecting to find him resting in bed. "We've got to rebuild the barn and the bunkhouse, not to mention patchin' a whole heap of bullet holes."

"And there's a contract to negotiate with Victor Magnusson, too," Dolores added.

Frank's eyebrows rose in surprise. "You're going to let Magnusson drill on your range?"

Dolores sighed and nodded. "Yes. I hope Francisco

understands, wherever he is. But you were right about there not being any way to turn back the clock, Mr. Morgan. Things will never be as they once were, and if I hadn't been so stubborn about insisting that they could be, Jorge wouldn't have been able to take advantage of the situation like he tried to."

Frank heard the catch in her voice when she mentioned Sandoval, and said gently, "I'm sorry about your brother."

"So am I, Mr. Morgan. So am I. But I'm not the only one who lost a loved one. The death of Astrid Magnusson is even more tragic because she didn't even have anything to do with all of this."

"I suppose so," Frank said. None of Sandoval's gun-wolves had survived the battle, so he was the only one who knew the truth about Astrid. Keeping it to himself was really more than she deserved . . . but after thinking it over, he still didn't see a good enough reason to heap even more grief on her brother's head. Let him mourn her, and let the truth be buried with her, Frank had decided.

"Say, we've got something for you, Morgan," Linderman said, speaking up. He turned to call to his nephew, who was over by one of the corrals with several other punchers. "Hey, Jeff, go fetch that surprise for Mr. Morgan."

Frank frowned. "I don't much cotton to surprises," he said.

"I don't figure you'll mind this one," Linderman said, and a moment later a grinning Jeff led Goldy out of a shed that hadn't burned.

Frank caught his breath as he saw the big, golden-hued stallion. Goldy was limping a little, but seemed to be all right otherwise.

"He came wandering in this morning," Linderman explained with a smile. "He's a little lame in one leg, like he fell and hurt it. You might want to have a horse doc take a look at it. But I've been around horses plenty and I think he'll be fine. He just needs plenty of rest and some good graze."

"He can get those things right here on Salida del Sol, Mr. Morgan," Dolores said. "If we can talk you into staying for a while, that is."

Frank went over to Goldy, stroked the stallion's shoulder, and let Goldy nuzzle his shoulder. "I reckon I could do that," he said as he grinned at Dolores, Linderman, and Jeff. "I can't think of anywhere I have to be."

The Drifter could drift on some other day.